Praise for *Delivering Hope*

"Somewhere in the world a pregnancy test is negative . . . and a woman weeps. Somewhere else in the world a pregnancy test is positive . . . and another woman weeps. In *Delivering Hope*, the miracle of adoption brings them together. Holt has masterfully crafted an astonishingly honest and gripping account of the journey, the joy, and the hope that is made possible through adoption and the Atonement of Jesus Christ. A must-read for anyone interested in adoption, and a page-turning, entertaining read for anyone interested in the real life drama we know as choice, consequences, sacrifice, selflessness, and pure love."

—**Wesley D. Hutchins, Esq.**, adoption attorney; adoptive father; president, Utah Adoption Council

"*Delivering Hope* is a great read! In addition, it's also a novel that daughters and their moms should each go through and then get together to discuss what they've learned. *Delivering Hope* lives up to its title."

—**Jack Weyland**, bestselling author of *Charly*

"An engaging and accurate account of individuals dealing with loss, grief, love, and hope through the adoption process. As someone who has worked with people on all sides of the adoption process, I would say *Delivering Hope* is a must-read for anyone whose life has been touched by infertility or adoption, as well as anyone who enjoys a well-written and uplifting story."

—**Sarah Burgess, Esq.**, MSW, LSW

JENNIFER ANN HOLT

delivering HOPE

JENNIFER ANN HOLT

delivering HOPE

Bonneville Books
An Imprint of Cedar Fort, Inc.
Springville, Utah

This is a work of fiction. The characters, names, incidents, places, and dialogue are products of the author's imagination and are not to be construed as real.

ISBN 13:978-1-59955-902-5

Published by Bonneville Books, an imprint of Cedar Fort, Inc.
2373 W. 700 S., Springville, UT 84663
Distributed by Cedar Fort, Inc., www.cedarfort.com

LIBRARY OF CONGRESS CATALOGING-IN-PUBLICATION DATA

Holt, Jennifer (Jennifer Ann), 1977-
  Delivering Hope / Jennifer Holt.
     pages cm
  Summary: A woman unable to have a baby yearns to have children, and an unwed mother chooses to put her baby up for adoption.
  ISBN 978-1-59955-902-5 (alk. paper)
  1. Adoption--Fiction. 2. Adoptive parents--Fiction. 3. Birthparents--Fiction. 4. Man-woman relationships--Fiction. 5. Christian fiction. 6. Domestic fiction, American. I. Title.

  PS3608.O4943593D45 2012
  813'.6--DC23

                    2011042269

Cover design by Angela D. Olsen
Cover design © 2012 by Lyle Mortimer
Edited and typeset by Emily S. Chambers

Printed in the United States of America

10 9 8 7 6 5 4 3 2 1

Printed on acid-free paper

To my husband, Shane,
for believing that I could

In adversity a man is saved by hope.
-Menander

Book One

OLIVIA

CHAPTER ONE

Olivia's hands were shaking as she opened the small, pink box containing the pregnancy test. She carefully unfolded the instructions, which she read every single time she was about to use one of these sticks. The familiar words raced through her mind without really registering, but she knew the important parts by heart. Accurate up to five days before your period, and then, the appearance of one line is a negative result, the appearance of two lines is a positive result. She took a deep breath, closed her eyes, and whispered, "Here it goes."

After placing the test stick face up on the counter and flushing the toilet, Olivia looked around her bathroom, studying the tiny purple flowers on her shower curtain and that place in the corner where the warm tan paint she had applied to the wall slightly overlapped the white baseboard. She noticed that they were running low on shampoo and that she needed to get a new bar of soap from the closet in the hall. She consciously kept her gaze away from the small piece of plastic lying on the corner of her counter while the required three minutes seemed to drag on for thirty. She checked her watch. Nope. One minute left to go. She knew if she glanced at the test, she would be able to get an idea of what the results were, since the lines would already be forming. Instead, Olivia directed her eyes to the laundry hamper and made a mental note that she would need to wash a load of whites today.

One more peek at her watch told Olivia that the time was up.

She could check the results. Her heart was racing, and her palms had become wet and sticky. She chided herself for getting so worked up. The results would be whatever they were, and she could not do anything about them now. Olivia did not realize that she was holding her breath as she reached over, gripped the test stick in her hand, and looked down. One line. Negative. She was not pregnant.

Olivia felt the air rush from her lungs as though she had been hit right in the belly. She dropped the stick with a little clatter on the tile floor and braced herself against the vanity cabinets as she slid down to sit on the plush bathroom rug. Olivia propped her elbows on her knees and buried her face in her hands. The tears came as they always did. Slowly at first, as the results of the pregnancy test sank in, then harder and harder until the sobs were bursting, uncontrolled, from her chest. She let herself have a good, hard cry, then rubbed her eyes in anger and frustration when the tears stopped coming and her eyes began to burn.

Partly, Olivia was angry with herself. Angry that she had let her hopes build up once again. Frustrated that the news was still affecting her in this way. This was, after all, the twelfth pregnancy test she had taken in as many months. Every month she told herself that she was *not* going to buy another test. She would just wait and let nature tell her whether she was pregnant or not, but the "not knowing" was almost as unbearable as finding out she wasn't.

Olivia also had to admit that she was getting frustrated with Heavenly Father. Having a family was her greatest desire, and she could not understand why that blessing was being withheld. Before her mind could wander too far in that direction, there was a soft knock on the bathroom door.

"Livvy, are you okay? I've got to leave or I'll be late for work." It was Michael. This was the part Olivia dreaded most of all. Michael wanted a child as much as she did, and it broke her heart to have to tell him month after month after month that there was still no baby on the way. She stood up and splashed a little cool water on her face. After a quick pat dry, she opened the door.

Before Olivia could even open her mouth, Michael knew. Her big blue eyes were not bright and vibrant as usual; they were darker—almost gray—a sure sign that she had been crying. She gave a nearly imperceptible shake of her head and attempted to shrug off the ache in her heart.

Michael tried to hide the disappointment that rushed through him. He knew that Livvy needed him to be strong right now. He opened his arms and said, "Oh, Livvy, I'm so sorry!"

As she buried her head in his shoulder and the tears started flowing again, she whispered, "Me too, Michael. Me too."

Michael drove until he knew that Livvy would not be able to see him from the house. Then he pulled the car to the side of the road and put it in park. He had to gather his thoughts and get his emotions in control before he could go to work. Michael was at a loss, a complete loss. He had never felt so helpless or hopeless in his entire life.

It had been over two years now that they had been trying to get pregnant. Twenty-seven long months, to be exact. And for every one of those months he'd had to look into the eyes of the woman who meant everything to him and see the hurt and disappointment and sadness that threatened to engulf her. Of course, he wanted a child too. He wanted one so badly that his heart physically seemed to ache, but even more than that, he wanted Livvy to be happy again. He thought back to their wedding day and the sparkle that had been in her eyes as they knelt across the altar of the temple to be sealed together as husband and wife for time and all eternity.

He smiled momentarily at the memory, and then Michael's brow furrowed as he remembered something having been said about "multiply and replenish the earth." Apparently that was easier said than done. No one ever talked about the "what ifs." What if you and your wife couldn't conceive? What if your wife cried every single month? What if you tried to find words to comfort her, but they all seemed hollow and meaningless compared to her pain? What if you sought out the best doctors and tried everything in your power, and nothing changed? What if he could never fix this? What if that sparkle never made its way back to Livvy's beautiful blue eyes? What if . . .

Michael stopped and took a deep breath. Tears had sprung to his eyes and his chest was pounding. Clearly, this train of thought was not going to help him calm down. He just needed to do what he had been doing for the past two years. He needed to be strong and he needed to be supportive. He needed to push his own pain aside and focus on helping Livvy. Then maybe, just maybe, they could find a way through this together. That was the only thing he knew to do right now. Michael rubbed his forearm across his face to remove any evidence of tears and then slammed the car into drive, took one last deep breath, and headed off to work.

Olivia watched from the window as Michael backed the car out of the garage and headed down the street. Once he was gone, she tried to focus on what needed to be done that day. She remembered the load of whites from the bathroom and made her way upstairs so she could get the laundry started. As she bent over to pick up the laundry basket, her eyes inadvertently found the plastic pregnancy test lying on the floor where she had dropped it. She picked it up and threw it into the trash can with all the force she could muster. The action cracked her carefully formed composure, and she moved quickly to her bed and dropped to her knees. She pounded her fists on the green bedspread and screamed, "It's NOT fair! It's NOT fair! It's NOT fair!" Olivia looked heavenward and, for the first time, allowed all of her frustrations to fully form in her mind and on her lips.

"Heavenly Father, I've always been taught that if I did what was right, if I followed the commandments, I would be blessed. Why are you withholding this, of all things, from me? What did I do that makes me unworthy to be a mom? What is it that would be beyond my capabilities that every other woman on earth seems to be able to do? It's NOT fair!" Olivia knew that she sounded like a spoiled child, but in that moment she just didn't care. She had always done what was right. She had always done what was expected of her. For what? If she was not going to be able to have a family, what was it all for?

Growing up, Olivia had always been taught that being a mother was the most important role that a woman could ever have in this life, and she believed that it was true. More important, having children was what Olivia had dreamed about for as long as she could remember. When she was in Primary, Olivia had stood up in the Mother's Day sacrament meeting program with several other girls holding dolls wrapped in blankets and had sung about growing up and becoming a mother. Even at the young age of nine, those words had touched Olivia's heart, and she knew that she was meant to be a mom. In the sixth grade, when she was supposed to write a report on what job she wanted when she grew up, Olivia wrote about motherhood and the challenges and responsibilities that a mom has.

As she progressed through the Young Women program, lesson after lesson taught the importance of motherhood and the need to prepare for that most sacred calling. Olivia couldn't wait. She couldn't wait for the little boys who looked like the man she loved, and the little girls with the same golden brown hair and big, blue eyes that Olivia's parents found so endearing. She couldn't wait for the joy and happiness that each child would add to their family. Now, all that had been ripped away from her, and to make everything worse, week after week after week she attended Relief Society, and all she heard was "children, children, children." Last week she'd wanted to yell, "What about me? Where do I fit in? Is there room in this church for a woman who may never be a mom?"

They had been seriously trying to get pregnant for over two years now, and Olivia didn't know what to do. They had started working with Dr. Collins nine months ago, but nothing had come of it so far. Michael had given her countless blessings, and Olivia always hoped to hear a blessing of healing pronounced on her body so that she could give him the child that she knew he wanted as badly as she did. But that pronouncement never came. The blessings were mostly of comfort and reminding her to continue in faith. *That's all well and good,* Olivia thought, *but faith is not going to conjure up a baby.*

These thoughts felt a little like mutiny, and while part of Olivia relished the feeling of freedom, she mostly felt guilty. *After all, I have a wonderful husband. We have a roof over our heads and plenty to eat. We live in a time and place of abundance . . . but what good is all of that if I don't have a family to share it with?* As Olivia allowed herself to indulge in her feelings of anger and resentment, she crawled up into her bed and cried until she fell back to sleep.

The first time that Olivia saw Michael was while she was playing basketball inside the Smith Fieldhouse at Brigham Young University.

It was fall semester of her senior year, and Olivia was, at the moment, involved in an intense game of intramural coed basketball. Normally while she was playing, she didn't notice anyone or anything that was going on off the court, but as the tall, dark-haired man strolled through the door, something about him caught her eye. He was good-looking, but it was more than that. As she tried to figure out what it was that made her notice him, Olivia realized—a split second too late—that the ball was coming her way at a very high speed. The next thing Olivia knew, her eyes were filled with tears and her nose was throbbing where the basketball had hit her. Olivia's best friend and teammate, Heather, came running over as the referee called for a time out. Heather's face was pretty serious as she surveyed Olivia's and then broke into a grin as she teased, "You're supposed to catch the ball, not kiss it."

"Thanks a lot. I'll try to remember that," Olivia groaned. "Is it bleeding?"

"Yep. You better go take care of it. We'll try to survive without you."

"Whatever."

Olivia and Heather were both laughing as Olivia jogged off the court and out the door to the indoor track that surrounded the gym, trying to catch the blood that was dripping from her nose as she went. The drinking fountain was closer than the bathroom, and Olivia's hand was getting pretty full of blood, so she stopped there to rinse the blood off her hand. Then she filled her palm with water and tried to wipe off her face. She was just wishing that she had thought to grab a towel off the bench before she left the gym when Olivia felt someone walk up behind her. "I thought maybe you could use this." The voice was clear and strong, and Olivia turned around to find herself face-to-face with the dark-haired man who had distracted her in the first place. He was holding out a towel, which she grate- fully took, and mopped at her nose and face, trying to clean all of the blood away.

He took a step back and watched as she pinched her nostrils in an effort to stem the flow of blood. She had beautiful, curly brown hair that was pulled back in a ponytail. It was not as dark as his own hair, more the color of a perfectly roasted marshmallow. There were several errant strands that had worked themselves loose from the rubber band,

and she kept pushing them away from her face with her free hand. When they stood side by side, he realized that she was taller than he had initially thought, being only a few inches shorter than his own height of six feet. She moved with the ease of an athlete, and aside from her efforts to clean her face, the fact that a basketball had just smashed into her nose didn't seem to phase her. He liked her at once.

When it appeared that the girl had the bleeding under control and her face was mostly clean, he stepped forward again. "Hi. My name's Michael." For the first time, Olivia looked at the man squarely in the face and realized that it was his eyes that made him stand out. Not necessarily the color—although she liked the deep, dark brown—but the twinkle in them. Here was someone who was truly happy, someone who loved life and wanted to make the most out of it. He carried himself like he was at ease in his own skin, like he was at peace. She liked him.

"Nice to meet you, Michael. I'm Olivia."

The two of them returned to the gym, where the game was just winding down. As it turned out, Michael had graduated several years earlier and was the football coach and biology teacher at a nearby high school. He was at the Fieldhouse to visit with one of his former professors about some new training activities he was thinking about using, and he had decided that it might be fun to watch the basketball games for a few minutes. After the final buzzer sounded, Heather and her husband, Greg, made their way over to the bleachers where Olivia and Michael were sitting.

"Is this a friend of yours?" Heather asked in a tone of mock innocence. Greg elbowed her and muttered that it was none of their business, but he grinned and gave a sly wink to the pair.

As Olivia felt her cheeks flush, Michael stepped up and reached out to shake Greg's hand. "I'm Michael Spencer, and if I have anything to say about it, Livvy and I will become great friends." Heather raised an eyebrow at Olivia. She had never heard anyone call her "Livvy" before. Olivia snuck a peek at Michael, *he was so . . . so, what?* she asked herself. *Confident? Relaxed? Handsome?* Whatever it was about Michael, it just felt right that he had called her "Livvy." She smiled at Heather and shrugged. Greg ignored their exchange. "Well, any friend of Olivia's is a friend of ours," he replied with a warm handshake. "Now, who wants pizza?

Olivia and Michael had been seeing each other for several weeks when he planned a special evening in Provo Canyon. He had been talking about it for three days, and Olivia knew he was very excited about it. They were only thirty minutes into the date when an unexpected thunderstorm effectively extinguished the charcoal that was cooking their dutch oven dinner. Michael laughed as they were running back to his old truck, and he hollered over the booming thunder, "I guess it's time for Plan B." As it turned out, "Plan B" was to hurry back to his house and try to finish cooking the chicken and potatoes in Michael's oven.

They were halfway down the canyon when a flat tire deflated Plan B. Olivia waited for some frustration to show. She knew from watching him coach that when Michael put a plan together, he expected it to succeed. Instead, Michael grinned and said, "Well, a little rain never hurt anyone," and they jumped out of the truck while he changed the tire in the rain and the mud. It was there, on the side of the road—when Michael crawled out from under the truck covered in mud, his dark hair wet and dripping, with a smile on his face—that Olivia began to fall in love.

When he looked at her and saw her wide blue eyes laughing at him, his smile broadened and he reached around her waist and pulled her close. "Livvy, you're really something special, you know that?" Being this close to him made her heart pound—or was that the thunder?

"You're getting me all muddy," she said grinning.

"I know," was all he said. Then Michael slowly reached up and touched her cheek. She closed her eyes and leaned closer, feeling the rain land on her hair, her face, her lips. That's when he kissed her for the first time, and Olivia knew that Michael would be the only man she would ever kiss from now on.

Olivia felt the sun streaming onto her face before she opened her eyes. She knew that it must be close to noon for the sun to be shining through her bedroom window. She groaned and rolled over. She just didn't want to face the day. She felt exhausted from finally vocalizing the feelings that floated around the edge of her mind and was glad that nobody had heard her outburst. Her mind told her that she was being irrational, but her heart told her it didn't matter. Whether it was true or not, Olivia believed that Heavenly Father was letting her down. She was upholding her end of the bargain, being a "good girl" and all, yet she was not allowed to have the one thing she wanted most of all.

The telephone rang and interrupted her thoughts. It was her boss.

"Shelly is sick. Can you please cover the rest of her shift?"

"Sure, I'll be right in," Olivia said before hanging up the phone. Olivia was a nurse in the local emergency room, and while she enjoyed her job, it was not what she envisioned for herself. She thought back to the day of her graduation from BYU almost three years earlier. She had been so pleased with the achievement of graduating with her nursing degree. She scanned the sea of faces in the crowd until she found Michael's beaming up at her next to her mom and dad. She remembered how it had felt to look at him then. They would be married in two weeks, and the thought of becoming his wife left her breathless.

The wedding and reception were beautiful—even better than she had hoped. She thought, with a sad smile, of the discussion she and Heather had before the reception started. Heather was still trying to persuade Olivia that a woman who was seven months pregnant had no business being a matron of honor. "Besides," Heather had quipped, "this belly will make all the pictures look unbalanced." But Olivia would have none of it. She and Heather had been inseparable throughout their college years, and she wanted her best friend by her side.

"Children are what marriage is all about anyway," Olivia had scolded her. "If someone doesn't like the way the pictures look, well that's just too bad for them!"

Olivia had taken the job at the ER upon graduation for "something to do until I have a baby." She didn't realize it would take so long. To date, there had been twenty-seven months of chances for her to get pregnant, all of them failures. *At least I'm good at my job,* Olivia thought as she got dressed and headed out the door.

Olivia arrived at work and jumped right in. It actually felt good to be busy as she tried not to think about the pregnancy test from that morning. Time passed quickly, and Olivia had just finished assisting on stitching up a little girl's chin when in walked Sister Ellis from her ward. Sister Ellis was in the Relief Society presidency, had six kids, and always seemed to be on the go. She was carrying her four-year-old son, Jace, who had jumped off the top of the slide in their backyard and landed with his arm at an odd angle. By the looks of it, it was broken. Jace was upset and in pain, so Olivia paid special attention to calming him during the X-rays and while his arm was being cast. By the end of his ER visit, Jace was smiling and proudly showing off his fluorescent orange cast to anyone who would look. As Olivia was walking them out of the exam room, Sister Ellis took Olivia by the arm and with her eyes shining said, "Thank you so much! You took such good care of him and were able to calm him down when I was too frazzled to be able to do it myself! You're really great with kids. It's too bad you've decided to pursue a career rather than have a family!" She gave Olivia's arm a warm squeeze, smiled, and hurried out the door.

Olivia stood there in shock—at first too surprised to feel any-thing else. But then the realization of what Sister Ellis said sunk in, and Olivia had to run into the bathroom before the tears of anger, pain, and resentment poured from her eyes. *TOO BAD . . . I'VE DECIDED . . .* Olivia was shaking now and getting more upset by the moment. Sister Ellis was always making comments in Relief Society about the nobleness of motherhood and how a woman cannot be truly fulfilled until she has given birth to a child (preferably many children). Sister Ellis constantly annoyed and often hurt Olivia with these comments, but Olivia never dreamed that Sister Ellis would be so insensitive. Not to mention nosy and completely out of line! What business was it of hers anyway? How could she possibly know of the countless hours, days, weeks, months, and years that the desire to have a family had burned in Olivia's heart?

Olivia forced her mind off that particular train of thought. She couldn't lose it here. She had to get back to work. After a few deep breaths and a little cool water, Olivia's mask of normalcy was back in place, and she stepped out of the bathroom and back into her charade of happiness.

CHAPTER TWO

Olivia woke up early. After lying in bed for twenty minutes, she still couldn't fall back asleep, so she got up and had a long, hot shower. She enjoyed the heat and the steam and tried to imagine that the nervous butterflies in her stomach were being washed down the drain with the soap bubbles. Today she would head to the doctor's office for their first try of artificial insemination. After trying various fertility pills and shots over the past nine months, and having no success in becoming pregnant in over two years, Olivia's doctor, Dr. Collins, felt that artificial insemination was the next step. She agreed. Olivia was eager to try something new, and she was excited at the idea that this might work. She had been taking hormone pills to ensure she would ovulate, and although they made her feel lousy, it would be worth it if she got pregnant. Besides, it was early spring. The season of new life. The timing felt serendipitous to Olivia. She smiled.

The ovulation test she had been taking each morning was positive yesterday, so she called and scheduled the appointment. Michael was going to meet her at the doctor's office on his lunch break, and make his "deposit" in a little plastic cup which the doctor would spin with whatever else, and then bring it back in a little tube to be "inserted" into Olivia. Not very romantic. Quite embarrassing. Definitely not the way Olivia had envisioned getting pregnant, but at this point, she didn't care how she got pregnant, only that she did get pregnant. She was praying and praying that this procedure would work. She had even taken the time to explain to Heavenly Father why she deserved to be pregnant and what a great mother she would be. Together with Michael, she had prayed and fasted and asked their family members to join in. Surely this was going to work.

Olivia turned off the hot water and reached for a towel. She took her time drying off and picking out her favorite khaki slacks and light blue button-up shirt. She spent a few extra minutes getting the curls in her hair to fall just right, and she even made the effort to add eyeliner to her regular makeup routine. At least she could look nice when she went to the infertility clinic. Somehow that seemed important—like compensation. Being unable to get pregnant made Olivia feel less like a woman, less beautiful, on the inside. She wanted to make up for that on the outside.

She went downstairs and poured herself a bowl of cold cereal and waited for Michael to come down. He hurried down a while later, grabbing a granola bar on his way out the door. "Don't forget. You have to be at the doctor's office by 11:30," Olivia reminded him as he blew by.

"I'll be there, Livvy. Don't worry." He gave her a kiss on the top of her head and was gone. Olivia was hurt. She had been pondering this all morning, thinking that today could be the day she would get pregnant. This was a big deal! Apparently, Michael did not share her feelings.

Michael knew that Olivia was disappointed when he left. He heard her wake up early, then get in the shower after tossing and turning for a while. He could see her contemplative mood when she came out of the bathroom, and it was hard to miss the care with which she had dressed and gotten ready for the day. This was a big day for her. He just didn't have the strength to get into a lengthy conversation about it again. Every time they had discussed artificial insemination, Livvy talked about it as a lifeline. This would save her. This would make her a mother.

Michael didn't want to be pessimistic, but he wasn't so sure. He didn't want to talk about and encourage and convince Livvy that this was going to work only to see her even more heartbroken if it didn't. Nor did he want to tell her to prepare to be disappointed. That definitely would not go over well. So, this morning he chose to avoid conversation altogether. He laid in bed much longer than necessary, even feigning sleep at times, and then ran out the door with barely six words spoken. He was pretty sure he had handled the situation poorly, but he was flying blind on this one. He just didn't know what to do or say that would help Livvy.

Olivia felt like the clocks were running in slow motion all morning. She tried to stay busy around the house but kept finding herself watching the clock or just sitting and daydreaming about what pregnancy would be like. When it was finally time to leave and Olivia got in her car, a fresh batch of butterflies emerged in her stomach. They became faster and more eager to break free as she drove across town. When she parked her car at the infertility clinic, Olivia had to stop and take several big breaths to calm herself down. Her hands were shaking as the butterflies made their way to her lungs. They were making it difficult to breathe.

Olivia walked into the waiting room and started to relax a little. That was the obvious intent of the décor, with the soothing pastel colors on the walls and the cushy furniture that reminded her of her mom's living room. A large aquarium in the corner bubbled soothingly, and several pictures of babies were hung strategically throughout the room. Olivia checked in at the front desk, and the receptionist smiled at her and said, "Let me know when your husband arrives, Mrs. Spencer, and we'll get you right back."

Olivia smiled, nodded, and settled into one of the soft pink chairs. She picked up a magazine and flipped through, finding an article entitled "How to Combat Morning Sickness (and Win!)." She started reading, making mental notes of the remedies she would try once she became pregnant. Olivia had made up her mind. This procedure was going to work. In a matter of a few hours, she would be pregnant.

Michael walked through the glass doors and scanned the room

until he found Olivia. He had decided to be more excited about the procedure for Livvy's sake, even though the doctor had told them there was only about a 10 to 20 percent chance of pregnancy each cycle. Olivia looked up from her magazine and saw Michael watching her. She waved him over and was glad to see that he was smiling. *Maybe he was just nervous. Maybe that's why he seemed distant this morning.* Michael gave her a peck on the cheek as he sat down next to her. "Are you ready?" he asked.

"Absolutely!" Olivia felt confident and happy. She thought she saw a flicker of doubt as Michael's dark eyes grew momentarily darker, but then he smiled and squeezed her hand. Everything was going to be fine.

Separated from the soft colors and sounds of the waiting room, Olivia's nerves were starting to reappear. The nurse led Michael to a private room and handed him a small plastic container. After a bit, he came out, cup in hand, and red in the face. The nurse took the cup and told them that things would be ready in about thirty minutes. After the longest twenty minutes that Olivia could remember, the nurse led them to a small, antiseptic room. Bright white tile and glistening stainless steel cupboards full of medical instruments did little to inspire tranquility. The fact that Olivia was sitting, half naked, on a narrow, cushioned table, covered up with what looked and felt like an oversized paper towel, extinguished any remaining calmness she had felt earlier. She could hear her heart pounding in her ears, her hands were shaking, and she was starting to sweat. She shifted her weight, and the paper covering the table crackled beneath her.

Michael was sitting in the lone chair in one corner of the room. He looked up and forced a bright smile. "It's going to be okay, Livvy. Try to relax." She took a deep breath and tried to release the growing anxiety. She knew there was nothing to worry about. The procedure itself was painless; she would only feel some minor discomfort. But what if it didn't work? What if she didn't get pregnant?

No. Olivia mentally scolded herself. *You've got to think positive. Just think positive and everything will be fine.* There was a knock on the door, and Dr. Collins opened it, followed by the same nurse from earlier. He greeted Michael, and they exchanged brief pleasantries that Olivia barely heard.

Dr. Collins turned to Olivia as he was pulling a pair of latex gloves onto his hands. He smiled a warm, comforting smile that was a little too practiced to be of any actual comfort and said, "Now, Olivia, just lie down and try to relax."

Two weeks later, Michael opened the bathroom door to find Olivia gasping for breath as her sobs threatened to overtake her. The artificial insemination had failed. There would be no baby in nine months. He reached for her, wanting to take her in his arms, to tell her that everything would be okay, that they would keep trying until something worked, but the words caught in his throat. They just didn't ring true. What if there was never going to be a baby in their lives?

Olivia read the emotions as they flickered across his face, and when he took a step closer, she turned her back on him. A sucker punch to the gut would have hurt less. Michael closed the door as he walked out.

CHAPTER THREE

Spring rain showers awake the world from its winter slumber, bringing the yellows and reds and purples of the earliest blooms. Grass turns green and leaves emerge from tiny buds. The sun grows hot and the smells of freshly cut grass and newly turned soil fill the air. Sprinklers bring relief to thirsty roots as the scorching heat reaches a climax. Lawns start to yellow, and so do leaves, as the world begins to surrender to the inevitability of winter. Nature knows that time marches on whether we want it to or not.

"Merry Christmas, Livvy." Michael handed his wife a small, delicately wrapped box. His brown eyes were sparkling as she unwrapped the little package. When she opened the box that obviously contained some kind of jewelry, she gasped as her eyes focused on the beautiful gold ring that had three small diamonds placed in a row. Michael couldn't wait. He took the ring out of the box and placed it on the third finger of Olivia's right hand. "It's technically an anniversary ring, but I wanted to give it to you now. The three diamonds symbolize our past, present, and future, because I'm going to love you forever!"

Olivia smiled and kissed her husband. In spite of the strain that their infertility had placed on their relationship, she knew that she loved him. He was a good man, and he loved her. They had both made mistakes in the way they had handled their emotions throughout the last nine months of failed artificial insemination attempts, from outbursts of yelling to times when they had gone days barely speaking to each other—not out of anger, but out of the fear that anything they said would trigger an argument.

Olivia admired the ring on her outstretched hand. "Thank you, Michael. I love it. And I love you too!" She fingered the third stone in the row. The stone that symbolized their future, and a familiar burn formed behind her eyelids. Michael's hand covered hers instantly.

"Whatever the future holds, Livvy." He paused and lifted her chin to be sure they were seeing eye to eye. "Whatever the future holds, we're in it together."

CHAPTER FOUR

"Well, it looks like you two have been trying to get pregnant for a little over three years now," Dr. Ball said as he looked over Olivia's medical charts.

"Thirty-eight months to be exact," Olivia said and then mentally added, *thirty-eight times I could have been pregnant and was not. Thirty-eight times I cried. Thirty-eight times the Lord told me, 'Nope. Not you. You don't get to be a mom.'*

"In that case, I think the next step for you is to try in vitro fertilization," Dr. Ball said, "which is why Dr. Collins referred you to us." Olivia started nodding, but Michael remained still. He was not sure he wanted to dive into something else that would get Livvy excited, only to have her be disappointed once again.

"What are the chances that would work? That Olivia would actually get pregnant?" Michael asked.

"That depends on several factors, but in general, there is about a 30 percent chance of a pregnancy. Of course, we'll have to do some fairly extensive testing before we begin, to be sure that you two are good candidates for in vitro. With all of the shots, plus the time and cost of collecting Olivia's eggs, combing them with your sperm, and then allowing the embryos to begin growing before placing them back inside Olivia, the procedure costs too much to just move forward blindly."

"Just how much will it cost?" Olivia thought they would be able to cover it with the money in their savings account, but she wanted to be sure.

"About ten thousand dollars," Dr. Ball answered.

Olivia nodded. They would be able to cover one cycle, but just barely.

"I think we need some time to talk about this," Michael said.

"Sure, take all the time you need," Dr. Ball replied. "When you've made your decision, just call and let the receptionist know. If you want to move forward, she'll schedule the necessary appointments." Dr. Ball stood, shook each of their hands, and then left the room.

"Do we really need time to think about this?" Olivia asked. "I think we need to try everything possible before we give up."

"Livvy, I love you. And I want you to be a mom, but I'm not sure we can make it through another round of excitement and the pain that follows. We've both been trying very hard lately to move past the strain that these months and months of treatments have put on our marriage, and I think things are starting to get better. I'm just not sure I want to risk jumping into the most stressful treatment yet." He paused and looked her in the eyes. "I don't want to lose you, Livvy, and I'm worried that if this doesn't work . . ."

"I'm not going anywhere." Olivia was hurt that Michael thought she would actually leave over this. He should know that she loved him and wanted to be with him.

"I'm not talking about losing you physically, Livvy. I'm talking about losing you emotionally. We've been drifting apart through all of this. I know we're both committed to each other, but I have watched as little by little you—the real you—has become lost in pain and anger and grief. Your eyes never sparkle anymore. You hardly ever smile. The worst part is, there's nothing I can do to change that. I can't fix this. I can't make it go away. I feel . . . lost."

"Michael, I've known for a while that the doctor was going to suggest in vitro sooner or later. It may seem like I'm making a quick decision, but I've actually thought this over and over and over. Part of me is scared—no, terrified—to try this. If we jump in and put all of our emotion, all of our time, not to mention all of our money into this, and it fails, we lose it all."

"That's my point exactly. Are you sure you can make it through that and come out okay on the other side?"

"But, on the other hand," Olivia continued, ignoring Michael's question, "if we don't try every single thing possible, I know that I will never be able to let it go. I'll always wonder if we would have had a baby if we had tried in vitro. Always. As hard as it will be if we try and fail, I know my mind will never rest if we don't try. I have to know, Michael. I have to."

Michael couldn't argue. It was clear that Livvy had put a lot of thought into this decision. He stood up and took her hand. "Let's go schedule those appointments then."

After years of being poked and prodded and probed like a lab rat, Olivia thought she should be used to it by now. She wasn't. The homey feel of the waiting rooms in these clinics didn't help anymore either. In fact, it kind of annoyed her. She wouldn't even look at the pictures of babies on the walls. They only represented something that continued to elude her. When the nurse called her name, Olivia was glad to enter the more familiar world of medical equipment and procedures. Once in her exam room, she undressed and tried to cover up as best she could with the napkins (as she had come to think of them) that were provided for that purpose. She fought back the butterflies that were a part of every doctor's visit, and concentrated on the idea that maybe this time they were trying something that would allow her to get pregnant.

Dr. Ball told Olivia and Michael that their test results would be ready in several days, and that they would know whether they could move forward with Olivia's shots for the in vitro fertilization process. Michael tried to keep Livvy's mind off it by taking her out to dinner and the movies, and while she seemed to appreciate the diversion, they were both more than ready for some news when the phone rang two nights later. The caller ID showed the number of the clinic, so Michael and Olivia each grabbed a phone and sat down on the couch.

"Hello?" Olivia was going to do the talking.

"Olivia? This is Dr. Ball."

"Hi. Do you have some results for us?"

"I do. Is Michael there with you?"

"Yes, I'm here," Michael answered the question.

"Good. I'm glad you're together. I'm afraid I have some bad news."

Olivia listened as Dr. Ball shared the results of the tests and examinations. Her clinical, nurse's mind knew what he was saying, but the other part of her, the young woman who just wanted a baby, refused to understand until the end of the conversation when Michael asked, "So what, exactly, does that mean for our pregnancy chances using in vitro?"

"It means your chances of a pregnancy, ever, using in vitro or anything else, are practically zero. We discovered some abnormalities with the shape of Olivia's uterus that will make it impossible for an embryo to implant itself. I would not recommend pursuing in vitro. There's no reason to when the embryo won't implant anyway. I'm sorry, Olivia. It appears that you will never get pregnant."

Olivia's hand that held the phone dropped to her side. She vaguely heard Michael thanking Dr. Ball and telling him good-bye. He reached down, took the phone out of her hand, and hung it up. He put his arms around her, and she buried her head in his shoulder. Then he held her while they cried.

CHAPTER FIVE

Michael left work early and hurried home, eager to see Livvy. He had been worried about her all day. The last couple months since learning she was not going to have a baby hadn't been easy, and he knew this was going to be an especially rough week for her. Mother's Day was coming up on Sunday, and he didn't know what to do. Church had become so hard for Livvy to bear on Mother's Day, she had actually stayed home last year. A lump formed in Michael's throat as he thought back to that day:

"I just can't stand it!" Livvy shouted at no one in particular. Michael cautiously peeked around the corner and into the bathroom where Livvy was standing in her old pink bathrobe. He thought about pretending he hadn't heard; he was sure a conversation now would only upset her. However, Michael's better judgment won out. He knew that Livvy knew he had heard her, and he also knew that she expected an answer.

"What can't you stand, Livvy?" Michael kept his voice cheerful in spite of the storm he knew was brewing.

"I can't stand sitting through another Mother's Day program and hearing everyone from the bishop to the primary kids gush on and on about motherhood and what an honor and blessing it is, and how that's what all the girls should be planning for, and how having children is what makes life complete and worthwhile." There were no tears in Livvy's voice, only anger, but Michael knew her well enough to know that her anger was a mask for her pain. "I can't stand the fact that everyone takes it as an opportunity to either offer me their advice on what I need to do to get pregnant, or to question me about why I've 'chosen' a career, or to tell me not to worry about it. 'You know, sweetie,'" Livvy's voice had now taken on a sappy undertone as she mimicked her advice-givers, "'you're just stressing too much about this. I have a cousin . . .' It's always some-one random—niece, friend, friend's daughter's cousin—'and as soon as she quit trying to get pregnant and stopped worrying about it, POOF! She just got pregnant!' or 'Well, dear, if you just take a baby aspirin every day, that'll do the trick! You'll be pregnant in no time.' Oh sure, I've been seeing the best doctors in the state for years, and all the while they've been pulling the wool over my eyes. In reality, all the medical reasons why I'm not pregnant just don't matter and all of my problems can be solved by a bottle of baby pills! It makes me want to scream!"

Livvy was all worked up now, so Michael began slowly, care-fully measuring each word. "You know, Livvy, they don't mean any harm. They're just trying to help, or else they feel like they should say something to you, but they just don't know what to say."

"Well, it *doesn't* help! Besides, if they really don't know what to say, maybe that's a clue that they should say nothing. If they really want to help, they could respect the fact that this is hard for me and just give me a hug or something."

So much for calming her down, Michael thought. *She's just building up a good head of steam.*

"And what about the flowers they pass out at the end of the pro-gram?" Olivia's mouth had curled up in disgust as if the word had a bad taste to it.

Michael was now at a complete loss as to what he should say, but he was in too deep to turn back now. "What about the flowers?" He sighed. "I always thought that was a nice gesture."

"A nice gesture?" Livvy was screaming now, actually screaming. Michael couldn't imagine what had become of his bride. "It's just a chance for all the moms to stand up and look down their noses at people like me!"

Michael was clearly exasperated now. Could his bright, intelligent wife really not hear how ridiculous she sounded right now? "Livvy, it's not like that, and you know it. They don't even ask all the 'moms' to stand. It's all the women—eighteen and older."

"And just how is that supposed to help me feel better?" Tears finally broke through Livvy's anger, and she was yelling and crying all at once. "It's like they're saying, 'This is a day all about mothers, but some of you—Olivia Spencer—clearly aren't good enough to fall into that category, but we don't want you to feel too bad, so . . . go ahead and stand too.' So then everyone stares at the back of my head wondering what's wrong with me that I don't have a child."

"Olivia!" Michael's voice had risen for the first time during this conversation. "You . . . are . . . being . . . ridiculous!" He was fighting to keep his voice even but was losing the battle. "I can't even talk to you when you're acting crazy like this!"

"Oh, so I'm crazy now, am I? Well fine. Don't talk to me then. You know what? I don't even care right now. But if you think that Mother's Day is so great, you can go sit through the stupid program without me. I'm staying home!" And with that, Olivia slammed the bathroom door.

Michael stood there staring at the door. He was too upset to speak but also too upset to keep quiet. He gave in to his emotions and let one loud roar escape his lips and then stormed out of their bedroom and slammed the door behind him.

When Olivia heard the bedroom door slam, she slowly opened the bathroom door and peeked out into the room. She felt like screaming herself! Didn't Michael know her at all? Didn't he realize that, deep down, she knew she was being unreasonable, but she just didn't care! It hurt badly enough on regular Sundays to sit and listen to all the talk about motherhood and women's roles and family and on and on and on. She just knew that today would be utterly unbearable. Her tears were flowing freely now, and she didn't even bother to kneel as she flung her thoughts heavenward. "Heavenly Father, this stinks! It's not fair, and I just can't handle going to church today. Now, to put the finishing touch on this horrible day, Michael and I are fighting—again!" Olivia threw herself onto her bed and sobbed into her pillow, but the tears did little to wash away her pain. Then the anger welled inside her so strongly that she could no longer contain it, and Olivia found herself punching her pillow and crying, "It's not fair! It's not fair! It's not fair!"

When the weeping fury began to exhaust her, Olivia curled up on her side and pulled the blankets up around her chin. As she was falling into the welcome numbness of sleep, Olivia had a fleeting thought that Michael might be hurting right now too, but she was too spent to really focus, and it hurt too bad to try, so she closed her eyes.

Michael sat at the bottom of the stairs listening to the tortured sobs of his wife for about thirty minutes before they finally subsided and he knew, from past experience, that she had fallen asleep. His heart and arms ached for Livvy, but he had no idea how to help her. It seemed that every time he tried, they ended up in a yelling match, with Livvy crying herself to sleep and him sitting downstairs staring blankly at the wall, wondering how he could be so completely helpless. There was no way for him to fix this or heal Livvy's hurt, and Michael had given up hope that there was any way to bring back the real Olivia. The Olivia that was buried deep beneath this grief.

He thought about getting up and going to church, but although he had tried to downplay Livvy's insecurities about people whispering about them, he knew that, to a small degree, there was some validity to her fears. He didn't believe, as Livvy did, that the whispers were intended to hurt or belittle; he truly felt that they were a result of well-meaning people who simply did not know what to say to her. Whatever the motive, he decided not to pour fuel on the fire by showing up alone. If neither of them were there, nobody would even notice. But, if he went alone, everyone was sure to be curious about Olivia's mysterious Mother's Day absence.

He tiptoed up the stairs and glanced into their bedroom. Livvy lay curled up on her side with the covers wound around her. She had a tight hold on the blanket as if it were the only thing keeping her from splitting wide open. Michael felt the tears fill his own eyes as he brushed a leftover tear from Livvy's cheek and smoothed an errant brown curl back off her forehead. "I'm sorry," he whispered and pressed a soft kiss to Livvy's brow. "I'm so, so sorry."

"Yeah," Michael murmured to himself, "Last Mother's Day was terrible, and that was before we found out that Livvy will never get pregnant." He couldn't imagine what this Mother's Day might have in store for them.

As he pulled up in front of their home, Michael noticed that all the blinds in the windows were closed. He thought that was odd because Livvy always opened up all the blinds in the house right after she ate breakfast. She loved to let the sunshine filter through their home, sweeping away every speck of darkness. That wasn't something she would have just forgotten to do. Michael pushed the button to open the garage door but felt a sudden urgency to get inside, so he did not wait to pull the car in. He jumped out and raced under the garage door, ducking his head because it was not fully up yet. He burst into the kitchen where all was quiet. He felt a momentary panic but then wondered if Livvy had got called into work that morning. *Of course. That must be it*, Michael thought. Her car had been in the garage, but on a nice day like today, she probably would have ridden her bike the two miles to the hospital.

Michael chided himself for allowing his imagination to run away with him. He took a breath to calm his racing heart and then heard the sound of muffled sobs coming from the top of the stairs. He raced up the steps two at a time and found Livvy kneeling by the side of their bed, her face buried in her hands while her body was heaving from the force of the sobs. She looked up as Michael burst into the room, and the sheer agony in her eyes hit Michael's heart like a dagger. He was at her side in an instant, wrapping her in his arms, trying to shield her from the unknown invader that was torturing her. "Livvy, Livvy, shh . . . shh . . . What's the matter? What is it?"

"Oh, Michael!" She threw her arms around his neck and clung to him as if he was her only hope for survival. "Heather is pregnant again." Michael grimaced and held her tighter. This was a touchy subject. This would be Heather's fourth baby, and although she and Livvy had remained good friends after graduation, it became increasingly difficult for Livvy to watch each successive pregnancy—not only Heather's, but all of her friends, acquaintances, and coworkers. Many days Olivia had come home quiet and sullen after someone announced their pregnancy or brought in ultrasound pictures, or any of the other hundred little milestones that go along with pregnancy and childbearing. To Livvy's credit, she always put on a brave front and smiled and congratulated whoever it was, but Michael knew her heart broke a fraction each time. He kissed the top of her head.

"I'm so sorry, Livvy." It seemed he was saying that a lot lately, but it was the only thing he could say that did not cause an explosion. "I wish there was some way I could make this better . . ." he trailed off into silence, wondering what else he could say that would not be a trigger. Olivia continued sobbing, and Michael wondered at this extreme outburst of emotion. Never had the pregnancy of a friend hit her this hard.

"There's nothing you can do. I was terrible. I just got so angry, and I . . . I . . ." Her words were strangled by sobs, and it took Michael a moment to compute what she had said.

"Wait a minute. YOU were terrible?"

"Yes! Heather is my best friend in the world, next to you, and I was terrible to her." Michael was blindsided by the curve this conversation had taken, and he was not sure how to respond. Finally he managed to speak.

"Do you want to tell me what happened?"

"Well, you know that I've been having a really rough time since the doctors said that we should give up on the idea of ever having a child. After all we've been through, for them to tell me to forget it because I will never get pregnant, . . . well, anyway, I haven't been doing so good since then."

"Yeah. I noticed." Michael risked a small grin, and to his relief Livvy managed a weak smile in return.

"Well, anyway, Heather came over this morning and was so excited and happy, but when she told me that she was expecting her fourth baby, I just lost it. I don't even remember exactly what I said, but I was screaming and crying, and I said something about her having her fair share and maybe she could leave some for the rest of us, and why on earth was she here rubbing my nose in the fact that she could have babies at will, and did she REALLY think that I would be happy about this, and how I was sick of her thinking she was better than me just because she could have kids." Olivia stopped short at the shocked expression on Michael's face.

"You actually said that?" Michael could see that Livvy was distraught, and he wanted to console her, but he was having a hard time not laughing. He could not believe that his Livvy had unleashed years of pent up fury on Heather. He could not help but feel that it would be good for her to have gotten it off her chest. Luckily, Heather had been the one to face the hurricane of emotion. Michael knew that she would understand and forgive Livvy.

Michael noticed that Olivia's sobs had quieted, and as he looked down at her, he realized she had been studying his face. "What's so funny?" she demanded, but there was no real anger behind her words, and Michael thought he saw the glimmer of a smile around the corners of her mouth.

"Actually, I was thinking that it must have felt good to get that off your chest."

Olivia sighed, and the frustration returned to her eyes. "It did feel good, but . . . poor Heather. She has always been so great and understanding. She knows how uncomfortable I get when people tiptoe around and try to keep their pregnancies secret from me so I don't feel bad, so she has always been open with me. Yet, she seems to understand that, at the same time, it is difficult for me to hear all the details and gushing, and on and on, so she keeps those things to herself. Of all people, she was least deserving of a tongue-lashing." Olivia looked down and shook her head.

"That's why she will forgive you," Michael comforted. Olivia nodded and tried to smile, but her eyes filled with tears again, and the anguish returned. "What else is going on, Livvy?"

Olivia took a deep breath as though steeling herself against something unpleasant. "It's just that, well, when I was unleashing my fury on Heather, I actually heard what I was saying." She sighed and looked expectantly at Michael, as if that explained everything.

Michael studied her face, searching for the hidden meaning, then finally had to admit, "I guess I'm not following you, Livvy."

"When I actually listened to those angry, mean words coming out of my mouth, it dawned on me that I have become an angry, and sometimes mean, person. I have allowed my sadness to make me bitter—bitter and angry to the point that I am lashing out and hurting the people who mean the most to me." She paused and looked markedly at Michael. "Heather isn't the only one who I have wrongfully unloaded on. I guess it's my turn to say I'm sorry." Livvy looked up into Michael's face, her blue eyes seeking forgiveness, and Michael felt his throat tighten.

"Livvy, of course I forgive you. I love you. I love you. I love you." Michael pulled Livvy close to him again and pressed his lips to the top of her forehead. He was seeing a glimmer of the woman he had married for the first time in months, maybe a year or more. He kissed her forehead again, then moved down and kissed across the bridge of her nose to her cheek. He caressed the curve of her neck with his lips and then moved up to her chin. Michael hesitated for a moment. It had been months since they had shared more than a quick peck on the lips, and owing to the fact that they were no longer trying to get pregnant, they had not been intimate in at least that long. Making love had become a means to an end—an end that never came and always ended in tears. So they had been drifting apart, both lost, both hurt, not knowing how to rescue one another. Michael loosened his arms and gazed into Olivia's eyes. They were filled with tears again, but not tears of heartache. Her eyes were glimmering with love and trust and even desire. That was all it took. Michael touched her cheek, then closed his eyes and pressed his lips to hers.

CHAPTER SIX

Olivia awoke in Michael's arms. She glanced at the clock on the bedside table. It was six o'clock—dinnertime. For the first time in a long while, Olivia sent a prayer of thanks heavenward. She was very upset by her outburst at Heather this morning and had spent the day in a reflective mood, only to become more distraught as she began to realize what she had allowed herself to become because of her infertility. Worse yet—and this was the thing she had not had a chance to tell Michael—she could see no way out. Olivia knew that she did not want to remain a bitter and angry person, but she didn't know what to do to fix it. That was the true cause behind the agony Michael witnessed when he first walked into their room and found her on her knees. She had been praying for help. For the first time, Olivia wasn't flinging accusations and shouts of unfairness to the heavens, she was pleading for help—for some way that she could raise herself out of this pit she was sinking in.

Michael moved beside her, and she raised her head from his shoulder to meet his gaze with a soft smile. A thrill ran through her as he brushed his fingers across her cheek. "I guess we fell asleep," Olivia murmured as she snuggled in closer to him. She had not realized how much she missed having his arms around her, holding her against his chest, until this moment.

"I guess we did." Michael smiled and kissed her softly on the lips. As he did, Olivia promised herself that she would do all she could to not let their infertility come between them again. She just prayed that she would be able to keep that promise.

"Now," Michael began as he stood up and started getting dressed, "I think there was something more you were going to say to me earlier before we . . ." he paused and grinned.

"Before we remembered that we really do love each other?" Olivia finished for him.

"Yes. Before we remembered that we love each other." They both smiled.

"Actually, there is more I want to talk about, but I'm too hungry to talk right now. Let's eat first." Olivia knew this conversation would be difficult enough without her stomach growling at her all through it.

"Good idea. Let's go out."

The waitress had just taken their dessert order when Michael broached the subject. "So, what else is going on?" He smiled, trying to convey that they could work through whatever it was.

Olivia took a deep breath. It felt good to admit that she was not happy with her attitude. The hard part was going to be finding a way out. She hoped that Michael would not downplay her feelings and just tell her to be happy and stop being angry. Olivia knew it was not going to be as easy as that. These emotions had become too much a part of who she was.

"Well?" Michael urged after Olivia remained silent for a few minutes.

"Okay," Olivia began. "I told you that I realized I have allowed my sadness to turn to anger and then allowed that anger to take a hold of me. It has changed my outlook on life, marriage, family, even the gospel." Michael nodded. "I also told you that I don't want to remain angry, and I certainly don't want to remain sad. The thing I didn't tell you is that I'm not sure there is any way out. I hadn't even noticed what I was becoming, and now that I have, it seems like these feelings are part of who I am. I can't separate what my true character is from the person I have become. I don't even know where to start." Olivia stopped and looked at her husband, her eyes pleading that he would somehow understand.

Michael was surveying Livvy closely. She was now clearly waiting for him to say something, but he had no idea what that "something" should be. He sensed that his long lost Livvy's return was still a little tenuous, and he did not want to say something that would send her plummeting back into the depths she was trying to emerge from. Finally, he decided to be honest and hope for the best. "You know, Livvy, as difficult as this is for you, you still have many things to be thankful for." Michael had wanted to talk about this many times before, but he knew it would lead to an argument. Tonight, however, he felt that Livvy was searching, grasping, trying to find some answer to cling to.

"I realize that," Olivia said. She paused, and Michael could tell she was trying to form her thoughts into a fluid sentence. He waited. "Believe it or not, I have tried the old 'count your blessings' routine so I would not feel so bad about the absence of this one blessing. It just doesn't work for this. As I start to think of what I am thankful for—you, a home, the safety and security we enjoy here, food on our table, the opportunities we have had for education—I always come back around to the lack of a family. Because without children, all of that other stuff doesn't matter all that much." Olivia's thoughts were really flowing now, and Michael just remained quiet and listened.

"This isn't something that I can just compartmentalize away, tuck aside, and look at everything else. I know that I've been blessed, but I can't separate those blessings from this huge void. This taints, distorts, everything else. It is something that never goes away. Never. It's there when I first wake up in the morning and when I lay my head on my pillow at night. It's even in my dreams a lot of the time. I can't tell you how many times I've woken up crying and shaking from discovering—in a dream, mind you—that I was not pregnant. Then when I do gather my wits, I realize that I still have two weeks of agony, of wondering. Two weeks of asking myself, 'Do I feel nauseous? Could I be pregnant?' During that time, if I get a headache, or a cough, or a stuffy nose, no matter how severe, I don't want to take anything to relieve the symptoms, just in case I might be pregnant. So, I suffer through for a while, then finally succumb and take some medicine, then worry about whether I did the baby harm if, by some miracle, I was actually pregnant. Then after all of that I find out, each and every month, that I'm not pregnant, and I begin this cycle all over." Olivia stopped, and once again her eyes met Michael's. He knew she was seeking understanding; acceptance. Also a response.

"Livvy, do you know who I was thinking about today?" Michael was surprised at these words coming out of his mouth, but as he paused, he felt sure that this was the direction the conversation needed to go. "I was thinking about Brother and Sister Willis, and their little girl, Angie. She's what, five years old?"

"Yes." Olivia's voice was guarded, but her face remained calm.

"She was diagnosed with juvenile diabetes three years ago. They have to test her blood several times a day and give her insulin shots to regulate things. They have to be so careful about what she eats, to make sure that she stays healthy. That would have to be pretty tough."

Olivia only nodded, and Michael sensed he was on shaky ground, but he felt the need to press forward. "I was also thinking about Sister Webster and her three little kids. I can't imagine how difficult things have been for her since Brother Webster died. I'll bet she is lonely a lot of the time, and I would also bet that she worries every moment about what her children will do without their daddy." The waitress brought their dessert, and Olivia was glad for the diversion. If she was poking at her cheesecake, she didn't have to meet Michael's eyes. She knew where this was heading, and she didn't like it. "Then there's Brother Andrew, who has been out of work for the last few months. I imagine that wondering where his family's next meal is going to come from is a burden that he carries with him every minute.

"Sister Roberts is what, about eighty-five? She is alone in this world. No husband, no children, no grandchildren. Never even had a chance for those things."

"I get it, okay?" Olivia looked up, her eyes blazing. "I know that things could always be worse. I know that I'm not the only one with challenges, but the truth is, I just don't care about those other problems. I'm sure they are difficult, maybe even harder than this infertility, but this is the one that I'm dealing with day in and day out, month after month. This is the one that affects me. I'm not trying to be mean, but this is my reality, this is where my focus is."

"Maybe, my love, maybe that's the problem."

Olivia's throat burned as the bile rushed up. Her heart started picking up speed, and she clasped her hands together to keep them from shaking. *Did Michael just say what I thought he said? Did he really tell me that my problem is that I am focusing too much on myself and my problems?* She opened her mouth to snap back at him, but before anything came out, she remembered the promise she made to herself just this afternoon that she would no longer let this infertility be a source of contention between them. That would be easier said than done. She closed her mouth and tried to think about why Michael said that. *Is he trying to be mean and hurtful? Of course not. That's ridiculous.* So Olivia tried to move the hurt to the back burner of her mind and look at things from Michael's point of view.

Olivia glanced up at him now, but he had gone back to eating his cheesecake. Apparently, he had said everything that he had to say and was going to let her figure it out from there. Great. Of course she realized that everyone had problems and hard times. She had just never thought about them as being as real as her own problems were. Did Sister Willis think about Angie's diabetes every time she went to the grocery store to buy food for their family the way Olivia thought about not being pregnant every time she passed the baby aisle? Probably. Did Sister Webster cry herself to sleep at night with loneliness and pain in her heart the way Olivia often did? Probably. Was Brother Andrew constantly carrying the feeling that he wasn't as good as their neighbors who did have jobs and were providing for their family the way Olivia felt inferior to the mothers in their neighborhood? Probably. And what about Sister Roberts? She had never been married. Never even had a chance to have children. She probably carried a pain that was very similar to Olivia's own. Mother's Day was probably even more difficult for her.

Olivia thought about the prayer for help she had offered this afternoon, and she had an idea. Maybe Michael was right. Maybe if she could make someone else's Mother's Day a little bit brighter, her own wouldn't seem quite so gloomy. She felt her brow furrow. It would be difficult to be happy for someone else on that day, but maybe the Lord would help her. Maybe this was the first step on her way back.

"Sister Roberts?" Olivia was careful that her voice did not betray her nervousness.

"Yes?" Sister Roberts's voice carried the cautiousness borne of a lifetime of the unexpected.

"This is Olivia Spencer, from your ward."

"Oh, hello, Olivia." The cautious tone vanished and was replaced by wrinkled enthusiasm. "How are you today, dear? What can I do for you?"

"Well, I was just calling to invite you over for a Mother's Day supper with me and my husband on Sunday." There was silence for a moment, so Olivia hurried on. "It won't be a big deal or anything, just some food and visiting. Can I pick you up around 3:00?"

The silence continued just long enough that Olivia started wondering if this was a mistake. Then Sister Roberts cleared her throat and Olivia thought she heard the trace of a tear as she replied, "That would be wonderful, dear. I can't wait."

CHAPTER SEVEN

O livia stretched and yawned as her alarm clock started playing her favorite radio station. She started to get up, then remembered it was Sunday and reached over to hit the snooze button. She must have forgotten to turn off her alarm from earlier in the week. She never set it on Sunday. Then she remembered what was special about this particular Sunday, and she pulled the covers up over her head and tried to go back to sleep. Maybe she could sleep through Mother's Day. Just skip it altogether. That was when she felt Michael's toe poking her calf.

"Time to wake up, Livvy."

"No. I changed my mind. I'm going back to sleep."

"You told me you might say that. You also told me not to let you change your mind." Olivia peeled the covers off her face and looked at him. He was grinning. Her blood started racing, and she wanted to tell him to wipe that smile off his face and leave her alone. She considered it for a minute but knew he was right. She had made him promise to help her follow through on her plans for today.

"Okay, fine. I'm getting up." Olivia rolled her legs out of bed and sat up. Then she couldn't help but add, "You don't have to look so happy about it though." Michael just shrugged and kept on smiling as Olivia pulled on a pair of sweatpants and a T-shirt and headed downstairs and into the kitchen.

She began rummaging through her cupboards, gathering the ingredients she would need for the oatmeal chocolate chip cookies she was going to bake. She checked the recipe, set the temperature on the oven, and was beating the butter and sugars together when Michael came downstairs. "I'm really proud of you for doing this, Livvy. I think it's going to be a good day."

"I don't know about that, but it definitely can't be any worse than the last couple of Mother's Days. Anyway, it seems like a good idea."

"Well, I'm still proud of you. And you're right. It is a good idea." Michael leaned across the counter to kiss her forehead, then went back upstairs to shower.

An hour later Olivia was pulling the last pan of cookies out of the oven. She placed them to cool on the wax paper on her counter and went upstairs for a quick shower. She was actually getting a little bit excited about this. Maybe it would be fun after all.

After getting dressed, Olivia plated the cookies on the flowery paper plates she had chosen and sat down at the table to write the notes. There were five women she was going to take cookies to. Sister Webster was the first one on the list. This was her first Mother's Day since her husband's passing, and maybe just knowing that someone was thinking about her would help a little. She started writing:

Dear Sister Webster,
This isn't much, but I want to let you know how much I admire you.
You are an amazing lady, and are doing a great job raising your
children. Mostly, I want you to know that someone is thinking of you
today. I hope you and your children enjoy the cookies!
You are loved.
Happy Mother's Day!
Love, Your Secret Friend

The next three women all had several young children. Olivia knew them, but not well. She had watched them in church and could see that they loved their children very much and were good moms. Over the last couple of months, Olivia had also seen tears of frustration and embarrassment in each of their eyes during church meetings. One when her baby just wouldn't stop crying, the second when her toddler threw a huge fit during sacrament meeting, and the third when her preschooler didn't quite make it to the potty in time and had an accident in Primary. All of these notes were the same:

Happy Mother's Day!
I have been watching you, and I think you are a terrific mom!
Remember, you don't have to be perfect. You're doing great!
I hope you enjoy the cookies! You are loved.
Love, Your Secret Friend

Olivia got out the fifth card to write her final note and couldn't decide what to put down. She ended up writing just "Happy Mother's Day!" and taped it to the last plate of cookies. Then she loaded everything in her car and headed out.

At each of the first four stops, she parked several houses away and tried to be tricky as she set the cookies on the doorstep, rang the doorbell, and hid out of sight but where she still had a slight view of the various porches. At first she felt a little silly sneaking around, but as the four moms answered their doors, Olivia found herself smiling along with them as they picked up their cookies and read the notes. Her eyes even welled up with Sister Webster's as she read her note, then held it tightly to her chest. Sister Webster looked around briefly, but when she didn't see anyone, she just called out, "Thank you! Whoever you are, thank you!"

Olivia was wiping her eyes and smiling as she drove across town to her final stop, but as she drew nearer to the familiar house, her palms started getting sweaty, and she almost turned around. "The sooner you do this, the better you'll feel," Olivia told herself as she pulled into the driveway. She needed to deliver this plate in person. She walked up the front steps, took a deep breath, and knocked on the door.

"Happy Mother's Day, Heather." Olivia smiled and tried to swallow the lump that was rising in her throat. She held the plate of cookies out in front of her. "I brought a peace offering." Heather took the cookies and nodded. When she didn't say anything more, Olivia continued. "I just wanted to tell you how sorry I am for the terrible things I said to you the other day. There was no excuse for any of it. You are an amazing mom, and my best friend, and I'm glad that you are having a baby." Olivia was crying now, but she didn't bother to wipe the tears. "I'm still sad for me; sad that I'm not having a baby, that I'll never have a baby . . . ," Olivia stopped herself and shook her head. She was not going to wallow today. "But I am happy for you, and I'm so sorry that I was not a good enough friend to tell you that the other day. Can you forgive me?"

Heather didn't say anything at first, but then she held open her arms, and Olivia gave her a hug. "I do forgive you, Olivia. I was hurt by what you said, but then I realized that your anger wasn't really directed at me."

"You don't need to make excuses for me." Olivia tried to laugh. "I was terrible, and I'm sorry, and although I don't know how I'll ever do it or where I'll even begin, I'm going to find a way out of this. I don't want to be angry anymore, Heather. I really don't. If I try to look at the silver lining, at least I have learned that through this experience. At least I learned that I want to change. I'm just sorry that I had to learn that lesson at your expense."

"Well," Heather was smiling through her own tears now, "I'm glad I could be of service."

"I'm not sure I deserve to have such a good friend as you," Olivia said.

"Oh, yes, you do, Olivia Ann. Yes, you do."

Olivia got home from her deliveries, and she felt better. A huge part of that was the relief of apologizing to Heather, and of being forgiven, but she also felt good about giving the other ladies something to feel good about. Maybe she was going to be able to survive this day after all.

"I don't think I'm going to be able to survive this after all." Olivia was sitting in the passenger seat of their car in the church parking lot. Michael had come around to open her door for her, and Olivia was being as obstinate as a two-year-old in refusing to get out. "I mean, I was feeling okay at home, staying busy making cookies and getting supper ready for after church, but I really don't think I can go sit through the Mother's Day program. Can't I just go home?"

"I guess you can if you want, but you are the one who told me you wanted to do this. You are the one who told me not to let you weasel your way out of it."

Olivia huffed at him. "I'm not sure I used the word 'weasel,' but you're right. Let's just go in and get this over with."

Michael helped her out of the car, and they walked hand in hand into the church building. They found a seat near the back of the chapel, and Olivia tried to avoid making eye contact with anyone. This would be easier if she didn't have to talk. And then . . .

"Olivia! I'm so glad to see you here today." The voice was too enthusiastic; this was going to be bad. Olivia inhaled and turned around to face Sister Ellis. She had a giant carnation corsage pinned to her shoulder. Of course. The enthusiasm continued, "I've been wanting to talk to you. You know, all these years I've just assumed you didn't want to have a baby, what with your work at the hospital and all."

"Yes, you mentioned that to me when you brought Jace in with his broken arm." Olivia meant to disarm Sister Ellis with the comment, or at the very least embarrass her, and it almost worked. Sister Ellis paused for a moment but then rushed on.

"Well, be that as it may, now I know that isn't the case."

"Oh, you do?"

"Yes, because a couple of months ago as I was leaving my dentist's office, I saw you and Michael coming out of the fertility clinic that's across the parking lot. So it turns out that you do want a baby and you're just having a little trouble getting pregnant."

Olivia felt as if she had been slapped. Sister Ellis didn't seem to notice.

"So, I put together a little something that might help you. I've been carrying it around for a month meaning to give it to you, and when I saw you sitting here, I decided that now was as good a time as any." She tossed a small stack of papers into Olivia's lap. There was a pink staple in the corner. Then she leaned closer and whispered, "It's all different things you can try that increase your chances of getting pregnant. It's good stuff. When we started trying for our fifth child, I wasn't getting pregnant as quickly as I would have liked. We had been trying for three months already, so I looked all this up. After another two months of trying these techniques . . . BAM! Number five." She flashed a conspiratorial smile at Olivia, then added, "You can thank me later," as she hustled back to her overflowing bench.

It all happened so quickly. Michael, who was visiting with the people on the bench in front of them, didn't even realize what conversation had just taken place. He settled back into his seat and noticed something was wrong when Olivia did not return the light squeeze he gave her hand. Her jaw was tight, tears of anger flashed in her eyes, and her hands were beginning to shake. She was breathing very deliberately trying to calm herself, but without much luck. Then the bishop stood up and began the meeting. Michael mouthed, "What happened?" and Olivia handed the stack of papers to him. He started flipping through them, and his eyebrows raised in surprise at the content. Then understanding came, and he put his arm around Livvy's shoulder. He forced himself to stay in control. He tried to calm Livvy's breathing by first matching hers, then gradually slowing down. It worked. He put his lips to her ear and whispered, "Who?" Livvy jerked her head in the direction of the Ellis's bench, and there sat Sister Ellis looking just like the proverbial kitten who had swallowed the canary. Michael didn't need to ask anything more.

Michael had a hard time focusing on the program. He just kept his arm tight around Livvy's shoulder and fumed. Just when it seemed they were going to make it through the day, Sister Ellis had to be overly "helpful." That was the worst part about it. Michael knew that she really believed she was helping them. She just didn't understand, and her ignorance was hurting his wife. He decided that he needed to talk to Sister Ellis after the meeting and let her know that they wouldn't be needing any more help, thank you very much. With this decision in mind, he chanced a sideways glance at Olivia, and to his surprise, she seemed to have relaxed. He watched her for the remainder of the program, and although her eyes welled up now and then at something she heard from the pulpit, she seemed to be doing pretty well.

When the meeting ended and the bishop asked all of the women to stand so the young men could give them each a small potted pansy, Olivia hesitated and then slowly stood with only a slight flush on her cheeks. She kept her eyes focused straight ahead until one of the boys approached their bench. He held out the small purple flower, and Olivia's hand clenched in a fist momentarily before she took a deep breath, opened her hand, and accepted the gift with a quiet "Thank you." Then she sat down, discreetly brushing the moisture from her eyes as she gathered up her things.

Michael again leaned over until his lips were brushing her ear. "Don't worry, I'm going to go have a little chat with Sister Ellis."

Olivia eyed him tenderly, then said, "Thanks. I love you so much, but actually, I want to go talk to her myself." Michael felt the panic rippling through him at the thought of the emotion Livvy had unloaded on Heather. Olivia must have recognized the look in his eyes, because she said, "Don't worry. I'll behave myself." Then she squeezed his hand and merged into the crowd.

"Sister Ellis, could I talk to you for a minute? Maybe outside?"

"Oh sure, Olivia! Sure, sure, sure!" They made their way to the front doors and stepped out into the bright, May sunlight. "So, Olivia, did you look over the papers? Do you have any questions?"

"I did look at them briefly," Olivia replied, "but I don't have any questions. Actually, I wanted to give them back to you, because they won't do me any good." Sister Ellis opened her mouth to interrupt, but Olivia continued on. "You see, Michael and I have been married for four years next month, and we have been trying nearly the entire time to get pregnant." Olivia was pleased with how level her voice was. She didn't want this to be a frosty conversation, but she did have a few things she needed to say.

"We have been working with the best specialists in the state for the last two years. We have tried everything that is available to try, short of in vitro fertilization. The only reason we have not done in vitro is that after the extensive testing to determine whether we had a chance of it working for us, our doctors discovered that I have some physical issues that will not allow an embryo to implant. It won't matter if I stand on my head while sipping herbal tea spiked with baby aspirin and stay in bed for two full weeks, I am not going to get pregnant. So while I understand that you are trying to help me, the reality is that you are only making a painful situation harder to bear. So, in the future, I would appreciate it if you would keep your fertility manuals, as well as your 'helpful' suggestions to yourself." Olivia smiled and squeezed Sister Ellis's arm as she turned and walked back into the building. Only then did her eyes begin to burn, and Olivia sought the refuge of a bathroom stall to silently let the tears flow.

It took Olivia some time to regain her composure. Then she splashed her face with cool water, wiped away the black mascara streaks on her face, and went to find Michael. He was standing outside the door of the Relief Society room, and when he saw Olivia, he quickly closed the distance between them and put his arms around her. Sunday school was still going on, so they had a few moments of relative privacy there in the hallway. "Are you okay?" he asked.

"You know, surprisingly, I think I *am* doing okay. That was a terrible curve ball Sister Ellis threw at me, but as I sat there being upset and angry, it came time for the sacrament to be passed. I started thinking about the Savior—really thinking about Him for the first time in quite a while. I got thinking about how He suffered, silently, alone. I have spent so much time and energy over the past years focusing on my suffering that I forgot about His. I have complained that I have done nothing to deserve this pain while overlooking that the Savior was also innocent of any offense. I have spent so much time demanding the blessing of being pregnant that I have forgotten the principle of 'Not my will, but Thine be done.' As those thoughts flooded through me, I realized that this is my starting point. I told you that I didn't even know where to begin to climb out of my own personal hole, but now I know. I have to begin with the Savior. I'm not sure how to do that because I'm still angry with Him. But I believe that He is the key." Olivia shrugged and ducked her head, a little embarrassed at her outburst of pure emotion.

Michael hugged her, then pushed her back to arm's length so he could look into her eyes. "Livvy, you're amazing. Really amazing." This time she blushed and buried her face in his shoulder for another squeeze. "So, my curiosity is getting the better of me. What did you say to Sister Ellis?"

"I just explained our situation to her and told her that her assistance would not be needed. I didn't even cry . . . until I left her." Olivia managed a grin, which broke into a smile and a sparkle in her eye as she thought of how good it felt to ask Sister Ellis to mind her own business.

Michael laughed. "Now that's the girl I married. I haven't seen the a-basketball-just-smashed-my-nose-but-I'm-going-to-be-fine-because-I'm-tough look in way too long!"

The last hour of church was uneventful. Sister Ellis would not look Olivia in the face throughout Relief Society, but Olivia wasn't too worried about that. She hadn't been rude or mean; she just said what needed to be said. For so long, Olivia's world had been spinning out of control, and it felt good to take control of her life, even in that small way.

Olivia caught Sister Roberts on the way out the door and said, "Remember, I'll be by to pick you up at 3:00!"

"I'll be ready. I can't wait!"

Michael and Olivia walked through the door to the sweet smell of pot roast, potatoes, and caramelized onions. That was the smell that reminded Olivia of her own mom on the Sunday afternoons from her childhood. She was excited to talk to her mom today. Olivia could call her in fifteen minutes. Her mom and dad were serving a mission in rural New England, and Olivia missed talking to her. She knew her mom felt bad about leaving in the middle of all of these treatments, but Olivia had assured her that a mission was where she wanted her to be. Olivia set the table, put the rolls in the oven, then picked up the phone to call her mom.

They had a great conversation. Olivia's mom mentioned that Olivia sounded happier than she had in a long time. Olivia didn't go into details but just told her mom that she had grown tired of being angry and sad and was trying to work her way out of that. Her mom didn't offer any trite advice; she just listened. After about thirty minutes, Olivia glanced at the clock, "I've got to go, Mom. I'm picking Sister Roberts up in ten minutes for a Mother's Day supper over here. I've told you about her."

"Is she the older lady who never married?"

"Yeah, that's her. I just thought she could use a little company today." Olivia's mom was quiet for a moment. When she started talking again, there was a slight quiver there.

"I'm really proud of you, Olivia. I think that was a great idea! I love you!"

"I love you too, Mom. Happy Mother's Day!"

Olivia knocked on Sister Roberts's door at 3:00 sharp. She answered it immediately. She was still in her Sunday dress, and Olivia was glad that she and Michael had stayed dressed up too. It was a little more special this way. Olivia produced a plastic box from behind her back. Sister Roberts smiled when Olivia opened it and said, "We got this corsage for you. Do you mind if I pin it on your dress?" Sister Roberts could only nod, and Olivia concentrated hard on the pin so Sister Roberts would not be embarrassed about the tears shining in her eyes.

They had a great supper. Sister Roberts loved hearing about Olivia's work at the hospital and was excited to learn that Michael taught school, as she herself had been a first grade teacher for many years. "I loved so many of the children who came through my class-room," she told them. "I always hoped that I would marry and have children myself, but as that never happened, I called my students my 'adopted' children. Doing something I loved and, hopefully, helping some of those kids along the way, saved me."

When the meal was over and the visiting was through, Olivia drove Sister Roberts home. As they walked to the front door, Sister Roberts turned to Olivia with her eyes glowing and said, "Thank you so much, Olivia! You know, I have long since gotten over the fact that I was not meant to marry and have children in this life, but I always wished that I could have a special Mother's Day. One where I was the guest of honor and felt important and loved." Her voice cracked as she continued. "You gave that to me today, and I want to thank you for the best Mother's Day of my life."

Olivia was surprised to find that she was smiling and humming as she drove home. Michael met her at the doorway with a grin of his own. "I thought that went well," he said.

"It did go well," Olivia responded.

Michael kept smiling and said, "I think we're on the road to recovery."

"Don't get too carried away," Olivia said as her smile faded and her brow furrowed. "I survived the day, but this doesn't solve anything. I'm afraid I've still got a long way to go."

"Well then, we'll just keep taking things one step at a time."

"Hey, Grandma. I just called to wish you a Happy Mother's Day. Sorry we couldn't make it down, but I'm still planning on coming tomorrow." Olivia's grandmother lived about forty-five miles away.

"Don't worry about it, Olivia. I had a great day—a full house. All of your cousins were here with their kids."

"Are they still there? Do I need to let you go?"

"No. They left about an hour ago. Actually, I was just thinking about you and wondering how your day was." Olivia's grandma was one of the few people who knew how rough things had been for Olivia over these last years. For some reason it was easy to talk to her. Easier than talking to Heather or her mom or anyone. Grandma never tried to fix anything. She never really even tried to make Olivia feel better. She just listened and said she was sorry that Olivia was sad.

"You'll never believe it, Grandma, but I'm feeling okay. Not terrific, but okay. My day wasn't too bad." Olivia knew that was not the answer her grandma had been expecting.

"Oh? What did you do?"

"Well, I got up early and made cookies, then secretly delivered them around to some of the moms in my ward. Church started out a little rough, but it ended up okay. Then we had an older lady from our ward who has no family come over for supper. It was nice."

"Hmm. Interesting."

"What's interesting?"

"I've been thinking about giving something to you for a while now, but the timing never seemed right. Maybe it is now."

"What is it?"

"It's something that's very important to me, very special. You will have to make me a promise before I give it to you, though."

"Sure, Grandma. Anything." Olivia was curious. She had no idea what it could be, or what kind of promise might be attached.

"You just have to promise to read it."

That was an easy promise to make. "Sure I'll read it." As she said it, Olivia thought about the stack of papers she had been handed this morning in church. "Wait! Unless it's some sort of fertility manual or a how-to guide to pregnancy. You know those won't help me."

Grandma laughed right out loud. "Give me a little credit, Olivia. It's your great-aunt Elizabeth's journal. I want you to read it."

Olivia paused, caught off guard. "What did you say?"

"I said that I want you to read your great-aunt Elizabeth's journal. Surely you remember her. You were sixteen when she died, after all."

"Of course I remember your older sister, Grandma. She moved in with you after Grandpa died, when I was ten. But I don't understand why you want me to read her journal. She and I are very different."

"Oh, you think so, do you?"

"Well, sure. I mean, I know that she never had any kids, but that was her choice. I know she had a lot of great experiences and helped a lot of people, just like she and Uncle Arthur planned. She was always talking about how her life had gone according to the plan and she was truly happy. I'm just not sure I'll be able to relate to her."

"Elizabeth was a very different person than you think she was. She was my best friend, and I just thought you might enjoy getting to know her a little better. You might find that you two have more in common than you think. Besides, she taught me a lot about life. Maybe there's something you could learn from her too." Grandma paused, but when Olivia didn't comment, she went on. "So, will you do it?"

"Of course, I'll read it, Grandma."

"Good. You can pick it up when you come and visit me tomorrow."

CHAPTER EIGHT

Olivia's eyes moved over the old, leather-bound journal that her grandma had given her. She carefully lifted the worn brown cover and was surprised to discover that the paper was in pretty good condition. She inhaled the "old" smell of the book and scanned the small, neat script that covered the pages.

Olivia wasn't sure what her first memory of Great-Aunt Elizabeth was. She was scattered throughout a lot of Olivia's childhood, mostly through letters and pictures. Great-Uncle Arthur had passed away when Olivia was just a baby, and Great-Aunt Elizabeth had spent the next years serving several missions for the Church all over the world. Olivia remembered her saying that the Lord had blessed her with the good health and the financial ability to go and serve, so she was going to take advantage of the opportunity.

Olivia had been ten years old when Great-Aunt Elizabeth came into her life full-time. She had shown up on Grandma's front porch the day of Grandpa's funeral and announced, "There's no sense in both of us being alone when we could just as easily be together." That sentence formed the framework for the way Olivia always perceived Great-Aunt Elizabeth. She always seemed to refuse to look at the down side of things and was constantly on the look out for something good or beautiful or hopeful. Olivia remembered many times when Great-Aunt Elizabeth would take the time to point out some tiny beauty to her: a ladybug under a leaf, the first tulips beginning to peek through the soil in early spring, or a rainbow that seemed magical as it glimmered through the dampness of a summer rain shower.

Reminiscing over her memories of Great-Aunt Elizabeth, Olivia decided that getting to know her a little better through the pages of this journal might be a nice way to spend her day off. She snuggled a little deeper into the overstuffed armchair, tucked a blanket around her knees, and began reading.

April 1, 1929

I am beginning today, on my eighteenth birthday to compile a journal of my life. I feel impressed to write down a little about my life and experiences. I do not claim that there has been anything significant or out of the ordinary to occur thus far, but somehow, it seems important that I write.

Olivia's eyes ran over several pages that contained a brief history of Elizabeth's life to that point as well as information about her parents and each of her siblings. They contained a treasure trove of information about these people, and Olivia was thoroughly enjoying herself when an entry caught her eye.

April 19, 1929

Tomorrow I will marry Arthur Morris, a kind and loving young man who has been courting me for the past year. He loves me, and I him, but most important, he loves the Lord and honors the priesthood that he bears. My family and I, along with Arthur and his family, arrived in St. George this afternoon, and we will be sealed together for time and all eternity tomorrow morning in the holy temple. I feel so blessed to be able to embark on this great journey of marriage and family with a good man who I truly love. I look forward with great anticipation to the day when, having taken part with God in the creation process, I bear our children. For me, there can be no name so noble as that of "mother" and I look forward with joy to the day when I will be called such by my own sweet children.

Olivia felt the air rush from her lungs. Her eyes jumped back to the top of the page and carefully re-read the entry she had just finished. If it were not written there by Elizabeth's own hand, Olivia would never have believed it. Great-Aunt Elizabeth had never had any children, but Olivia was always under the impression that that was the way she wanted it. Whenever the topic came up, Elizabeth commented that children had not been in the plan for her. As a young woman with many hopes, dreams, and plans for her own future, Olivia always assumed that Great-Aunt Elizabeth meant that children were not a part of the life she wanted. Surely that was the case—how else could she have been so happy, so hopeful, and so full of peace, with no children? And yet . . . the words written on this page conveyed a great desire for children. Maybe these were just the sentimental words of a young woman on the night before her wedding. Whatever the case, Olivia was now extremely interested in what surprises this journal might contain, and continued reading eagerly.

It wasn't until her stomach growled that Olivia realized how absorbed she had been in the journal. A quick glance at the clock told her it was nearly two o'clock in the afternoon, and her body was scolding her for missing lunch. She placed a small paper bookmark in the journal and closed it, carefully marking her place for when lunch was over. She was tempted to read while she ate, but thought better of it, knowing that with her "natural grace," as she liked to call it, she would probably drip mustard or spill milk all over the priceless pages.

Olivia's hands worked automatically as she quickly prepared a ham and cheese sandwich and grabbed a bag of potato chips from the pantry shelf, but her mind was spinning. She sat down on a barstool at the kitchen counter to eat, allowing her mind to wander back over the words she had been reading all morning. As Olivia delved further and further into the journal, she found that Great-Aunt Elizabeth had hoped and prayed and longed for a child as much as Olivia herself did. In the beginning of her marriage to Arthur, Elizabeth tried to brush aside the fears that began surfacing when month after month passed without a pregnancy, but as the first twelve months and then twenty-four and then thirty passed without so much as a single conception, Elizabeth had progressively become more absorbed in grief and anger.

Olivia was anxious to continue reading, so she quickly downed the remainder of her sandwich and popped a few more chips into her mouth before wiping her hands on the bright yellow towel hanging from the oven door and resuming her position in her favorite armchair. She carefully opened the journal and immersed herself in a world that was eighty years (give or take) removed from the time in which she lived, but felt eerily familiar.

March 15, 1932

Today I discovered, as I have each and every month since Arthur and I were married, that I am not pregnant. Words cannot accurately express the depths of sorrow and despair that I find myself sinking into. Some days the pain and heartache is so severe that I wonder if I will ever be able to drag myself out. To make matters worse, I said some terrible things to Arthur today. As he tried to console me, I'm afraid that I turned on him. I told him that he had no idea how it felt to be broken, both physically and emotionally. Although I could tell by the hurt in his eyes that my words had stung him, he remained calm and composed. After a few moments, he replied, "I suppose you're right, Elizabeth. Although I grieve every month for your pain, as well as for our unfulfilled dreams, I do not know how this must make you feel."

He paused for a moment, and I used the silence to snap back at him, "Then I suggest you keep your sympathy to yourself!"

To my immense surprise, Arthur's eyes filled with tears as he gazed at me, searching my eyes. "My dear, sweet Elizabeth. While I cannot imagine the depths of pain and anguish that have caused you—my beautiful bride—to become so angry, I know that the Savior can. He has suffered all, so that He can succor you, even through this sorrow. Please turn to Him. Please seek His strength. The heartache of not having children is one that I believe I can overcome in time, but the thought of losing you to this anger brings a pain that I cannot even bear to think about. Please." And with that, he sadly left the room.

That all happened this morning, and although I want to heed his words, I cannot. How can I turn this over to the Savior, when He is the one withholding the blessing of children from me? Arthur is right about one thing, though. I have become angry—angry with God, angry with myself, angry with other women who are bearing children, and even angry with Arthur. I don't want to feel this way, but I just don't know how to let it go. I don't know what to do.

April 20, 1932

I started planting my garden today. Some may say that it's too early, but mother always said that as soon as the oak trees in the north hills get their buds, it's time to plant. Well, I was wandering through the hills yesterday trying to sort through my feelings and emotions, and I noticed that the oak buds were growing, so I planted today. There were also tiny sprigs of green trying to push their way up through the earth, and I saw a pair of robins building a nest in one of the trees. Signs of spring and new life are all around me. All around me . . . but not in me. Many people have tried to tell me not to think or worry about getting pregnant, that it will happen in the Lord's own time. They tell me to "count my blessings." I do know that I have been blessed. While so much of the country is in turmoil at this time, and so many people are suffering for lack of the bare necessities of life, life is continuing on as usual in this beautiful little valley we call home. Maybe that's because the people here have never had much in the way of worldly possessions; nobody had much to lose. But I just can't count my blessings when I do not have the one thing that everybody else here does have: a family.

"Family is what really matters." That's what my neighbor Edith told me yesterday, after confiding in me that she was expecting their first child. She has been married for three months, and is giddy with the idea of being a mother. I could only nod and mutter my congratulations before stumbling into my house clutching my sides, trying to lessen the feeling that my chest might tear wide open. I know she was just caught up in her own excitement and probably had no idea how her words would cut through me, but I can't help but feeling that she should have been more considerate!

Today was also my third wedding anniversary. I told Arthur that I did not want to make a fuss over it. I don't want to commemorate thirty-six times of failing to get pregnant. He wished me a happy anniversary this morning, then set out to mend some fence. I know that he is unhappy because I am sad and angry, but I don't know what to do. Mother Morris did stop by with an anniversary wish, but she took the chance (as she always does) to give me "helpful" suggestions for getting pregnant. "Eat this, stay in bed, lie down in this position," and so on and so on. I wanted to tell her that she needed to accept the fact that Arthur and I are never going to have kids. I didn't actually say anything, but I am starting to believe that I will never be blessed with a child, and all of her well-meaning advice is just awkward and embarrassing and makes me feel worse.

At least the day ended well with Arthur and I enjoying a nice meal together and some conversation. I just pray he doesn't give up on me before I can get my emotions figured out. Everything else aside, I know that I love him, and I cannot begin to imagine my life without him. I hope that my anger has not caused irreparable damage to our relationship.

April 28, 1932

I have never been angrier than I am right now! We were enjoying a nice visit with Arthur's family at Mother Morris's home when Arthur's younger sister Emily and her husband Jacob announced that they were expecting their first child. They believe the baby will be born in November. I am only a little ashamed to admit that when I heard the news, rather than being happy for them, I was upset. I was upset that it was them and not us. They were only just married in February! Besides, Emily is three years younger than me. I should have been first! I think that Arthur must have known that this news would be difficult for me, because he gently reached over and took my hand. Apparently, the gesture did not go unnoticed by Mother Morris, because she blurted out—right there in front of all eight of Arthur's siblings and all of our nieces and nephews—"You shouldn't be consoling her, Arthur. If Elizabeth was living her life in a pleasing manner to Heavenly Father, she would be blessed with a child too." For a moment, I just sat there staring at her, too stunned to speak. The room had gone silent, and every eye was now on me. I opened my mouth to speak but no words would come out. The lump in my throat was making speech impossible. As I stood, I felt the hot, wet tears begin to stream down my cheeks. I did the only thing I could think of in the moment. I turned around and walked out the door. But as the door was closing behind me, I heard her voice say, "See, she knows that it's true!" The sobs tore from my chest as I ran, blindly, the few blocks to my home. How, how, how could she have discovered the innermost thoughts of my mind? How could she have possibly guessed that this is the very thing that eats at my soul day in and day out? My dark, secret fear: that I'm just not good enough. That somewhere, at some time, in some phase of my existence, I must have done something that so disappointed my Father in Heaven that I am now unworthy to bear a child. It is a fear that I have never disclosed to anyone. Not even Arthur, and now his mother has just pronounced it as truth in front of the entire family. How dare she? She has no right! How could she be so thoughtless and cruel? She has to have known how that would hurt. Doesn't she realize the pain and heartache I go through each and every month? Doesn't she know the longing

I feel . . . not only for a baby for myself, but also for a child for my dear husband? Doesn't she know that it haunts me that I am apparently unable to perform this one supreme act of creation? It all makes me so angry! Why is Heavenly Father doing this to me? He could make this better if He wanted to! Why won't He help me?

Olivia had to stop reading. Her vision was lost in the sea of tears that was threatening to overtake her. She was gulping for air, as though her pain was drowning her. She closed the journal and leaned her head into the palms of her hands and let the sobs rack her body. Olivia cried long and hard as she allowed herself to admit her own feelings of self-doubt. She knew well the secret that Great-Aunt Elizabeth had kept locked in her heart; for Olivia was keeping the same one.

As the tears of anguish slowly began to subside, they were replaced by tears of relief. Olivia had always believed herself to be alone in her feelings. Until just recently when she revealed a few things to Michael, she was never able to share them with anyone and had kept them tucked neatly away. But Elizabeth had felt the same agony, the same heartache, the same disappointment, and the same anger. It was a glimmer of support when Olivia most needed it.

Olivia allowed her tears and emotions to run their course, finally ending in the dull ache she had grown accustomed to. Then she took a few steadying breaths and let her mind wander. *Could these really be the words of Great-Aunt Elizabeth? My great-aunt Elizabeth?* Olivia was having difficulty reconciling her own memories of the happy, easy going, elderly woman who was always at peace, with the picture painted by the journal: that of a heartsick and agonized young woman groping desperately to discover some shred of hope or help that would bring meaning to her own personal agony. A woman, Olivia was reluctant to admit, who was far too similar to the one reflected in the mirror over the last few years.

CHAPTER NINE

Great-Aunt Elizabeth's journal had dug up some of Olivia's own painful realities and forced her to look at them in the light. Somehow, just knowing that she wasn't alone in her feelings made things seem a little brighter. She was also starting to feel something new. Not hope, exactly, more the desire for hope; the belief that maybe in the future she could learn to hope again. After all, somewhere in the pages of the journal, Elizabeth began her journey from the anguished and angry young bride into the peaceful, mature woman that Olivia remembered. Maybe, just maybe, the journal could help Olivia make a similar transformation.

On her next day off Olivia again snuggled into her favorite chair by the window and started to read. Elizabeth had pressed forward as best she could, but when month after month after month passed with no pregnancy, she began distancing herself from everyone, including, and especially, the Savior. Olivia cried with Elizabeth as she read of the despair and hopelessness that had gripped them both. And then . . .

November 15, 1932
Arthur spent the afternoon at his sister Sarah's home. It is Sarah's oldest daughter Jane's fourteenth birthday. I, of course, passed on the celebration.

It's just easier that way. When he returned home, he told me something that I have been unable to put out of my mind. He said, "I observed something very interesting today while I was with all my nieces and nephews. All of their parents love them very much. They want them to be happy. If it were up to my sisters and brothers, their children would never be sad, mad, angry, upset, or hurt in any way. However, because the parents are wiser and can look ahead farther than their children can, they often have to do things that upset the children, but are for their own good." I was just getting ready to tell Arthur to quit rambling, but he did not give me the chance. He simply pressed forward. "For example," he said, "Sarah's twelve-year-old son, Joseph, wanted to leave in the late afternoon to head out to the old mill with some friends. Joseph is a good boy, and so are his friends. Sarah knows there would be no serious mischief, but she also knows that the weather is unpredictable this time of year, and she did not want the boys getting trapped in a storm. Also, as it was rather late in the day, Sarah knew there was a chance that it would get dark before the boys returned home and that the temperature would become frigid after sundown. Consequently, she told Joseph that he had to stay home. He was angry, and I could see in Sarah's eyes that she wished it could be different, but ultimately she knew what was best for him in that situation. After that happened, I started watching closely to see if this pattern repeated itself.

"I was not disappointed. Before long, Sarah and Peter's two-year-old daughter Charlotte became very interested in the fireplace. She wanted to be right next to it and kept running over to it whenever she was not on Peter's lap. Peter kept trying to explain that it was hot and would hurt her, but she did not understand. Ultimately, Peter had to hold Charlotte for the remainder of the evening to keep her safe. Charlotte was not happy about that and could not understand that this experience was really helping her. Peter felt bad that Charlotte was sad, but he knows that his job as her father is to protect her and teach her." I asked Arthur what he was getting at, but he told me to keep listening and I would see.

He continued. "There were several more similar situations that occurred throughout the afternoon, but I will tell you just one more. Sarah's seven-year-old daughter, Mary, was upset at all of the attention her sister Jane was getting. It did not matter to Mary that today was Jane's birthday, and that there were many children there who all needed to be cared for. Mary wanted her mother's undivided attention and she wanted it all afternoon. Mary began yelling at the younger children and even pushing some of them.

I suspected that was Mary's way of gaining the desired attention, and I wondered if it would work. When Sarah realized what was going on, she came and gently took Mary's hand and led her out of the room. Sarah came back a moment later without Mary, and because of what I had been observing, I was curious to know what had happened. So I took Sarah aside and asked her. Tears filled her eyes as she told me that she had taken Mary to the little storage room at the back of the house and told her that she could not come out until she could stop pushing and yelling. I told Sarah that I thought that she had done a great job, and asked her why she was crying. 'Because,' she replied, 'I hate to discipline my children. Joseph is mad that we will not let him go to the mill. Charlotte is upset that she can't play near the fire. Mary is in there crying right now. I wish I could give them everything they want and everything they ask for right in the moment that they ask. But I cannot. It is my job to help them to learn what is and is not appropriate. It is my job to help them learn what is and is not safe. It is my job to help them learn what is right and what is wrong. There are lessons that they need to learn, which they would not learn if I gave them everything they wanted. So, although it makes me sad to see them unhappy, I discipline them and tell them no and teach them even when it is difficult because as much as I want them to be happy right now, there is something I want more than that. I want them to be happy as adults. I want them to learn the lessons they need to now, so that they can grow up to be happy and healthy people and good members of the community.'

"I gave Sarah a hug and told her she was a very good mom, and then I started thinking." Arthur stopped and waited for me to comment, so I gave in and asked him what he was thinking about.

"Well, I got wondering if that is how Heavenly Father feels about His children. I think that our loving Heavenly Father would like to give all of His children everything that they want and ask for. I think that He wants all of His children to be happy. I think it makes Him sad when His children are sad. I also got thinking that maybe, like Sarah, there is something that our Heavenly Father wants more than He wants His children to be happy right now. Maybe He wants His children to learn the things they need to learn on this earth and gain the knowledge and experience that they will need so that they can be happy forever. Even if it means some disappointment and sadness right now."

When Arthur got done with his story, I asked him what he was getting at. He just hugged me and told me that he loved me, and then went out to chop the firewood. As I mentioned earlier, I have not been able to let this go. I have been thinking and thinking about it, and I am beginning to wonder if Arthur is right. All of these years that we have been married, I have been wondering why Heavenly Father is punishing me, why He will not allow me to have a family, why He has turned His back on me. Now, I am not sure that is the case. What if the things I need to learn in order for me to be happy in the eternities require that I go through this now? What if Heavenly Father has another mission on this earth for me? What if conceiving and giving birth to lots of babies is my own will, and not necessarily the plan that Heavenly Father has for me? What if He, as a loving and all-knowing parent, is allowing me to have these sad experiences now, so that I may come through them and be the woman He needs me to be on the other side? What if He has been saddened each time I have turned away from Him in my grief and anger? What if His arms are open and He has blessings that He is waiting to give me that I am not willing to seek because I am too focused on what I want? What if being barren is simply some part of living in a mortal world with a mortal body, and my task now, is to learn to turn to the Savior and be happy in spite of it?

Right now, I do not have any answers, but I believe that for the first time, I am finally asking the right questions.

Olivia closed the book. She had never even considered the questions that Elizabeth had penned, but there was a familiarity about them that struck a chord with Olivia. Could she be right? Could this be her starting point? Maybe if Olivia quit blaming Heavenly Father and Jesus, maybe if she quit blaming herself, maybe if she laid aside blame all together, she could begin to let go of the anger. Maybe if she stopped pleading and demanding and bargaining for a pregnancy, and instead asked Heavenly Father concerning His will for her, she would receive the answers she needed. She felt certain that moving forward would be difficult, but the shadow of a path seemed to be forming in her mind. Up until now, there had been only blackness, anger, and confusion. Olivia still couldn't see very far into the distance, but thanks to Great-Aunt Elizabeth, she could now see just enough to take the first step. It felt like the right way to go.

Olivia consumed the remainder of Elizabeth's journal. It was amazing to watch a transformation that took years to be completed, transpire over the course of several afternoons of reading. The anger did not go away overnight and neither did the pain. The difference was that Elizabeth was now turning to the source of truth and light and hope and healing, the Savior, instead of away from Him. She wrote of hours and hours of earnest prayer where she pled for relief from the anger and help in overcoming her own insecurities and shortcomings. Elizabeth prayed to understand Heavenly Father's will for her and for the strength to move forward and accomplish it.

She began immersing herself in the scriptures and was over-whelmed at the Spirit that flowed into her life as a result. And Elizabeth began serving. She offered to tend her neighbor Edith's baby for a few hours several times a week. Whenever one of her sisters-in-law had a baby (which seemed to happen quite often), she went to work taking care of the other children, cleaning the house, baking bread, making meals, doing anything that needed to be done. It wasn't always fun, and sometimes being around the children was sharply painful, but over time, as Elizabeth began to realize that she was having a positive influence on her nieces and nephews, as well as other children in the community, that pain began to dull around the edges. As Elizabeth turned to the Savior and fully embraced the Atonement, the healing came.

Elizabeth became a friend to everyone. She searched out oppor-tunities to help, and then followed through, often with no one else knowing. She had served in the Church, mostly in the Primary. Olivia read of the love she had for so many Primary children over the years, and smiled as Elizabeth would rejoice in their small successes.

She and Arthur had served a mission together before he died, and she served three more after. When the opportunity arose to come live with her younger sister Anna (Olivia's grandma) she helped Anna through the death of her husband, and the two of them became very close.

Olivia was surprised to find her own name sprinkled through-out those last years of Great-Aunt Elizabeth's life, and it made her happy to read of the joy that being with Olivia and her brother had brought. She had loved them as if they were her own grandchildren.

The last entry of Great-Aunt Elizabeth's journal was dated the week before she died. The penmanship had grown shaky, but the spirit was clearer than ever.

I believe that my time on this earth is coming to a close. As I have looked back over my life, I feel satisfied that I have, indeed, become the woman that my Heavenly Father intended me to be. The way was not always easy, but I know that through the Savior and His Atonement, ALL things can be made well. I know that at the times when my heart ached in loneliness, my Savior became my dearest friend. When my arms seemed utterly empty, He filled them through giving me the strength to serve others. At the times when I felt abandoned, it was not the Savior who had turned His back; it was me.

Now, I do not know if anyone will ever read this journal, but I hope that in some future day one of the children that I have loved over the years will be able to find some comfort and solace in knowing that I was able to overcome. Not alone—no not ever alone—but with the help of my dear Elder Brother.

I feel to rejoice for soon, I believe very soon, I will be reunited with my sweet Arthur. The love of my life—the man who had the patience and the courage to reach out and save me when I had no desire to be saved. I think he will be proud of me. And my soul burns within me as I anticipate the moment when I will meet my Savior once again. For it was He that made me whole.

Yes, my life has indeed gone according to the plan. The peace and joy I have felt would not have been possible otherwise. I will be forever grateful that I was able to give up my own plan for life and embrace my Heavenly Father's. May you, dear reader, whoever you are, have the courage to do the same.

Olivia reverently closed the journal and squeezed it to her chest as the tears rolled down her cheeks. She determined that she would do as Elizabeth had. She would seek out Heavenly Father's will for her, and she would serve. She had read first-hand that it would not be easy, but Olivia knew it was right. Yes, if Elizabeth could do it, so could she! At that thought, Olivia felt a warmth flow through her and she knew that Great-Aunt Elizabeth was very close by, and that she was smiling.

CHAPTER TEN

Over the next few days, Olivia tried to consider what Heavenly Father's plan for her own life was. She was a very good nurse, and there were lots of ways she could help other people in that capacity. She could also serve in the Church as Elizabeth had done, and she could continue to look for ways to help her friends and neighbors.

Olivia hadn't prayed that she would be able to get pregnant since Dr. Ball had called with the news that a pregnancy wasn't in her future, but no matter how she tried, she couldn't get the thought of being a mother out of her mind. In fact, as Olivia prayed to know Heavenly Father's will, the idea of her with a baby in her arms seemed to become more clearly formed. Olivia was frustrated by the image, and after several days, voiced those feelings to Heather as they were visiting on the phone.

"I'm trying to move past this, but the thought of me as a mother seems to be getting stronger. I don't know how that can be after what my test results showed," Olivia said.

"Do you think there's any way the results were wrong?" Heather asked.

"No," Olivia said. "After my initial shock I requested the results and went over them myself. It all looked right. When you add that to the years we've spent trying to get pregnant with no luck . . ." Olivia shrugged. "I feel certain that I'll never get pregnant. I wish I could accept that I'm not going to be a mom and move forward."

"I don't know what to say," Heather replied.

"Me neither."

It had been several weeks since finishing Elizabeth's journal, and Olivia was no closer to discovering an answer than she had been the day she closed the old book. In fact, some of the peace she had felt at realizing that someone else had been in her same situation and had experienced similar feelings, was beginning to leave.

"Grandma, the journal helped for all of two weeks, and now I'm as frustrated as ever!" Olivia complained over the telephone one afternoon. "Elizabeth and I had so many of the same feelings and heartaches, and when she finally accepted that she wasn't going to have a baby, she was able to press forward and work through her trials with faith. I thought it would be the same for me, but no matter how I try, I can't get away from the feeling that I'm going to be a mom. And not only in the next life, which I considered, but here. In this life."

Grandma was silent for a moment—long enough that Olivia finally asked, "Did I lose you?"

"No, Olivia, I'm still here. I'm just thinking."

"About?" Olivia prompted when the silence continued.

"You've been praying to know Heavenly Father's will concerning your life?"

"Yes. But like I said, I keep coming back to motherhood."

"Hmm. Interesting."

"Thanks, Grandma. You always say that and it's always very helpful." Olivia laughed.

"I just mean that if you've truly been praying and being humble and are willing to do whatever God asks of you, and you keep coming back to being a mom, then . . ."

Olivia knew her grandma was waiting for her to come up with the answer on her own, but she had no idea where she was headed this time. "Then what, Grandma? I'm not following you."

"Then there must be a way for you to be a mom," Grandma replied matter-of-factly.

Olivia sighed. Her grandmother didn't fully understand the medical side of this. "Grandma," Olivia continued softly, "I'm never going to get pregnant. We've tried everything, including priesthood blessings, and it is not Heavenly Father's will for me to be healed. There will be no pregnancies for me."

"Olivia," Grandma pressed, "I didn't say you would get pregnant. I said there must be a way for you to be a mom, if that's the answer you keep getting."

Olivia started to protest, but her grandma stopped her. "Just think about it, Olivia. I'm sure you'll figure something out."

"Okay," Olivia conceded. "I'll think about it. Bye. I love you."

"Bye, Olivia. Love you, too."

Olivia did think about it—a lot—for the rest of that day and the next, but couldn't see any way she could be a mom without getting pregnant. As she knelt to say her nighttime prayers, Olivia stopped. If anyone could figure this out . . . well . . . it was worth a shot.

"Heavenly Father," she began. "I have been feeling that thy will for me on this earth includes motherhood, but is there any way that I can be a mom when I can't get pregnant?"

Olivia paused as she felt a familiar warmth envelop her heart and then begin to spread. She focused on the feeling of love that accompanied the sensation and the comfort it always brought. Then when her mind was clear, a conversation she had with Sister Roberts back on Mother's Day replayed in her head.

"I loved so many of the children who came through my classroom," Sister Roberts said. *"I always hoped that I would marry and have children myself, but as that never happened, I called my students my 'adopted' children."*

The warmth and love surged through Olivia's soul, and she knew she had found her answer. She basked in the glow of the Spirit for a few moments longer, and then concluded her prayer as she felt Michael kneel down beside her. She reached for his hand, but her mind was spinning as he voiced their family prayer. *Adoption! I have never even considered adoption before. It's never crossed my mind! That's crazy! We don't know one thing about adoption. Will we be able to love a baby that isn't genetically ours? What if we do get a baby, but I don't feel like a mom? What if we can't bond with the child? What if the mother takes the baby back? What if . . . what if . . . ? I don't even know enough to know what else to ask!*

Olivia realized that Michael had finished the prayer and was staring at her. She mumbled a quick "amen" and climbed into bed, only giving him a smile in answer to his questioning gaze. She wasn't ready to talk about this with him yet. She had no idea how Michael would respond. She wasn't even sure what her response was. There were so many unanswered questions. But as Olivia lay in bed reflecting on the idea of adopting a child, a sense of hope filled her, and the burning of the Spirit coursed through her again. She knew this was the right path, even if all she could see was the first step.

By the next evening, Olivia felt more certain than ever that she and Michael needed to try to adopt a baby. None of the questions in her mind had been answered, but every time she prayed or thought about them, she felt at peace. She knew that it would all be okay. She didn't know how or why it would be okay—Heavenly Father wasn't passing those details along—she just knew.

Michael worked alongside Olivia as they cleaned up the kitchen from supper, and when they both settled into the couch to read, Olivia was ready to broach the subject.

"So," she began, "I've been thinking a lot over the last few weeks."

"Oh?" Michael answered. Olivia knew he had been waiting for her to come to some kind of resolution about what direction she was going to take now that pregnancy was out of the picture. "What about?"

Olivia took a deep breath. She knew this would not be the answer Michael was expecting. "About having a family."

Michael exhaled forcefully. "Olivia, I thought we were past this. You know what the doctors said. You're not going to get pregnant."

"I know that," Olivia said. She was pleased that there was no sarcasm in her response. She had to keep her emotions in check. "I haven't been thinking about getting pregnant, I've been thinking about being a mom and having a family."

"Livvy, you can't have one without the other."

"I think we can."

Michael was shaking his head. "Livvy, you've got to move past this. Our family is here. Me and you. That's all. This," he waved his arm to indicate the two of them, "is our family. It's time to accept that and let the other go." Olivia sensed that there was more Michael wanted to say, so she waited. "I thought . . ." he hesitated.

"Yes?" Olivia prompted.

"I thought that over these last weeks you had been praying to know what Heavenly Father's will for your life was, not trying to convince yourself that there is a baby on the way when there is not." Michael crossed his arms and looked up at Olivia.

She felt the challenge in his words, but it didn't upset her. "That is what I have been doing, Michael, and the answer I received is that there is a way for us to have a family." Olivia didn't wait for him to disagree, she just pressed forward. "I think we should try to adopt a baby."

Olivia watched the surprise on Michael's face. Clearly, the idea of adoption had never crossed his mind. She waited for the understanding and acceptance that she hoped would come, but then Michael's eyebrows creased, and his voice was tight. "I don't know, Livvy. I'm not sure that's a good idea. We don't know the first thing about adoption. Plus, I've heard of people waiting years before they get a baby. What if that happens to us? I don't want you going through all of the ups and downs this is sure to bring." Michael stopped and Olivia could see his mind racing—working through possible scenarios and their outcomes. His eyes softened momentarily, but then he shook his head—pushing whatever the hopeful thought had been aside. "No, I don't think we should do it," he concluded.

Olivia was prepared for a little resistance, but she hadn't expected him to flat-out refuse. The hurt must have been evident on her face because Michael spoke more softly. "Come on, Livvy. I'm just starting to get you back, and I don't want to risk losing you again. I can't watch you suffer any more."

Olivia could see the pain in her husband's eyes. He was being sincere. It wasn't that he didn't want a baby. He was just afraid that they would get their hopes up, only to have their hearts broken once again. Olivia reached out and took Michael's hand as she spoke. "I know that these years of trying to get pregnant have been extremely difficult for both of us."

Michael started to speak but Olivia reached up and gently touched his lips with her finger as she continued. "And you're right about something. We don't know anything about adoption. I don't know where to begin either. I've asked myself so many questions about this, and I still don't have answers, but I do know one thing: I have been chasing my plan, my will, for the last few years, and it hasn't gotten us anywhere. As I prayed about understanding Heavenly Father's will, adoption is the answer I got. The Spirit I felt was undeniable. Specific answers to my questions haven't come, but peace has. I don't know exactly how this path will go, but I do know that I've finally found the right one." Olivia paused and looked at the man she loved. "Please pray about it. I know your answer will be the same."

Several mornings later, Michael came down the stairs and gave Olivia a weak smile. "Okay. I feel like it is fine to check into adoption." Olivia's face lit up. "But," Michael broke in before she could get too excited, "I'm still nervous about it. I don't like having all of these unanswered questions."

"I know, Michael. But I think that as we begin moving forward, the answers will start coming. I feel so strongly that this is what we should do."

Michael nodded and Olivia began putting bowls on the table for their breakfast. She couldn't help but smile and hum to herself. After stumbling around in the darkness for so long, she was beginning to see a glimmer of hope.

CHAPTER ELEVEN

G reat news, Michael," Olivia said as Michael walked through the front door. "I called several different adoption agencies today, and we can go through LDS Family Services. Besides the background checks and home study that all agencies require, Family Services requires that adoptive parents have been married for two years, be sealed, and have current temple recommends so the baby can be sealed to you."

"First, where on earth did you find several adoption agencies to call, and second, how much is this going to cost?" was Michael's response.

"The yellow pages, and actually, they are less expensive than the other agencies I spoke with. Their fee is on a sliding scale, and then we will have to pay our attorney fees and any travel expenses. Our savings account should be able to cover all of it."

"How long until we would have a baby?"

"Well, some of the other agencies guarantee a baby within one year or two years. Adoptive parents are put on a waiting list and it's kind of 'first come, first served.'"

"And what about Family Services?"

"They wouldn't give me a timeline. They said there's no way to know how long, because the birth parents choose the family. It could be a few months, or it could be several years . . . or more."

"I'm not sure I like that—no timetable at all."

"To be honest, Michael, I wasn't sure about it either at first, but I've been praying about this all day, and even though a few of the other agencies seem okay too, I really feel like LDS Family Services is the right choice for us." Olivia waited. She could see Michael trying to wrap his mind around all of this. Finally, he spoke, and there was only a little grumble in his voice.

"Okay. So, what do we do now?"

Olivia smiled, relieved. "Well, I made an appointment for us to meet with a social worker next week. In the meantime, the receptionist suggested we check out their website. She said there's some good information there and it can answer a lot of our questions."

That evening after supper, Michael and Olivia went online to see if the website for LDS Family Services could answer any of their questions. Olivia felt optimistic that there would be some information there that would help ease Michael's anxiety. She suspected that his reluctance to adopt stemmed mostly from not knowing anything about it, and if he could get some of his questions out of the way, he would feel better about it.

They read through some adoption myths that addressed several of Michael's big fears: not being able to love a child that Olivia didn't give birth to, and the concern of the birth mother trying to take the baby back after adoption.

"I really like what it says about love not being based on biology, but on serving and taking care of each other," Olivia offered.

"Yeah, I never really thought about how much I love you—more than anyone else in the world—yet we're not genetically related," Michael replied.

"And look," Olivia continued, pointing to the screen, "birth parents cannot reclaim the child once their rights have been terminated. I always wondered if those stories we see once in a while on the television news programs are very rare and a little exaggerated, and apparently they are."

"Hmm. I guess so," Michael said.

Olivia was enjoying reading the real-life stories about other couples who were blessed by the miracle of adoption. Some of the situations were similar to hers and once they had turned to following Heavenly Father's will instead of their own, adoption was the answer they received. Some couples were hesitant in the beginning and worried about having an open adoption, but they all expressed so much love for their children's birth moms, and they shared that they enjoyed exchanging letters, pictures, emails, and—in a few cases—even occasional visits.

Michael wasn't saying a lot, but Olivia watched as the muscles of his jawline began to relax, and he uncrossed his arms and intermittently leaned forward to read a passage more intently. After over an hour of reading everything they could find on the website, Michael pushed his chair back from the computer desk and asked, "Did you see that part about adoption not curing the pain of infertility?"

Olivia nodded. That had stuck out to her also. "I did. But I'm not thinking it will. I already figured out that those feelings will be healed in time by serving, turning my life over to the Lord, and allowing my pain to be swallowed up in the Atonement."

"It's going to be difficult," Michael said.

"Lots of good things are," Olivia replied.

"Then let's move forward." Michael nodded, firming things up in his own mind. "It sounds like a lot of work and my brain is still a little unsure, but my heart is telling me that this is what Heavenly Father wants us to do. This is the way our family is meant to come."

Olivia felt good about the things they learned from the LDS Family Services website, but after she and Michael met with their social worker, Kevin, the following week, she was feeling overwhelmed. There was so much they needed to do from attending a series of adoption classes offered by the agency, to ordering an FBI background check, to filling out seemingly endless forms and questionnaires about every aspect of their life—past, present, and plans for the future. Olivia insisted they go get started this very day.

"You heard what Kevin said, Michael. The faster we get all of this stuff done, the faster our profile will be out there where birth mothers can see it. I think the sooner our file is complete, the better."

They got all of the information turned in for their background checks and were driving back toward home when Michael finally said what had been gnawing at him all afternoon. "Aren't you a little bit worried about all of this 'open adoption' business and having contact with the birth mother and everything? I mean, this will be our baby when it's all said and done, and I'm not sure I want someone else meddling in our lives."

Olivia bit her lip nervously and then sighed. "To be honest, I was a little worried when we found out about all of the adoptions being open to some degree or other and, no, I don't like the idea about someone else meddling in our lives . . ." Michael started to nod, satisfied. "But," Olivia pushed, "I really don't think it will be that way. After reading all those true stories on the website, I believe that the birth mother will truly consider us to be the baby's parents. How could she go through with the placement otherwise?"

"Maybe," Michael agreed, "but I don't want to come home from work and find our baby's birth mom sitting on the front porch waiting for us."

"That's not fair, Michael," Olivia countered. "Kevin says that we can set boundaries, and if we're not comfortable having live meetings after the placement, we just put that in our file. We don't have to do it." Olivia paused, and then nodded, confirming something in her own mind. "Besides, our baby will know that she is adopted right from the beginning, and I want her, or him, to understand that that is a good thing—an amazing gift given by her birth mother. I think that after being part of an adoption, we will love our baby's birth mom, and she will always have a special place in our hearts."

"But you really won't mind if our baby has another mom out there?" Michael pressed.

"Initially, I thought I would be bothered by that, but for some reason, I'm not. I just don't think it will be that way. I will be our baby's mom, and once we are sealed in the temple, that binds us as a family forever. Anyway, in the crazy world we live in today, can a child ever have too many people who love her?"

Michael was silent, and Olivia knew he wasn't convinced. She was actually surprised that she felt so calm about this facet of adoption. She didn't know exactly how everything would go in this process, but she felt at peace with their decision. Whatever happened, it would all work out.

A few days later, after spending hours and hours on the Internet filling out all the required forms, the peace she felt was fading. Michael was grumbling about the nature of some of the questions they each had to answer. "I can't believe they want to know about the intimacy in our marriage or the challenges we have and how I feel about all of that. I may just as well put down how many times I use the bathroom each day and how many squares of toilet paper I use and how I feel about that. It's about the only thing they haven't asked for."

Olivia was on the verge of tears. She wasn't completely comfortable divulging her deepest emotions to virtual strangers, either. She was just trying to get through the questionnaire quickly and honestly. "Michael, don't be a smart aleck. I'm sure there's a reason for all of these questions, and if you don't take it seriously, we're never going to get a baby!" Michael didn't comment but went back to answering his questions.

With school now over for the year, Michael had some free days before his summer commitments with the football team started. Olivia took a couple days off work so the two of them could get their adoption file put together as quickly as possible. By the end of the fourth day, however, they were both at the end of their rope. The forms seemed unending, and there was the constant discussion about their preferences for everything from the gender and race of the baby to whether they would accept a special needs baby to the type and amount of contact they wanted with the birth mom. Then there was the stress of trying to write a letter to potential birth mothers and sift through years' worth of photos trying to find a handful that would portray Olivia and Michael's life together.

"How in the world do you ask a young woman to give you her baby?" Michael complained. "I don't even know where to begin." He tossed his pencil in frustration, which broke Olivia's last shreds of patience.

"I don't know either!" Olivia shouted at Michael.

"Hey, don't yell at me—this was your idea, remember?" he snapped back.

That only inflamed Olivia's temper. "Well, you're free to leave any time you want! Better yet, I'll leave and then you can go find another wife who isn't broken and can give you a family the old-fashioned way! Then you won't have to be dragged through all of this trouble. You can find a perfect little wife who will give you perfect little children!" And with that, Olivia stormed out the front door, slamming it behind her.

Michael stared at the door, dazed. What on earth just happened? The thing he was most worried about was that Olivia seemed completely sincere. She wasn't even crying when she left. Since he didn't know what to do, Michael just waited. *Maybe Livvy needs to let off a little steam. Emotions had been running pretty high as they sorted through all of this adoption stuff. And maybe,* he scolded himself, *you could be a little more supportive and do a little less complaining.* He had not even considered how his grumpy remarks might be affecting his wife. Sure, all of this had added tension to the strain that years of infertility had placed on their relationship, and he could see that his attitude wasn't helping anything, but it was crazy for Livvy to think that Michael wanted—could ever want—anyone but her. She knew that . . . didn't she?

Suppertime came and went, and Michael was really starting to get worried, but he had no idea where Olivia could be. She left in such a hurry that her cell phone was still sitting on the kitchen counter, so he had no way to contact her. With her parents gone on their mission, Olivia wouldn't have gone home, and her brother lived too far away to drive to his house. Michael had a sudden flash of inspiration, and picked up the telephone.

"Hello?"

"Hi, Heather, it's Michael." He didn't wait for her to respond, he just plunged forward. "Have you heard from Livvy this afternoon? She left a while ago and I'm really starting to get worried."

Heather hesitated just a moment before she answered. "Yeah, she's here. Look, I know it's none of my business, but she's really upset, Michael. She seems to think that you don't want to be married to her anymore. I told her I didn't think that was true . . . is it?"

"Of course it's not true, Heather! I love her more than anything. Things are just nuts right now." Michael paused, but Heather didn't say anything. "Does she want to talk to me?" he said.

Michael heard a muffled conversation, and then Olivia's voice on the other end of the line. "Hi, Michael." Her tone was flat.

"Livvy," Michael thought of everything he wanted to tell her, but then simply said, "Will you please come home? I miss you."

He heard Olivia choke back some tears, and then she said, "I'll be there in five minutes."

When Olivia opened the front door, her blue eyes, once so bright and shiny, looked lifeless—hopeless. It was obvious that she had been crying, and the agony that was looking out at Michael was almost more than he could bear. He rushed forward and took his wife in his arms. "Livvy, I'm so sorry. I'm sorry that I was being grumpy and insensitive. I'm sorry that I haven't been as supportive of this adoption as I should be. I just . . . I'm just scared to get my hopes up that we will actually get a baby, and I really don't want you to get your hopes up. My heart would barely survive another disappointment, and I'm not sure yours would survive at all."

Olivia opened her mouth to protest, but Michael softly covered it with his fingers. "But none of that can excuse my behavior. I can't believe that you would actually think that I don't love you, that I don't want to be with you. Livvy, if I lose you, nothing else matters. Nothing. We can sit down right now and finish every last bit of our adoption portfolio if that's what you want to do."

Olivia smiled, but there was no humor behind it. "This isn't just about tonight, Michael. I've wondered for years if you secretly wished you could be married to someone else; someone who could get pregnant; someone who wasn't crying half the time; someone who wasn't a failure as a woman." Olivia looked up and her eyes were hollow. "I've tried to push those thoughts aside, because I love you more than I can explain. I can't even begin to imagine my life without you, but I've often wondered if you would wake up one morning and think 'I could do a lot better than her—she can't even give me a family' and then you would just be gone." Olivia shrugged. It was finally out there. Now Michael was free to leave if he wanted to.

Michael buried his face in his hands for a long moment, and when he finally looked up, the agony Olivia was feeling was reflected back at her from Michael's eyes. She looked away. "I have a lot more to apologize for than I thought." Olivia was surprised at this response, but Michael didn't give her a chance to question him. "If you truly believe that I could ever leave you, then I'm the one who has failed. Let me say this one time, and then I will work every day to help you believe that it's true." Michael put both his hands on Olivia's shoulders and turned her so she was looking straight at him. "I love you, Olivia Ann Spencer. You. Just as you are. You are my family. You are the only person I can't live without. There's no doubt that I would love to bring children into our family, but if that never happens, you are enough for me now, and forever. I'm not going anywhere." Michael's eyes were shining, and before Olivia could respond, he pulled her to him and was kissing her with an urgency that Olivia had never felt before. She was pressed against him and was returning the emotion as she clung to him. When they were both out of breath, Michael moved his head slightly so he could see into Olivia's eyes. "I love you, Livvy," he whispered as he wiped the tears from her cheeks.

"I love you too, Michael," she said.

"Now, do you want to stay up and finish our portfolio tonight?" Michael asked.

"Actually," Olivia grinned, "I think the portfolio can wait until tomorrow. Tonight I want you to keep showing me how much you love me." And before Livvy knew what was happening, Michael swept her up in his arms and was carrying her up the stairs like they were newlyweds.

CHAPTER TWELVE

O ver the next few weeks, Michael was much more engaged in the adoption process. He and Olivia began the adoption classes at LDS Family Services and completed their adoption portfolio. Kevin was amazed that they had finished all of the paperwork so quickly since it often took couples months and months to get to that point. "Well, we're very serious about this," Olivia told him. "We're not fooling around." Kevin agreed and scheduled their home visit and final interviews for the following week.

The day before Kevin would be coming to inspect their home, Olivia was running around the house, once again on pins and needles. Michael was having no luck in reassuring her. "Livvy, all he's looking for are a few basic safety items. You know, smoke detectors, a couple fire extinguishers, a carbon monoxide detector. We've got all of that. We're covered."

"No, the receptionist told me that the social worker will be making sure that the home is safe for a baby. We need to have safety covers on all of the electrical outlets and child locks on all of the cupboards and drawers." Olivia was frantic and on the verge of tears.

"Okay, I'll give you the outlet covers if you really want them, but I don't think we need to install child locks on everything. Our home is safe. It's clean. We have plenty of space for a child. We're not hiding a stockpile of guns in the closet, and there's not a meth lab in the kitchen." Michael's last statement was an attempt to get Olivia to smile and relax, but instead she burst into tears.

He gathered Olivia into his arms. "I'm sorry, Livvy. I didn't mean to upset you. You've done a great job on our house, and Kevin is going to think it's terrific. I'll go to the store right now and get the outlet covers. I'll even get the child locks if you really want them, but I don't think they're necessary."

"I know I'm going a little overboard," Olivia sniffed. "It's just that I want everything to be perfect."

"It is perfect, Livvy. It really is."

"I know you're right," Olivia replied.

"Then . . . why are you still crying?" Michael was worried that he had messed up again. "Is it because of my bad meth lab joke?"

"Yes—I mean no—I mean . . . oh, I don't know what I mean!" Olivia was frustrated. "It's just not fair, you know?"

"What's not fair, Livvy?"

"It's not fair that you and I, who would be terrific parents, have to go through this huge process and all of this stress and worry to try and get 'qualified' for a baby that might take years to arrive, when there are women out there getting pregnant every day who are a disaster, and some who probably actually have meth labs in their kitchens, and they get to have a baby . . . no questions asked. How is that right? How is that fair?"

Part of Michael wanted to smile at his wife and tell her to relax, but a larger part of him felt the pain of what she was saying. He had experienced similar thoughts himself back when they were going through all of the fertility treatments. It wasn't fair that it was so easy for some people, and so very, very difficult for others.

"It's not fair, Livvy," he said gently. "You're right, it's not fair. But where is the promise that life was going to be fair? There is none. Is it fair that you and I never have to worry about where our next meal is coming from when there are people all over the world going to bed hungry every night? Is it fair that we are both healthy and strong when there are so many others who suffer from sickness and disease? Is it fair that we live in a free country surrounded by safety and security when the world is full of so much turmoil? Life isn't fair. It isn't supposed to be."

"How is that right?" Olivia demanded. "How can that ever be made right?"

"There's only one way," Michael said. "Through the Atonement of Jesus Christ. I don't have all the answers, but I know that somehow, some way, at some future time, all will be made well through the Atonement. Every pain, every heartache, every sadness, every sickness, every broken dream will be swallowed up in the Atonement."

"And what do we do until that happens?"

"We have to believe that Heavenly Father is in control. We have to believe that our Savior loves us and will never leave us alone. In short, we have to have faith."

"I have a feeling that's easier said than done," Olivia said, but she had a faint smile on her face again. "I'll just have to take things a day at a time and do my best to follow the Savior."

"That's all He asks of you, Olivia. That's all He asks."

In the end, Kevin's home visit and final interview went great, even without the child locks. He was impressed and pleased with how quickly Michael and Olivia had plowed through the process and, when the background checks came back several weeks later, Michael and Olivia received a letter in the mail telling them that their application for adoption was approved and their file would be posted on the Internet and sent out to the surrounding agencies as well. There was nothing left to do now but pray and wait.

Book Two
ALLISON

CHAPTER ONE

Allison Campbell looked at the little pink box in her hand. The packaging was innocent enough, but Ally had felt like a bright red "A" was emblazoned across her chest while she shopped for it at the grocery store. She had intentionally traveled to a store that was all the way across town so she wouldn't run into anyone she knew and had then purchased eight other items that she did *not* need so she wouldn't look too conspicuous.

"Well, here it goes," Ally murmured to herself as she ripped the box open. Ally carefully read, and then re-read, the instructions for the pregnancy test. Of course she understood them the first time, but she liked to be thorough. She didn't want to miss even the smallest detail that could compromise the test results. Ally realized that her hands were shaking as she popped the clear, plastic cover off the end of the stick.

Ally's mind was reeling, but then focused in on the thought that this couldn't possibly be happening to her. "After all, I'm supposed to be a 'good' girl," she mumbled. In truth, Ally was a good girl by just about anyone's standards. She had graduated high school on the high honor roll less than a month ago. She was involved in the student council and enjoyed going to church. Although her high school basketball team just missed winning the state championship this year,

Ally was named to the All-State team. She had a full academic schol-arship to the best medical university in the state where she was going to pursue a nursing degree. Her life was cruising along, and she liked where it was headed.

Then life came to a screeching halt when she made one huge mistake. As Ally considered the repercussions of her actions, preg-nancy did not, initially, fit into the equation. Surely, she wouldn't get pregnant after only one time. At least it was the guy's first time too, so disease wasn't an issue either. But the emotional consequences were really devastating. Ally always believed that this kind of rela-tionship should be saved for marriage. She had planned on waiting. She had wanted to wait. Then this . . . just . . . happened. She had cried more in the last three weeks than in the last three years com-bined.

Ally knew that what she did was wrong, but she was too embar-rassed to talk to anyone about it. She felt guilty and ashamed and as if a piece of her was missing. A piece that she had intended to hold on to but in one careless moment had given it away. Ally had gone to sleep every night since "the night" wishing that this all was a bad dream and she would wake up in the morning and feel whole and right again. But of course it wasn't a dream, and yesterday things had become all too real when it dawned on her that she was over a week late. Time had been passing in such a blur that she hadn't realized it at first, and that was what propelled her out the door and to the grocery store.

Well, I'll know one way or the other in three minutes, Ally thought as she carefully laid the pregnancy test face-up on the bathroom counter and looked at her watch. She studied every detail of the familiar bathroom from the deep red rugs, to the navy blue towels on the rack, to the wooden representation of the flag of the United States that she helped her mom paint six years ago. One of the stars was half blue where Ally's hand got a little shaky. "Oh, well," her mom had said. "Mistakes happen." Ally wondered how her mom would react if and when Ally had to tell her about this mistake. The thought triggered a sigh.

Ally checked her watch to find that only two minutes had passed. It felt like a lot longer than that. She thought about peeking at the test stick to see if she could make out what the result was, but decided against it. Better to wait and be sure, than guess and get it wrong, even for a few moments. She forced herself to count slowly to thirty in her mind, and then ventured a peek at her watch. Time was up. Ally took a deep breath trying to calm her nerves and steady the trembling in her hands long enough to pick up the test stick. She reached for it and closed her eyes.

Ally felt her clammy fingers close around the cool plastic and opened her eyes. Two lines. Positive. She was pregnant. Ally squeezed her eyes tightly shut and opened them once more, just to be sure. She felt her breathing becoming ragged as her chest threatened to explode and her eyes began to burn. Ally tipped to one side and caught herself on the bathroom vanity as the test stick clattered to the floor. The sob erupted from her chest and the tears began to pour as Ally slid to the floor and dropped her face into her hands.

CHAPTER TWO

Allison wished she could shrink into invisibility as she sat outside the bishop's office. The reality was that no one was giving her so much as a second glance, but Ally felt like there were neon arrows pointing down at her, letting all the world know that she had sinned. Was it her imagination, or could she already see a small bump forming on her belly? Allison shook her head. Of course it was her imagination. She was only about six weeks along, so there was no way she would be showing yet. She was having a hard time wrapping her mind around that one. That she would be "showing" before long. Ally knew that she was in trouble. Big trouble. Not only with the Church, but with her parents, her family. They were going to be so disappointed and ashamed of her. She was feeling overwhelmed and hopeless. She didn't know what she was going to do! In fact, the only thing she knew right now was that she had to talk to someone or she was going to explode! She couldn't face her parents yet, although she was pretty sure her mom knew that something was wrong, and she didn't feel right about talking to Amy and Hannah before she told Brandon. At the thought of Brandon, her eyes welled up with shame and embarrassment. He hadn't said more than a few words to her since the night they had . . .

"Ally?" Allison jumped as Bishop Jenkins opened his office door. She blinked back the tears, determined to maintain her composure, and stood up to shake his hand. The way Bishop Jenkins's eyes crinkled as he smiled at her reminded Allison why she decided that he was the one she was going to confide in. He had always been so kind and understanding. Ever since the day Ally crashed her bike in front of his house when she was six years old and he came out and carefully wiped the blood from her knees and carried her home, she had known that Brother Jenkins was someone she could trust. Since he became the bishop, the love and kindness in his face had only grown. She knew he was going to be disappointed in her, but she also knew that he wasn't going to be angry with her. He opened the door a little wider and motioned for Ally to come in and sit down. Once she was seated, he moved around the shiny, brown desk and settled himself into his chair facing her. Then he smiled and waited. When Ally didn't say anything, Bishop finally began. "Since you are the one who scheduled this appointment, I'm guessing there's something you wanted to talk to me about."

"Well actually, Bishop, I guess there is." Ally's voice sounded much more quavery than she had hoped it would be. She took a deep breath and got ready to begin the speech she had been rehearsing in her mind for the past week, but as she opened her mouth, her voice cracked and the floodgates opened.

Ally hadn't allowed herself a good cry about this since the morning she took the pregnancy test a few weeks ago, and now all the pent up emotion came crashing through. Bishop Jenkins waited patiently, and aside from passing a box of tissues across the desk to her, he remained still and quiet while Ally worked to regain her composure. After several minutes, the sobs began to subside, and Ally was once again able to look into the bishop's face. To her surprise, he didn't seem shocked or worried by her outburst. He only smiled his kindly, crinkle-eyed smile again and said, "What is it, Ally? Whatever it is, we can work through it with the Lord's help."

"I'm not so sure, Bishop," Ally managed to squeak. "This is pretty bad."

"Do you believe that the Lord can help you, Ally?"

"I don't know. I used to, but that was before . . ." she sighed. "I guess it's possible that He can help me, I'm just not sure that He will."

"Okay, fair enough. What makes you say that?"

"Because if He would have helped me to begin with, I wouldn't be in this mess!"

"So, you feel like the Lord has let you down?"

"Not when you put it like that, but let me ask you a question, Bishop."

"I'm all ears." He smiled.

"I thought that the Lord would not allow us to be tempted above that which we could bear."

"That's not a question, Ally."

"Okay, well, if the Lord will not allow us to be tempted above that which we can bear, then why am I in here? He should have helped me to overcome the temptation in the first place! Since He didn't do that, I'm not sure He will really help me now."

"Ally, have you had a problem with the Word of Wisdom?"

"No."

"Then, is this a morality issue?" Ally felt like the air was frozen in her lungs. She opened her mouth to answer but found that the words wouldn't come. She just looked up at Bishop Jenkins's face and slowly nodded as she felt silent tears begin streaming down her cheeks.

"I see. We'll talk more about that in a minute, but first I want to address your concern about the Lord not helping you overcome this temptation to begin with. If it's okay with you, I'd like to tell you a story from my own life."

"Sure, I've got nowhere else to go." Ally managed a small smile.

"Ally, there's something that I don't think you know about me. When I was in high school and college, I rode bulls."

"What? You were a bull rider?"

"I know, I know, it sounds crazy, but it was a lot of fun, and it put me through college. That's not really the point, though," he said, grinning. "Anyway, there was this one bull that no one ever wanted to have to ride. His brand was K-5 and his name was Mr. Rat. He was mean, he was ornery, he was incredibly hard to ride, and chances were that if you got on his back, you were going to end up hurt. However, if you were good enough and happened to get lucky and make the full eight seconds on K-5 Mr. Rat, you were probably going to win the first place money at the rodeo. I always wondered what I would do if I ever drew K-5 Mr. Rat. Then, the day finally arrived. My buddies and I called the rodeo secretary a couple days before the big fourth of July rodeo to find out which bulls we had drawn. A knot immediately formed in my stomach when I heard her say, 'Cody Jenkins, you'll be on K-5 Mr. Rat.'

"Well, now I had a decision to make. You see, when you find out which bull you will have to ride, you have the option to tell the secretary that you're going to 'turn out.' That means that you are basically going to forfeit that rodeo. You still have to pay your entry fee money, but you are not going to get on the bull because you don't think you can win or place on him, and you don't want to risk an injury."

"Okay, but I'm not sure where you're going with this," Ally commented.

"Just keep listening, and you'll see. Now, where was I?"

"You had a decision to make. Whether to try and ride K-5 Mr. Rat, or to turn out of that rodeo."

"Right. Well, immediately, my friend told me that I should turn out, and in that moment it would have been pretty easy for me to tell the rodeo secretary that. After all, it was just me and two other guys sitting in our apartment. No pressure. But I still had lots of time. The rodeo was several days away. I decided that I would wait and think about it for a little bit before I decided what to do.

"The next day, I was with the rest of my traveling partners, and my roommate told them that I had drawn K-5 Mr. Rat for Saturday's rodeo. Now, all of my friends knew about the choice I had to make. They kept asking me if I was going to ride. I was kind of leaning toward not getting on him, because if I got injured it could mess up the rest of the season for me. But now, it was a little harder to say that I wasn't going to ride. They all wanted to see me try. I still could have turned out, and they would have understood because everyone knew it was dangerous to get on K-5 Mr. Rat, but I kept rationalizing things in my head. I was a good rider, and I might be okay . . . I might even ride him and win. So I just told my friends that I hadn't decided yet, and left it at that.

"Now, at any time during the following two days I could have called the rodeo secretary and told her that I was going to turn out. My traveling partners might have been a little disappointed, but they would have understood. I felt like I probably should not get on K-5 Mr. Rat, but I reminded myself that I could turn out at any time, but once I called the secretary and turned out I would not be able to change my mind and decide to ride him. So I chose to wait until I got to the rodeo and see how I felt then.

"When we arrived at the rodeo late Saturday afternoon, I was pretty sure that I would turn out, but when I went into the secretary's office to tell her and pay my fees and turn-out fine, it was packed full of cowboys from all over. My pride wouldn't let me tell the secretary that I was turning out in front of all those other cowboys. They would assume that I didn't have the guts it took to try and ride K-5 Mr. Rat. So I just paid my entry fee and decided that I would go back later, after the rodeo had started, and tell her.

"The rodeo began and I knew that I had to go to the secretary's office now and tell her that I was going to turn out. I started heading that direction when I heard the rodeo announcer declare to the crowd that 'the featured match-up in the bull riding tonight will be Cody Jenkins versus K-5 Mr. Rat.' You see, I was one of the top riders in the circuit, and nobody had been able to stay on K-5 Mr. Rat in over a year. The crowd went wild. I stopped. If I went and turned out now, the entire audience, not to mention the announcer, stock contractor, and every single cowboy and cowgirl in the arena would know that I had backed out. Technically, I still had the choice not to get on the bull, but it was becoming more and more difficult the farther I let things go.

"I returned to the warm-up area behind the bucking chutes and decided to try and make the best of the situation. After all, I was a good rider, and even if I got bucked off, I could probably keep myself safe. The stock contractor had just started loading the bulls into the bucking chutes when the thought occurred to me that this was my last chance to choose what I was going to do. Once I climbed onto the back of K-5 Mr. Rat and nodded my head, the chute gate would open and I would be faced with the consequences of my action. I almost told the contractor not to load my bull, but the pressure had become too strong for me to bear. I couldn't walk away now that I had reached this point. I just wasn't strong enough."

Finally Ally could see where Bishop Jenkins was going with this experience. She started to nod her head as she realized that there had been several times the night she got pregnant that the Spirit had warned her. *Don't go to the party. Don't leave with Brandon. Don't go into his parents' house while nobody is home.* At any one of those moments she could have walked away. But she believed that she would stay in control of herself and her emotions, that the temptation would not become too severe. She hadn't counted on there coming a point where the excitement would overcome her determination to stop before she went too far.

Ally realized that Bishop Jenkins had stopped talking and was watching her. She was sure he could hear the gears turning in her mind as she realized that the Lord had tried to help her. In fact, He had tried several times to help her, and if she would have made a good choice at any one of those moments, the temptation never would have become more than she could bear. But when she continued to ignore the promptings, thinking that she was good enough and strong enough to keep pushing the limit, she chose to put herself in a situation that she couldn't handle.

"So you got on K-5 Mr. Rat?" Ally asked.

"Yep. I made choices that took me to a place where I wasn't strong enough to walk away."

"So what happened?" To Ally's surprise, Bishop Jenkins reached up and rubbed his nose. For the first time, she noticed that it was a little crooked.

"I don't quite remember what happened. The last thing I do remember was nodding my head and the chute gate opening. My friends tell me that on the second jump out of the gate, K-5 Mr. Rat jerked me down and my face smashed into the back of his head. That knocked me out, and while he was flipping me around, my arm was broken before anyone could get him away from me. Besides my arm, I had a broken nose and a concussion. I was lucky, though. I only spent two days in the hospital. However, I missed the rest of the season because I couldn't ride with my arm in a cast from my hand up to my shoulder. Those were my consequences."

Ally looked up and was glad that she had come to talk to Bishop Jenkins. She was ready to take some of this weight off of her own shoulders, if only for a few minutes. "So, Ally, are you ready to talk about your consequences?"

She squared her shoulders, took a deep breath, and for the first time said the words out loud. "Bishop, I'm pregnant."

CHAPTER THREE

When Allison left the bishop's office, she was relieved at having finally gotten her secret off her chest. On one hand, her burden felt a little lighter. On the other hand, she was feeling more overwhelmed and hopeless than ever. Bishop Jenkins was kind and understanding, but also very firm. What she had done was very serious, and there would be a number of steps she would need to take to work through the mistakes she had made. Then came the question that Ally had been trying not to think about. The question that made all of this seem totally and completely real. "Ally, what are you going to do about the baby?" For the first time Ally pushed aside the walls she had built in her head over the past few weeks, and allowed her mind to really make the connection between being pregnant and having a baby. A baby. My baby.

As she unlocked the door to her little green Volkswagen Beetle, Allison forced the thoughts of the baby to the sideline of her mind. Right now she needed to focus. Bishop Jenkins had counseled her to go home and talk to her parents tonight. The idea of telling her parents what she had done, and what happened as a result, filled her with dread, but she also felt that Bishop was probably right. He told her that she would need their support right now, more than ever. Ally just prayed that "support" would be what they would give her.

Ally pulled into the driveway of the only home she had ever known and turned off the key. The upstairs windows were all dark except for the third one over. Her sixteen-year-old brother, Charlie, was still awake, probably reading a book he couldn't wait to discuss with her in the morning. She enjoyed those conversations. Charlie was much more mature than the boys his age—or Ally's age for that matter. He always thought things through very carefully and had very keen insights about things. She wondered what his reaction would be when he found out she was pregnant. She shook her head. Right now she needed to think about how she was going to tell her parents.

It looked as though her twelve-year-old twin sisters, Emma and Elsie, were already asleep. Thank goodness! She hoped that the worst part of her parents' reaction would have blown over by morning so "the girls," as they were affectionately known, wouldn't have to witness the initial disgrace of their big sister firsthand.

Ally felt as though her shoes were full of cement. It was much easier to just sit here in the dark car than to try to open the door and move her feet to the front porch. Her hands were sweaty and her heart was pounding. *You'd think that after all the bawling I've done tonight, my eyes would be dry,* Ally thought. But she could feel her emotions burning in her throat, threatening to explode again. Ally saw the curtains covering the front window move and her mother's face emerged on the other side. She had heard the car pull up and was wondering who was sitting out there in the driveway. Allison knew that if she didn't go in now, her mom would be out soon to see what the hold-up was. So, she tried to steel herself against the reaction she knew would be coming, opened the door to the warm night air (which did nothing to dispel the chill of fear that had settled in Ally's stomach) and headed up the front steps and through the door.

The sounds and smells of home hit Allison as she stepped into the living room. Apple crisp. It was one of her mom's specialties. Ally could still smell the warm cinnamon underneath the clean aroma of dishwashing liquid. The soft "swoosh swoosh" of the dishwasher and the rustling of her dad's newspaper provided a quiet backdrop to the picture of peace and serenity that Ally was trying to ingrain into her memory. This was the "before" picture. She was sure that the "after" would not look so good. "Hey, sweetie." Dad looked up and smiled. His eyes stopped and searched her face, and Ally realized that her eyes were probably still red and puffy.

She decided to act before he could question her. "Hi, Dad. Can I talk to you and Mom for a minute?"

"Sure, Ally." Then a little louder, "Julie, come on in here. Ally has something to tell us." His dark brown eyes never left hers. That was the one feature Allison had gotten from her dad. Her eyes. They were just like his. Ally could tell that he knew something was really wrong. That was clear from the way his eyes probed hers, looking for answers. But there was also a calmness in his eyes that surprised and encouraged Ally. Maybe this would go better than she thought.

"What did you say, Steve?" Ally's mom had walked in wiping her hands on a dish towel but stopped when she saw the quiet exchange between father and daughter.

"I said that Ally has something to tell us." Ally nodded and sat down opposite her father in the glider rocker that Ally knew her mother had rocked her in when she was a baby. A baby.

Ally gave a quick shake of her head to clear her thoughts and then looked up. "Mom, I think you'd better sit down for this."

"What's wrong, Allison?" Julie's jaw tightened as she sat down on the sofa next to her husband of twenty years. "What has happened?"

"Mom, Dad, I've been visiting with Bishop Jenkins tonight."

"And?" Julie pushed when Ally hesitated.

"And there's something that I need to tell you guys." Ally paused again, and Julie opened her mouth to start talking, but Steve stopped her with a gentle touch to the arm.

"Let's let Ally do this her way, okay, hon?" Julie hesitated at Steve's suggestion, then gave a stiff nod and turned her attention back to Allison. Ally tried to swallow the lump that was threatening to burst from her throat but had no luck.

"There's no easy way to tell you guys this, so I'll just say it. I . . . I made a mistake. A really, really big mistake." The tears she had been fighting back since leaving the bishop's office now spilled over onto Ally's cheeks. "You remember that graduation party I went to?" Ally didn't wait for a reply but decided to hurry through her confession. Maybe that would be less painful, like quickly ripping a Band-Aid off. "Well, anyway, I made some bad decisions that night. I left the party with Brandon, and one thing led to another, and we ended up, well we . . ." She choked back a sob and cried, "We ended up sleeping together!" Ally looked up and saw the sadness engulf her dad's face. She felt like her heart was about to rip right out of her chest. "I'm so sorry, Daddy! I know I messed up big time, but I talked to Bishop Jenkins, and—"

"Allison Jane Campbell! How could you?" The outburst came, not from her dad, but from Ally's mom. "What on earth were you thinking? Obviously you weren't! Is this how we raised you?"

"Julie, lower your voice, please." Dad was sad—his voice soft. His hand was still on his wife's arm, and she whirled around and turned on him.

"Are you defending her? Are you defending what she did?"

"No, I'm not defending her actions, but I don't think that yelling is going to help anything right now. Besides," and at this he turned back and gave an encouraging nod to Ally, "I think there's more that Ally wants to say."

"You're right, Dad. There is more." Suddenly all of Ally's tears seemed to dry up and her mouth felt like it was full of cotton. Her tongue was thick and heavy, but there was no turning back now, so Ally forced the words out. "I'm pregnant." Her mom looked as though she were about to protest, so Ally hurried on. "I took a pregnancy test a couple weeks ago when I realized there might be a problem. It was positive. I'm pregnant. I'm pregnant, and I'm scared and I don't know what to do and I know that I messed up but I really need some support from you guys right now because otherwise I don't know how I'll ever make it through." Ally stopped and took a deep, shuddering breath. The words had spilled out uncontrolled and now she sat looking at her parents, waiting to know when, or if, they would ever be able to forgive her.

"Now you've really done it, Allison! You've ruined everything! What about your plans, your future?"

"Julie!" Steve hadn't yelled, but his tone carried enough authority that Julie stopped her tirade and turned to look at him. "I think you should stop talking now before you say something that you're really going to regret." Julie's face turned red as her anger boiled inside her. Steve and Ally both knew there was more she wanted to say, but Steve gave a curt shake of his head, and Julie closed her mouth and folded her arms. She quit yelling but would not look up at Ally. She kept her eyes focused on an invisible spot on the rug.

Steve looked up at his daughter. Tears were rolling down his cheeks. Ally didn't even realize that she was crying again, but as she touched her fingertips to her cheek, they came away wet. "I'm glad you went to Bishop Jenkins," Dad said. "He's a good man."

Ally nodded and her father continued, his words coming slowly and carefully. "What you are going to do about the baby?"

Ally didn't trust her voice right now, so she just shrugged. "Does Brandon know that you're pregnant?" Ally silently shook her head. "Well, it's too late to go over there tonight, but I think you should arrange a meeting with him tomorrow morning and let him know. After you see what he says, we can move forward from there."

Ally nodded again and her dad reached out his arms. Ally felt his tears on her cheek as she hugged him.

CHAPTER FOUR

Ally muttered under her breath when she accidentally dropped the cordless phone and it banged around on the hardwood floor beneath her bare feet. Her hands were shaking so hard that she barely managed to pick it up. At least she did manage to get the phone gathered up. That was more than she could say for her thoughts and emotions.

She was still unsure what she was going to say to Brandon as she dialed his cell number and waited for one, two, three rings. Maybe he was sleeping in. It was summer vacation, after all. But that really wasn't like Brandon. More likely he had been up since the crack of dawn running ten miles or doing a hundred push-ups or some other athletically challenging activity designed to keep him in peak condition. After all, he was heading out to California on a football scholarship to play for one of the best college teams in the nation. As she thought of this, Ally's resolve almost faltered, but after the fifth ring—and just as she was about to hang up—she heard Brandon's voice on the other end of the line. He was out of breath. He had probably been on his ninety-fifth push-up and wanted to quickly finish before answering the phone.

"Hey, Ally. I've been meaning to call you, but I've been really busy with training, and trying to get packed, and, well, you know . . ." As his voice trailed off, Ally found that she was glad to hear him sounding sincerely sorry, or at the very least, sincerely sheepish for having spent so little time with her since the night they, well, since the night of the graduation party.

"Hi, Brandon. Yeah, I know things have been crazy for you. I've been pretty busy myself." What was she doing? Maybe she should just hang up and not tell him anything. Maybe he never had to know. Maybe she could just act as though nothing at all had changed. Maybe she could just tell him good-bye and wish him good luck. Maybe she could just pretend that they never had sex, that they were still just the good friends they had been from the moment he moved here at the beginning of junior year. Maybe . . .

"Are you still there, Ally?" His voice rattled Ally's mind back to the conversation at hand, and she knew what she had to do. No matter what, she had to tell Brandon. They had been too good of friends to keep something this big from him. Maybe he would understand. Maybe he would want to help her. Maybe he would even want to marry her. Maybe then he would become interested in the Church. Maybe she could still have her happily ever after. Maybe . . .

"Ally?"

"What? Oh, yeah, I'm still here. Hey, um, I was thinking. Can I come over and talk to you, you know, for old time's sake? To, uh, say good-bye? Besides, there's kind of something I want to tell you."

Brandon hesitated for only a moment, then replied, "Sure, Ally. I'd love to say good-bye to you in person. Anyway, my mom wants to say good-bye to you too. She's worried that once I leave and you're off to college, she won't get to see you much anymore."

"Okay. Sounds good. I'll be there in fifteen minutes."

As Ally drove across town to Brandon's house, she let her mind wander over the past two years since the first day of junior year when he sauntered into her first hour biology class, and into her life. His blond, curly hair and big blue eyes caught the attention of nearly every girl in the classroom. Not to mention his athletically built body that made his jeans and T-shirt seem so much better than every other guy's in the room. The classroom had been about three-quarters of the way full when he arrived, with plenty of seats to choose from. He stood in the doorway momentarily, surveying the room. Then his face broke into a huge smile, and he started making his way toward the empty seat directly behind Ally. She hadn't even dared look up from her book, once she realized he was moving in her direction. She heard him settle into the desk behind her, and just as she was about to risk a glance over her shoulder, he spoke. His voice was music to her ears, but somehow the lyrics were all wrong. "Hey, man. Good to see ya! How's that throwing arm?" Ally suddenly sat up straight and felt her cheeks color as she realized that he had not come over to sit behind her, but to sit next to Jeff Richards, who was behind and to the left of Ally. Jeff had been the football team's starting quarterback last year as a junior, and the school and community were expecting great things from him in this, his senior year. Jeff also happened to be in Ally's ward at church, and they had known each other since she was twelve.

Of course he would be coming to sit by Jeff! He was obviously a football player, and football practice had started a week ago. *Duh!* The two guys were carrying on a conversation behind her, which she tried to tune out, her embarrassment still too strong to turn around and actually say anything. Finally, to her relief, class started and she turned her full attention to Mr. Herman's lecture. When the bell rang, Ally jumped as Jeff reached forward and put his hand on her shoulder. "Hey, Ally!" She turned around and was face-to-face with Mr. Blond Curls.

She forced herself to shift her gaze to Jeff's face as she responded. "Hey, Jeff. What's up?" She was trying to sound casual. She hoped she sounded casual.

"Well, we were just wondering if you would be part of our study group for this class. Oh, by the way, this is Brandon White. He just moved here from Texas. He's going to be my star wide receiver." Jeff high-fived Brandon, then gestured toward Ally. "This is Ally. Ally Campbell. She's the starting point guard on the girls' basketball team, and she probably understands biology better than old Mr. Herman up there."

Ally grinned as she consciously tried to divert the blood from her cheeks. "Nice to meet you, Brandon." She stuck her hand out, glad that it wasn't cold and clammy for once. They shook hands, and Brandon smiled. Then she turned to Jeff and, mustering all of the swagger she could, Ally replied, "Sure, I'll help you guys study. Someone needs to make sure you hotshot football jocks keep your grades up!"

That's where it all began. Much to Ally's surprise, Brandon was easy to talk to and a lot of fun to be around. Somewhere around the third week of class they moved past the awkward "is he going to ask me out/should I ask her out" stage, and became fast friends. They never looked back. They had hung out a lot over the past two years, usually just at one of their houses, doing homework, playing Rook, or even just talking. She had cheered him on at all of the football games, and he had driven all over the state to watch her play basketball. Somehow, through all of that, they had always stayed "just friends." Very close friends, to be sure. Ally's mom often commented on the nature of their relationship, and how familiar and casual they were with each other.

Whenever Brandon came to Ally's house, her mom never left them alone. Ally always tried to convince her mom that Brandon wasn't her "boyfriend" so she didn't need to worry.

"Call it what you want, Ally," her mom told her. "You two spend so much time together and are closer than most couples your age. You just need to be careful."

Ally always thought she was being silly, but as it turned out, Mom was right, and everything changed at the end of May, two nights after graduation. For Ally, it was the realization that after this night (and the few others that would follow), after he left and headed out to California, she would probably never see Brandon White again. Of course there was email and texting, and a hundred different online ways to keep in touch, but none of them could make it so she could be with him. And let's face it—the reality was that they would both move forward in their lives. In the beginning it would be stuff like his football and her academics. Meeting new people and having new experiences. But eventually, he would fall in love with someone and marry her. At this thought, Ally suddenly wanted Brandon to be hers. She didn't want to share him with anyone, especially not some nameless, faceless girl.

They were dancing together at a party when these thoughts occurred to her. Maybe Brandon noticed that she was now pulling him toward her, maybe he had been having some of the same sort of thoughts about losing her, maybe they just finally let their guard down. Whatever happened in those brief seconds, it changed everything. Brandon stopped dancing and looked down into Ally's face.

It was impossible to resist the emotion that clouded his blue eyes. She didn't even want to resist. As he touched her cheek with his fingertips, it felt right. It felt like this was how it should have been all along. Why had they wasted all of this time, not realizing that they were meant to be together? When he started pulling her face toward his, she didn't hesitate. She just kissed him. He kissed her softly at first, both of them savoring the moment, the sensation. Then came the memories of all the laughter, all the tears, all the talks, all the games of one-on-one basketball, and the dinners with family, all the studying and reading, all the hope of going to college and fulfilling dreams, all the hours spent together. As these came flooding in, Ally realized he was holding her tighter, kissing her harder, and she didn't want him to stop. He turned his head slightly and whispered in her ear, "No one is at my house, let's go."

For the first time Ally hesitated just momentarily. Maybe she shouldn't. But she wanted to. It would be all right. She turned his face back toward hers and gave him a slow, soft kiss. Then she breathed, "Okay."

As Ally eased her "Green Giant"—as Brandon had nicknamed her little, green Volkswagen—up alongside the curb in front of Brandon's house, she forced her mind back to the present. She hadn't completely abandoned the thought that maybe, just maybe, he wouldn't see this as bad news. She was still holding onto the slightest glimmer of hope that maybe Brandon would be glad all of this had happened. She had already decided that she would move to California with him if he asked her to. She would have to take a year off of school if she went because she hadn't applied to any colleges in California, and the application deadlines were past, but that would give her and Brandon time to get settled, time for her to . . . have the baby. That wouldn't be so bad. She took a few calming breaths, glad that she wasn't feeling too nauseous this morning and opened her car door.

Stephanie White met Ally at the door. Brandon's mom was not like a second mom to her—but more like an older sister. Someone who loved and accepted you the way you were, not feeling responsible for your behavior, but still urging and encouraging you in the right direction. She gave Ally a big squeeze.

"Hey, sweetie. How have you been? Are you all ready to move and start school?"

"Not quite. I, uh, might have a little change of plans. I've had some things come up, and now I'm not exactly sure what I'm going to do." Stephanie raised a quizzical eyebrow, but thankfully chose not to pursue the topic further.

"Well, if you stay around here, you know that you're always welcome."

"Yeah, I know. Thanks, Steph." Ally wondered if that invitation would still be valid after she talked with Brandon. She hoped so.

As if summoned by her thought of him, Brandon appeared around the corner and gave his mom a quick hug as he moved past her and out the door. "Ally and I are gonna visit out here for a little while, okay?"

"Sure thing. Now Ally, don't you dare leave without saying good-bye." Ally managed to smile and nod, but her voice had suddenly become unavailable to her. All of her ideas that this conversation might go smoothly just gave way to the idea that Brandon would probably, understandably, freak out.

He motioned to the huge oak tree in their side yard, and Ally turned and headed that direction without meeting his eyes. They had sat under the sweeping branches many times over the past two years, sometimes alone, and sometimes with the whole family, just laughing and enjoying each other's company. This time was going to be different. This time was going to change everything.

There was a brief moment of awkward silence as they sat down. The memory of the last time they had been alone together loomed between them. Ally tried to swallow but couldn't, so she tried to talk. Brandon put his hand up and softly covered her lips. "Let me start, okay? I wanted to say that I'm sorry. I'm so, so sorry for what happened. I know that you have always wanted to wait until you were married, and I'm sorry that I'm the one who messed that up for you. I never should have suggested coming back here when I knew that everyone else was gone. I really didn't think things would go so far. I have always really respected you and I feel like I let you down." The words flowed so smoothly that Ally knew Brandon had been thinking a lot about this, but the sincerity and depth of emotion was impossible to miss. He was truly sorry. He looked up and met her gaze, his perfect blue eyes hoping for forgiveness. This was going to be even harder than Ally had imagined.

"Of course I forgive you, Brandon. Anyway, I'm a big girl, and I didn't exactly discourage you, did I?" Ally saw the relief start to soften his features. She was going to have to say this now, or she would never get it out. "But there is something you should know. There have been some,"—*how should I say this?*—"um, consequences, to our actions that night." She stopped, unable to say more. Ally watched the range of emotions flood through Brandon's eyes. She could tell that her statement puzzled him. Then came a flash of understanding, and Ally couldn't bear to keep eye contact. She ducked her head as the tears began falling into her lap.

Brandon's mind was reeling. *Did Ally just say what I think she said? Is she really pregnant? How can this be? We only did it once. Just one time that one night. You can't get pregnant by doing it one time!* But even as he thought it, he knew he was wrong. *Of course somebody can get pregnant after only one time. Ally is proof of that. I'm sure there's no mistake, either. Ally wouldn't get this wrong. If she was telling him that she was pregnant, then it is true. No mistake.*

Brandon reached out and put the tips of his fingers under Ally's chin. He gently lifted until she was facing him again. The sight of her big brown eyes drowning in hurt, embarrassment, pain, and anxiety was almost more than he could stand. His hand moved from her chin up to her cheek, wiping the tears away.

"Have you been to see anyone yet?" That was not the response Ally was dreading. He didn't seem to be too angry.

"A doctor, you mean?"

"Yeah." Brandon put his arm around her. "Have you been in to see a doctor, yet?"

"No, I wanted to talk to you first. You know, see how you felt about all of this. I guess I really wanted to see if you would come with me."

"Of course I'll come with you, Ally," Brandon said.

Did I hear him correctly? He wants to come! He wants to be involved! Ally threw both arms around Brandon's neck. She didn't know what would happen from here, but Brandon would be with her. Helping her. Supporting her. She felt a smile flickering on the corners of her mouth. Maybe everything would be okay, in the end.

"We need to get an appointment sooner than later, though. We'll need to get this taken care of before I leave for California. I want to make sure you're okay and that this is behind us before I take off. I'll have to rearrange a few things, but I'm sure I can push things back. After all, football practice doesn't actually start for several more weeks, I was just going early to get settled in." Brandon sounded so confident, so sure, but suddenly Ally was unsure.

"What do you mean 'you want to make sure this is behind us'? Look, if you don't want me to come to California, I guess I can understand that, but I'm not going to be able to just 'put this behind' me! This is my life we're talking about!"

"Ally, why on earth would you come to California? You've got your whole future planned out, and it definitely never included California. Don't look so upset. I know this is going to take some time for you to get over. That's why I think the sooner we take care of it, the better. I'll stick around as long as I can afterwards but then I've got to go."

Something about the way Brandon said, "the sooner we take care of it" just caught Ally's attention. The house of cards she was building her hopes on came tumbling down around her, followed by a wave of nausea that had nothing to do with the pregnancy hormones. Brandon did not want to support her and help her through this pregnancy or with raising a child. He wanted to support her and help her through an abortion! He wouldn't come with her to a doctor's appointment to hear the tiny heartbeat and find out the due date. He would only come to discuss ways to silence the new life growing inside her. Ally's stomach lurched and she jumped up to run to the edge of the lawn where the little bit of breakfast she had been able to choke down was deposited on the grass.

She remained frozen where she was, bent over with her hands resting on her knees. She was frantically trying to stop the spinning in her head, the ringing in her ears. She had to calm down. Ally took a couple of deep breaths and turned her back on the remains of her breakfast, careful to keep her eyes away from Brandon. Once her pulse began slowing, Ally felt that she must have misunderstood. Brandon hadn't been talking about an abortion. She knew he didn't share her particular religious convictions, but he must know that she would never consider that. Slowly Ally straightened her back and wiped her mouth with the back of her hand. She turned to face Brandon, but found that she couldn't quite meet his eyes. She resumed her seat across from him under the tree, and waited.

They sat in silence for a few moments, then Brandon tentatively reached up and touched her cheek. "Ally, I'm so sorry for putting you through all of this. You are one of my very best friends, and I don't like to see you hurting. I know this must be so overwhelming for you, so I'll handle everything. I'll call and set up the appointment myself. You're over eighteen, so you don't even have to tell your parents if you don't want to. We could tell them that you're coming with my family on one last trip . . . camping or something. My parents will support us in this, and I will even pay for it. You won't have to worry about anything." *So, she hadn't misunderstood.* The way he talked so matter-of-factly about ending a life shattered any silly hopes Ally had about the two of them making a life together with this child as the center of it. She knew she was going to be on her own in this, and somehow, with the knowing, came the strength to walk away from him.

Ally stood up and brushed her hair out of her eyes. Brandon took that as a sign of agreement and said, "It'll be okay, Ally. Don't worry. I'll make the call first thing Monday morning."

"Don't bother, Brandon. As it turns out, I'm not going to need your help. I'll make my own doctor appointment, and it will not be to destroy an innocent life."

"What? You can't possibly be thinking about actually having this baby?" His voice was rising now. "What will you do? Throw all your plans away? Well, you can count me out! You might be willing to toss aside all of your hopes and dreams, but I'm not! I'm going to California, and I will be moving on with my life. Look, I think you're great, and we've had some really good times together, but you are not my future, just like I'm not yours. If you go through with this, you'll be doing it without me!"

Ally didn't trust herself to speak. She was hurting too deeply. Besides, she had no answers for him. After all, she didn't know what she was going to do, or how she was going to do it. The only thing she knew was that this tiny, unborn, helpless little being was not going to be purposely snuffed out. She gave one quick nod to show that she understood. Brandon's eyes bored into hers, demanding answers, but when he got none, he turned and stormed back into the house. Ally fled to her car and made it several blocks before she could no longer choke back the sobs and had to pull over.

The next week, Ally knocked on the White's familiar hardwood door once again. Stephanie opened it and motioned her to come in. Ally's eyes flickered quickly around the entryway and into the living room, and then she exhaled. She didn't even realize that she'd been holding her breath. Ally was surprised at how relieved she was to discover that Brandon was not, in fact, anywhere around. When Stephanie called and asked Ally to come over and talk, Ally hesitated until Stephanie assured her that Brandon wouldn't be in on their conversation. Ally just couldn't bear to argue with him anymore. She had tried to talk with him once more, but it ended with Ally in tears and Brandon turning his back on her and walking away. Ally was sure that her eyes were now permanently red and puffy from all the crying, but she had come to terms with the fact that she was on her own in this. Brandon would not be swayed.

Then Stephanie called this morning asking Ally to come over and talk about the pregnancy, and Allison wondered if maybe she wouldn't have to do this completely without the White family. After all, this baby—she had finally allowed herself to start thinking of her pregnancy in terms of a baby—this baby would be Stephanie's grandchild. Perhaps she would want to be involved. These thoughts were swirling through Ally's mind as Stephanie invited her in and they sat down in the living room. Ally absorbed the familiarity of this house, this room. The tan carpet and off-white walls, the large, stone fireplace in the corner, and the antique upright piano that had been Stephanie's grandmother's. Ally had spent a lot of fun times with Stephanie and her family in this room. Then as Ally focused on Stephanie's face, she knew that this conversation would not be so fun. Stephanie was smiling, but the smile didn't extend to her eyes. They were bright blue, like her son's, but the little crinkles around the corners that meant she was sincerely happy were missing.

Instead, Stephanie's eyes were full of weariness. Just as the silence was starting to get awkward, Stephanie broke it with a sigh. "Hey, sweetie. How are you feeling?"

Allison managed a small smile. "Oh, I've been better."

"Yeah. Well, that's what I wanted to talk to you about." Ally just nodded. She was not yet sure what direction this conversation was going to take, and she wanted to know where Stephanie stood before she said too much. "I know that you and Brandon have been unable to get on the same page about this pregnancy. Sometimes men just don't have the tact or understanding that women need." Stephanie paused, obviously waiting for a response, but Ally just shrugged.

Another sigh escaped Stephanie's lips, then she tried a different approach, and Ally knew exactly where Stephanie stood and the course that this conversation was going to take. "Look, Ally. I know that your church disapproves of abortion, but I want you to take a minute and think about what having a baby would mean. Really think about it. Are you prepared to sacrifice everything you've ever hoped and dreamed for in order to take care of a baby?" Ally opened her mouth to protest, but Stephanie held up her hand. "We've always been able to talk openly and freely, Ally. Please just hear me out on this and then I'll do the same for you. I didn't invite you over to fight with you, okay?"

Ally nodded and took a deep breath. She made a quick decision to listen to what Stephanie had to say. After all, she had always given her good advice in the past. Stephanie noticed the slight softening of Ally's features and took it as a sign to continue.

"I want you to understand the amount of time and effort and sacrifice that a baby takes. School will be terribly difficult at best, and chances are you probably won't even be able to go, at least not right away, because now you've got to support a baby. You can't very well move into the dorms with a newborn. How will that impact your future and the life you've always wanted? And what about your social life? You won't have the time or energy to date anyone, and besides there aren't a lot of nineteen-year-old guys who want to get serious with someone who has a baby."

Ally opened her mouth with the intent to comment that not even this baby's father wanted to have anything to do with them, but Stephanie hurried on. "I know what you're thinking, but can you blame Brandon? He's thinking about your future as much as his. You guys are too young, and even though you are good friends, you know as well as he does that you could never make a marriage work. He is never going to share your religious beliefs, and he knows that those are too important to you to compromise on." Stephanie was gathering steam in her argument and paused momentarily to peer at Ally.

"I'm not convinced, yet, if that's what you're waiting for. But I did make a decision to hear you out, so if there's anything else you want to say, now is the time." Ally was pleased that her voice remained calm while she spoke.

"Well, it's plain to see from what Brandon told me and from what you just said that your mind is pretty closed on the subject of abortion. I have been thinking about why that is, when we live in a country that is based on freedom of choice. I also happen to know that your church puts great stock in 'free agency,' or the ability to choose for yourself. It seems to me that they have indoctrinated you to the point that your ability to choose is gone. But this isn't about some religious ideal. This is about your body. Your future. Your life. This is as real as it gets, Ally." Stephanie stood up and began pacing.

"Having a baby will change your life forever, and Brandon's as well. Even if he's not involved in your life, he will always know that he has a child somewhere in the world. You can make a responsible choice that will save yourself a lot of hard times, and both you and Brandon a lot of worry and heartache. Or you can choose to be self-ish, and think only about what your parents or neighbors will think. Just remember, you are the one that will have to deal with a child day in and day out, night after night." Ally fidgeted. That thought had crossed her mind.

"And don't think," Stephanie continued, "that Brandon's going to change his mind, or that I'm going to step in and help you with this. Brandon wants nothing to do with a baby right now, and I'm going to support him in that. You are not going to ruin his future over one mistake, one night. If you choose an abortion, we will help and support you in every possible way we can. If you choose to carry this fetus to full term, you do it without us." The atmosphere in the room turned from cool to frigid as Stephanie concluded her outburst. Her blue eyes were colder than Ally had ever seen them before. The weariness that was there earlier was replaced with anger.

Ally was angry too, but there was something she needed to say to Stephanie, though she didn't know how she would ever get through it. She took a deep breath and hoped it would come out right. "Stephanie, I can see that you're very upset, and I am sorry about that." She wanted to tell Stephanie that clearly her statement about not wanting to fight with Ally was only true as long as Ally would agree with her, but she checked herself, knowing that would only add fuel to the smoldering flames of this conversation. "I've listened very carefully to everything you wanted to say, and now it's time for me to tell you what I think about all this. Do you really believe that you've told me anything that I haven't already thought about over and over and over again until my mind is spinning?"

Stephanie sat back down and crossed her arms.

"I know that having a baby will change everything. I don't know all the particulars, but I realize that my life will never be the same again. And my decision not to kill this baby is not just based on some random religious ideal. To have an abortion would go against everything that I am. You talk about choices and agency, but you don't fully understand it. Of course we all have agency, we all have the gift to choose what we will do. But it's not really 'free'—not like you think it is. It comes with a price, and that price is that there is a consequence to every choice. The night that Brandon and I made our 'mistake,' as you call it, I could have used my agency differently. I could have used the gift of choice to make a decision not to kiss him, not to come back here, not to sleep with him. But I didn't. Instead I used my agency to choose to do all of those things. It's true that this is about my body, my life, and my future, and in the moment that I gave in to temptation with Brandon, I made my choice. I know what causes pregnancy. I was not forced against my will. I chose."

Stephanie was looking at the ground. Ally's words echoed of truth and she couldn't argue with them.

"Now, I'm facing the consequences of that choice," Ally said. "A pregnancy. A baby. A life. My choice about whether or not to be pregnant is over. There is a new life growing and developing inside me, and now it's not just about me, and my life. It's about this baby, and the life that it will have. The life that I have already given it, and that is as real as it gets." Ally paused, and when she began speaking again her voice was softer, but full of the strength of conviction.

"You've always given me good advice, Stephanie, and you've even given some today. You told me to be responsible. Well, I am. A responsible person doesn't run from the consequences of their actions. They take them and face them one day, one hour, one moment, at a time, and that is what I plan on doing. It's not just about me anymore, it's about my baby and what will be best for her." Ally felt the tears running down her cheeks, but her voice was calm and sure. "I can't say that I'm not disappointed that Brandon doesn't want to have anything to do with this baby, but I understand, and I will respect his decision. I'll leave now, and I won't be bothering any of your family anymore. I'm sorry that it's all ended this way. You and Brandon and your whole family have meant a lot to me over the last couple years, and I wish it didn't have to end this way. Good-bye, Stephanie."

As Ally stood up, she realized that Brandon was standing in the doorway to the living room. She didn't know how long he had been there, but it didn't matter. She held her head high as she approached him. "I'm really sorry about all of this, Brandon."

"Me too, Ally." His eyes were filling with tears, but Ally couldn't wait around any longer; her sobs were threatening to explode. All she could do was give him a quick hug.

"Good-bye, Brandon."

"Bye, Ally. I wish it could be different, but it just can't."

Ally nodded, no longer trusting her voice, and she walked past him and out of his front door for the last time.

CHAPTER FIVE

Allison sat nervously in the waiting room of the doctor's office. Her mom had offered to come with her, but Ally wanted to do this on her own. She had already filled out the mountain of paperwork for a new patient and a pregnancy and was glancing around at the homey office. She liked the large fish tank in the corner. *Did every doctor I've ever been to have a fish tank?* Ally thought so. There must be something soothing about the soft gurgling of the water, although the sound was doing little to dispel the nerves that were causing Ally's hands to shake.

She started looking around the room at the women in varying degrees of pregnancy. There was one with a small tummy just beginning to show, several who looked big, but not yet miserable, and one poor woman who looked like she was about to pop. There was also a young couple sitting in the corner, whispering excitedly to each other. The girl didn't look pregnant yet, but judging by the fact that they were here, in this office, Ally was sure she was. The girl seemed to be only a few years older than Ally, but she had a diamond ring on her ring finger, and she and her husband were obviously in love and very happy about the prospect of bringing a child into their family.

Ally wondered if anyone noticed that there was no wedding ring on her finger. She was trying to blink back the burn in her eyes when the nurse poked her head into the waiting room and called, "Allison

Campbell?" Ally stood up and mentally shook off the tears. She could make it through this appointment, and she could do it without crying. Somehow that seemed important.

The nurse was friendly and efficient. She weighed Ally and took her blood pressure. She handed Ally a cup and pointed her to a small bathroom. When Ally emerged the nurse dipped a paper strip into the cup, made a note on the chart, and showed Ally to an exam room. "Dr. Broadbent will be just a few minutes. Since you will be getting a full physical today, you will need to remove all your clothing. Put the robe on top with the opening toward the front. The sheet is to cover your lower half." She smiled somewhat apologetically as she handed Ally a stack of what appeared to be large paper towels, and left the room.

Ally looked around for the aforementioned robe and sheet and then realized, to her dismay, that that was what she was holding in her sweating hands. She was grumbling to herself as she undressed and tried to drape the flimsy coverings over and around her so that nothing was showing. She wasn't positive she had much luck in the back because the "sheet" as the nurse called it, didn't wrap all the way around her. At least Dr. Broadbent was a girl. That would make this all slightly less embarrassing.

Ally tried to sit still on the exam table. She was worried that if she moved too much, her careful job of covering up would be undone. She stared at a picture of a mother and baby on the wall opposite her, trying to imagine herself as a mom. She was having a hard time thinking of herself that way, because it was still hard to believe that there was actually a baby growing inside of her.

Allison jumped as Dr. Broadbent knocked on the door and entered the room. As they began talking, Ally was happy to find that Dr. Broadbent was sensitive to the fact that Ally didn't have a husband, or even a boyfriend, to help her through this. She asked whether Ally's parents knew she was pregnant and seemed relieved that they did. Dr. Broadbent asked a lot of questions about Ally's overall health and emotional state as she performed the exam, and Ally was glad to have something to think about besides the exam itself.

At the end of the appointment, Dr. Broadbent made some notes on the chart and then said, "Well, Ally, from what I can see here,

I'll put your due date at February eighteenth. That would make you about seven weeks along right now. That's far enough that we should be able to hear a heartbeat. Do you want to give it a try?"

Ally was surprised. She hadn't realized there would be a tiny heart beating already. "Sure. I'd like to hear that."

Dr. Broadbent got out her equipment, and after just a moment, she smiled as Allison heard a quick thub, thub, thub, thub, thub, thub, thub. "That's my baby?" Allison asked.

"It sure is, Ally. That's your baby."

Allison could no longer hold back her tears, but for the first time since she had discovered she was pregnant, these were happy tears.

"So, Ally, it's been several weeks since we last talked. How did it go with telling the baby's father?" Bishop Jenkins knew immediately that it hadn't gone well by the way Ally's eyes welled up. She could only manage to shake her head. "I'll take it from your response that a successful marriage does not look possible."

"Oh, Bishop," Ally managed as her tears began flowing again. "A marriage is impossible. First off, he's not a member of the Church, and has flat out stated that he never will be. But mostly, a marriage is impossible because I don't think I'll ever see him again."

Bishop Jenkins raised an eyebrow, "Never?"

"Never. He essentially told me that unless I had an abortion, we had nothing more to say to each other." Bishop Jenkins looked momentarily alarmed but quickly regained his composure.

"I see. And what did you say to that?" His words seemed measured, careful.

"Well, it's a long story, but basically, when he wouldn't budge on his position after a couple conversations, I said 'Good-bye.'" Ally could see the relief wash across Bishop Jenkins' face.

"That must have been very difficult for you." It wasn't a question.

"It was one of the hardest things I've ever done, next to telling my parents that I was pregnant. But what else could I do? This isn't just about me, and what I want to do or be. It's about this baby. It doesn't matter what sacrifices I have to make, I need to take care of this baby. The hard part was realizing that I will have to do it alone, without him." Ally wiped her tears and squared her shoulders as though mentally preparing to take on this huge responsibility.

"Well, Ally, I don't need to tell you that you made the right decision about not having an abortion. Unless you have anything else to say on that subject, I suggest we move forward."

"Please do. I don't ever want to hear the word again."

"Okay, and since the father does not even want to discuss the possibility of being a parent and has removed himself from the picture, I don't think we need to dwell any further on him, either." Ally was surprised that when the bishop said these words, she felt a tiny stirring of peace within her, as if his words confirmed that her choices in handling this pregnancy had been good so far.

"I would like that. I'm ready to quit looking back and start looking forward. I don't have any idea what I'm going to do or how I'm going to raise this baby, but I know that my main priority right now needs to be this child." Ally realized as she was saying the words that this was how she truly felt. She would do whatever was needed to make sure this baby would be okay.

"I'm glad to hear you say that, Ally. Now, what do you know about LDS Family Services?"

"LDS Family Services?" Ally had seen some commercials, but surely Bishop Jenkins wasn't suggesting she go talk to them. "I've heard of them, but Bishop, I am *not* interested in giving my baby up! I know this is going to be difficult, but this is my responsibility and my baby!"

"Whoa, whoa! Slow down, Ally. Adoption is only one part of what they do. They have a support group for unwed pregnant women, and they can also help you and teach you what you need to know about being a single mom."

"Well, I am *not* interested in talking about adoption!" Ally's mind was spinning once again. That was happening a lot lately. After having spent several weeks of sheer agony when she knew that she was pregnant, but had not yet told anyone, she thought much of the load would be relieved when her secret was finally out. Not so. She spent the next week or so arguing with Brandon—fighting for this baby's life—and was only now starting to feel like she could start looking toward the future, only to have the bishop throw this at her.

"Ally." The bishop's voice startled her from her thoughts. "Ally, the social workers at LDS Family Services will certainly mention an adoption plan as one option for you, but they will not force it on you. If you're not interested in that, just tell them. There are still lots of things they can help you with." Bishop Jenkins smiled and Ally knew he was about to play his trump card. "Besides, wouldn't it be nice to talk with some other girls who are in a similar situation to you? Some friends that could go through this with you and understand where you are coming from? With them, at least you won't have to do this part of things all alone."

"Well, I have to admit that it would be nice to talk to someone who understands my situation. I have been feeling alone in this. Even though my dad is being very supportive, and my mom is trying to be, they can't possibly know how I am actually feeling." Ally could feel her features softening, and Bishop Jenkins's smile widened.

"I might go and talk to them," she conceded, "but not about adoption. Bishop, something has happened over these past few weeks. After the shock and fear that I initially felt subsided, I went to the baby's father hoping to make a family. Even though I knew it would not be the kind of family I have always dreamed of, I still thought that would be better for my child than no family. Then, when he turned his back on us and I started fighting for this child's life, something happened that I never imagined would happen so soon. I fell in love with my baby, Bishop. I know that sounds silly when I'm only a few months along, but it's true. I love my baby! I love her more than I ever dreamed possible, and I'm going to do everything in my power to give her the best chance in life. After all, I was the one who made the mistake, not her. I want her to be happy and I will do whatever it takes to give her all the love and joy and learning and experiences that this world has to offer."

Ally expected the bishop to try to talk about adoption again. He was still smiling that crinkly-eyed smile of his, and Ally was sure there was more he wanted to say on the subject. Instead she was caught off guard when he replied, "Isn't it still too early to find out the gender of the baby?'

"What? Oh, yeah, the doctor said not until I was twenty weeks along. Why?"

Bishop Jenkins was still smiling.

"You just keep referring to the baby as 'she' and 'her.'"

"I don't know . . . I think of the baby as a girl. It just feels right. I guess I'll find out for sure in another couple months."

He nodded and then changed the subject. They read a few scriptures, and he asked Ally how she felt about the book he had recommended to her. "When I first started reading, it made me feel more lousy about what I've done," Ally said. "But, as I kept going and finished the book, I was comforted by the Spirit. I want to believe that this can all be made right. I'm still not sure, though."

"Well, Ally, I think you're doing good. You're truly sorry for the wrong choices you have made. That is definitely the first step. I want you to keep working on believing that you can be forgiven for this, and that the Savior will help you through what lies ahead."

"I'll keep trying. I just feel so hopeless sometimes. The idea of the Atonement sounds good, and I always thought I had a testimony of it. I'm just having a hard time believing that it applies to me. Mostly I'm so overwhelmed about all of this, and I'm struggling just to keep my world from crashing down around me." The bishop looked thoughtful for a moment, then his easy smile faded, and when he looked up at her, his eyes were wet.

"Ally, I can't understand what your emotions and feelings are right now, but I think you'll find the road that lies ahead of you to be the most difficult you have yet traveled in your life, and the only way you will be able to make it through is with the help of the Savior. Don't give up. Turn to Him. Turn more earnestly to the scriptures and to your Heavenly Father. Don't give up your hope in the Atonement. It is real, and our Savior can help you . . . if you let Him."

Ally found herself choked up again, and she could only nod. He made it sound so simple, so true. She could almost begin to hope . . . almost. Bishop Jenkins stood and reached across his desk to shake Ally's hand. She took a brief moment to clear her mind and was relieved that he hadn't mentioned LDS Family Services again. Maybe he had realized that she didn't need them after all. Then Bishop Jenkins reached into his desk, pulled out a business card, and handed it to her. "I won't tell you that you have to go see them yet, but I do think it would be a good idea."

Ally tucked the card in her back pocket and tried to smile at the bishop. "I'll think about it."

"That's all I'm asking."

When Ally arrived home from the bishop's office, her dad was waiting for her in the living room.

"How did it go tonight?" Ally was thankful that her father was being supportive of her. She knew he was disappointed in the mistakes she had made, but he was putting his own feelings aside to do what was best for Ally. She made a quick mental note that that was how she wanted to be as a parent.

"It was pretty good, but I'm starving! Come in the kitchen and I'll tell you more about it." Ally was filling a plate with leftover chicken and mashed potatoes and gravy as she spoke. "Now he wants me to read a book that's about believing that Christ will do what He has promised." Ally took a big bite of chicken. "I guess he thinks I'm skeptical because when he had me read Isaiah 1:18 where it says 'though your sins be as scarlet, they shall be white as snow,' I asked him how that was possible."

"What did he say?"

Ally's mouth was full of potatoes, but she swallowed and looked up at her dad. "He read another scripture, and it hit me pretty hard. It's in Ephesians . . . I wrote it down." Ally reached into her pocket for the piece of paper. "It's Ephesians 1:7. It says—speaking of Jesus— 'In whom we have redemption through his blood, the forgiveness of sins, according to the riches of his grace.'"

"Why did that hit you so hard, Ally," Dad asked. Ally was quiet for a few minutes, thinking and eating.

"I guess because whenever I've thought about the Atonement, it's always been an abstract idea. It has never occurred to me that Jesus bled—actually offered His own blood—for my redemption. He paid the price for my mistakes. Not in some far-off mythical way, but with His own blood. It's starting to seem real to me for the first time."

"Well, Ally, it is real and the Atonement can make things right between you and Heavenly Father, just as it has started doing with me. You just have to be willing to allow it to work in your life."

"Wait a minute, Dad. How has the Atonement made things right with you? You didn't do anything wrong."

"I'm not sure that's entirely true, but it doesn't matter now. Anyway, you know I was upset with your actions, but I knew that harboring those angry feelings would not help either of us. So I decided to turn them over to the Lord. It isn't easy, and I'm still working on it, but because I'm willing to let those feelings go, and to put in the effort to truly let the Atonement in, Christ has begun to take those angry feelings from me. I'm still sad, but I think that in time, the Savior can ease those feelings as well."

Ally felt the familiar wetness begin to gather in the corners of her eyes.

"Dad, I don't know what I'd do without you!" She threw her arms around him and cried on his shoulder; something she hadn't done since she was seven and her cat died. She cried over her mistakes, and the disappointment and hurt she had caused for so many people. She cried over the loss of her best friend, because that's what Brandon had been. She cried over her uncertain future. Would she ever graduate from college, get married, or have more children? Most of all, she cried for her baby. This little life growing inside her. She cried over the difficulties that would be in this child's life because of Ally's choices, and when the heartache became almost more than she could bear, her dad squeezed her tighter, and Ally's heart broke as she realized that her baby would not have the safety of a father's arms to be held in when she cried.

CHAPTER SIX

"Hey, Amy, it's Ally."

"Hi, Ally! I've been trying to call you, but maybe my messages haven't been getting through or something. It's been forever since I've talked to you."

"Yeah, well, I actually have been getting your messages, and Hannah's, but I've just been going through . . . something. Anyway, I was trying to get things sorted out before I said anything."

"That sounds pretty serious. So what's going on?" Amy was curious.

"Well, I'd rather not tell you over the phone." Ally paused, but she was past the point of no return now. Besides, they were going to find out about Ally's pregnancy sooner or later. It would be better if they heard it from her. "I invited Hannah to come over this afternoon. Can you come too? Then we can talk about it all together."

"Sure. I get off work at three."

"Could you come to my house around four?" Ally asked.

"That'll be great. See you then! Bye."

"Bye, Amy. See you later."

Allison was nervous. She had been doing a good job at avoiding all of her friends. It was easy during the week, now that they were all graduated and moving forward with their lives. Sundays were a little trickier, but she had been going to Relief Society with her mom, and her friends were staying in Young Women's through the summer. That really cut down on opportunities to visit at church, which was just what Ally wanted. Apparently, Bishop Jenkins noticed Ally sep-arating herself, because after several interviews, he encouraged her not to shut her friends out of her life.

"Your friends are not as emotionally tied to the situation as your family is, so they might be able to help you in ways that your parents can't," he told her. "Besides, Amy and Hannah are terrific girls. I think they'll support you."

Ally hoped so. Hannah and Amy had been her friends since they were all five years old. Their two families moved into Ally's ward within three months of each other, and the girls developed a friend-ship that remained strong. Ally took a little courage in that thought. Surely they wouldn't turn their backs on her now. Maybe Amy could even give her advice on being a single mom. After all, Amy was the only child of a single, never-been-married mom. Funny, how she hadn't thought about that before. Amy turned out great, and her mom seemed fairly happy, although she did worry throughout their senior year about what she would do if Amy went away to college.

Ally jumped as the doorbell rang. Hannah and Amy were stand-ing on the front porch looking worried. "Hi guys," Ally began. "Thanks for coming over. Let's go up to my room."

Hannah and Amy exchanged glances as they followed Ally up the stairs. They all sat cross-legged on Ally's fuzzy, pink bedspread, and there was silence. After a moment, it was Amy that spoke up. "So, Ally, what's going on? Why have you been avoiding us?"

Ally had been thinking about what to say to them all day and decided that a quick, direct approach would be the least painful. "Well, guys, I did something really crazy after graduation, and there were some . . . unexpected consequences. I've spent the last couple months trying to figure out what to do."

"Wait a minute." It was Hannah that spoke up. "I thought your plans about college were solid. Did you change your mind?"

"Not really," Ally said. "I still want to go to college, but it doesn't look like I'll be going right away." Her heart was pounding and her hands were starting to shake. Ally knew she had to tell them now, before she chickened out.

"What are you talking about?" Amy asked.

"Hold on a second," Ally responded. "This is going to be hard to tell you, but just let me get it out, and then you can ask questions, okay?" Hannah and Amy both nodded. "Okay, well, the thing is," Ally took a deep breath and then blurted out, "Remember our graduation party? Well, Brandon and I left together and one thing led to another . . . and we slept together and now I'm pregnant and Brandon wanted me to have an abortion, and when I said no, he told me that he wanted nothing to do with me or the baby and now I don't know what I'm going to do and I'm scared and I'm worried and I feel like I've messed everything up, and there's nothing I can do to make things right."

Hannah and Amy stared at Allison for a split second while the news sunk in, and then Amy squealed, "You're going to have a baby! Oh, congratulations, Ally! That's terrific! A baby will be so much fun! Are you going to stay here?" Ally was surprised by Amy's excitement. She was hoping for acceptance and support, but she sure wasn't overflowing with excitement. It took her a moment to recover, then Ally nodded.

"Oh good," Amy continued. "Now I'm glad I decided to stay here and work instead of going off to school because I can be here and see you and the baby all the time! It's going to be great!" Amy reached over and hugged Allison.

Ally's surprise was turning to confusion and she didn't know why. She was hoping that the girls would still be her friends after she told them. Amy had taken it amazingly well, but the way she was talking made it sound like they were little girls who would be playing house with a new doll. That just didn't feel right.

Hannah cleared her throat, and Amy stopped gushing. Hannah looked down and Ally knew she was thinking very hard. Then she nodded her head once. Just a quick bob, like she had made a decision. Then Hannah looked up at Ally. "Do your parents know?"

"Yeah. I actually told them before I told Brandon. Bishop Jenkins knows too. He was the first one I talked to about it, and I've been meeting with him regularly ever since."

"And what do your mom and dad think?"

"My dad actually took it pretty well. I mean, he was sad, and disappointed, but he didn't get angry with me. Mom didn't handle it quite so good. She was very angry at first, but she's been coming around. I think she's even starting to get the tiniest bit excited about the thought of having a grandbaby."

"So, you're going to raise the baby yourself then?"

"And what's wrong with that?" Amy interjected. "My mom has managed just fine, and I've turned out all right. Of course Ally's going to raise the baby. What kind of question is that?"

Hannah didn't comment on Amy's outburst. Instead she turned back to Ally and said, "So? Are you?"

"I have to, Hannah. Besides the fact that I'm responsible for this baby, I'm already attached. I love her more than anything else."

Hannah hesitated. She opened her mouth to say something and then shut it. She shook her head, opened her mouth again, and closed it again. In spite of the serious conversation they were having, Ally had to smile at her friend. "Go on and say it, Hannah. I want to hear what you think. That's why you're here."

"Well, I was just wondering if you have considered adoption." Allison started shaking her head, but Hannah held up her hand and continued. "Look, Ally, I have no doubt that you would be a great mom. But can you be a mom and a dad? Can you, on your own, give your baby the blessing of being sealed in the temple to her parents?"

"Hannah, that's not fair!" It was Amy that had spoken. "Of course Ally can't be a mom and a dad. And she can't be sealed in the temple right now, but maybe in the future she will meet a great guy and they will all be sealed together." Amy's voice was starting to shake. Allison knew that tears were close to the surface.

Hannah remained calm and turned to Amy. "I know that your mom has done a great job raising you, and I have all the respect in the world for her for that. She made the decision that was right for her. I'm just wondering . . . well, I don't know . . . I've often wondered if you could have everything you have with your mom, *plus* have a dad . . . ?" Hannah's question trailed off as the tears spilled over onto Amy's cheeks.

"Well, I don't have a dad, and nothing can change that." Amy's voice was soft, but there was no bitterness in it. "I won't lie to you.

There have been times when I've wished for a dad, but this is the life I've always known, and it's been good."

"I didn't mean to upset you, Amy," Hannah responded. "Ally asked what I thought, so I told her. I'm not saying that your mom was wrong for doing what she did, any more than any of the other women who choose to raise a child on their own. I'm just saying that there is another choice. I don't know what Ally should do." Hannah turned to Ally and shrugged her shoulders as she continued. "I really don't. That's between you and Heavenly Father. I'm just wondering if you have given Him the chance to let you know how He feels about it."

Hannah and Amy left Allison with a lot to think about. On the one hand, Amy was right. Her mom had done a good job, and Amy was a terrific person. Plus, there was always the chance that within a couple years Allison would meet a wonderful man who would accept and love her and her child and they could all be sealed together, just as Amy said. Maybe she could still have the family she'd always dreamed of, temple marriage and all. But if that didn't happen, even if she never married, she was willing to make that sacrifice for her baby.

On the other hand, Hannah said some things that Allison had never considered. She had been dead set against adoption, but maybe it wouldn't hurt to just look into it. Besides, Hannah was right too. Through all the prayers that Ally had sent heavenward lately, she had never asked Heavenly Father what His will concerning this situation was. She wasn't ready to do that yet, but it was something to think about.

Later that evening, after the dinner dishes were washed and Allison's younger sisters were in bed, the phone rang. It was Hannah. "Hey, Ally, how are you doing?"

"Honestly? I feel lousy. I feel like I'm going to puke, and my brain hasn't stopped spinning since you guys left."

"I'm sorry about that. I've been afraid that I made things worse for you, and that's not what I wanted to do."

"No need to apologize, Hannah. I said I wanted to know how

you felt, and I meant it. It did seem like you have given adoption a lot of thought, though. Much more than most eighteen-year-olds, anyway," Ally said.

"Well, that's actually why I called," Hannah continued. "I was wondering if you could come over to my house tonight."

"Right now?"

"Yeah, if it's okay."

"All right. I'll double-check with my parents, but it should be fine. I'll see you in a minute."

"Okay, bye."

Allison hung up the phone and realized there must have been more Hannah wanted to say this afternoon but didn't when Amy was getting so upset. She walked down the stairs. Her dad was sitting on the couch reading his newspaper.

"Dad, that was Hannah. I think she wants to talk a little more. I told her I would come over, if that's okay."

Dad smiled. "Sure, Ally. I'm glad to see you talking to her again, anyway. You'll need her support."

"Thanks, Dad. See you later."

Allison decided to walk to Hannah's house. She only lived a couple blocks away, and the warm evening air felt good. She knocked on the door, and Hannah answered right away. "Mom, Ally's here," she called as they sat down in the formal living room. Ally looked around and smiled. They were never allowed to play in here when they were little, but as the girls grew, they spent more and more time in this room—studying, laughing, pretending to study, laughing some more. The flower patterns on the couch had faded over the years, and now more often than not, a thin layer of dust covered the china cabinet in the corner, but it was definitely a happy room. Happy and comfortable. Just like Hannah's family.

Hannah's mom, Melanie, walked in pushing a loose strand of hair behind her ear and wiping her hands on the blue apron that Hannah had made in the eighth grade home economics class. Allison stood and gave Melanie a squeeze, then they settled in to the overstuffed furniture.

"Ally, I hope you don't mind, but Hannah told me about what is going on in your life right now." Melanie spoke matter-of-factly, but with kindness and no judgment in her voice.

"No, I don't mind. Everyone's going to know sooner or later, anyway," Ally said.

"After telling me about your conversation this afternoon, Hannah asked me if I would share my story with you. I told her she was welcome to tell you herself," Melanie smiled at her daughter, "but she thinks I tell it so much better."

"You do," Hannah responded. "Besides, the timing wasn't right this afternoon. I didn't want to upset Amy any more."

"Okay." Ally was interested. "I'm all ears."

"I won't go into all the details," Melanie began, "but suffice it to say that when I was just the age you and Hannah are now, I made some decisions that led to me getting pregnant."

Allison was stunned. She had no idea! Hannah was the oldest in the family, but Ally also knew that Melanie had celebrated her fortieth birthday just before school got out. There had been a big party. Ally quickly did the math in her head; there was no way that Melanie gave birth to Hannah when she herself was only eighteen or nineteen! Which meant . . .

Melanie only paused for a moment. "I'm sure you've done the math, Ally, and I'll bet that brought up a question. The answer is yes. I gave birth to a baby boy when I was nineteen years old, and I placed him for adoption." Melanie's voice was steady, but there was a hint of moisture in her eyes as she continued. "Now, I don't want to preach adoption to you because I know, better than most, what a personal decision you are faced with. I will simply tell you my story and how I came to make the decision that I did." Melanie leaned forward and Ally mirrored the action.

"After I figured out I was pregnant," Melanie continued, "and found that the biological father wanted nothing to do with me now that I was carrying his child, I turned to my parents. They immediately started talking about adoption and sent me to the bishop for instructions on how to proceed. Luckily, I had a wonderful bishop who listened to my worries and concerns about adoption, and did not tell me that I had to do what my parents were recommending. He told me that this was a decision that would affect the rest of my life, and that I was the one who needed to make it. He helped set my feet on the road of repentance, and he sent me to talk to a social worker at LDS Social Services. That was before the name change to LDS Family Services," Melanie explained. "Anyway, Deborah explained all my options to me and we spent hours in counseling sessions as I tried to determine what I needed to do. I wanted to keep my baby and raise him. I was smart and resourceful. I believed we could make it on our own. I would do whatever it took to make a happy life. I was willing to make the sacrifices necessary to take care of him." Ally was nodding. She could relate.

"Two months before my due date, I was explaining all of this to Heavenly Father in my prayers, and I heard how often I was saying 'I, I, I.' This realization stopped me for a moment, and there was a whisper from the Spirit to my heart that said, 'But what about the baby?' My answer was ready. 'I love him. I want him. I need him.' The whisper repeated itself, 'But what about the baby? What is best for him?'

"I opened my mouth but didn't quite know how to respond. I had never considered that there might be something better for him. Although my entire being fought against the idea of not raising him myself, I began thinking of him at two years, three years, five years, twelve years old. I could be a great mom, but I could not be a dad. Who would teach him to fish? Who would play catch with him? Who would show him that a man can be loving and kind, and still be a man? Who would take him to Scout camp? Who would baptize him? Who would give him the priesthood? Who would bless him when he was sick or scared? In short, who would be his dad?

"As my mind whirred through these questions, I felt the sobs building up, and as they exploded, I felt as though my heart had done so as well, for at that moment I knew what I had to do. I did not know how I would ever be able to manage it, but I knew that adoption was the answer—for me and for my little boy. 'How, Heavenly Father?' I pleaded, 'How can I ever give him away?' I was surprised by the answer, but it filled me with love. Adoption was not 'giving him away.' Instead I was giving him the most precious gift that anyone could give. I was giving him a family. I was giving him a dad. I was giving him the blessings of being raised under the sealing covenant of the temple." Melanie paused, smiled, and brushed a tear from her cheek with the back of her hand before she continued.

"So I went to Deborah and told her I had decided to place him for adoption. I picked an amazing couple that had been married for four years. The woman had experienced some health troubles in her teenage years and ended up having to have a hysterectomy. She had known for years that her only hope of having a family was through adoption, and she had been praying for all those years that a birth mom somewhere would be able to give her a child. The child that she could not bear.

"Adoptions were closed then, so I never got to meet them, but Deborah told me that when she placed my three-day-old little boy in the arms of his mom, she held him to her heart and cried and cried and cried while my baby's daddy wrapped his arms around his wife and his son and held them as tears ran down his cheeks as well." Melanie's eyes were wet as she concluded her story, but they were also filled with peace.

"But how did you manage to go through with it?" Ally couldn't help but ask.

"There is only one Being that made it possible for me to sign the papers and release my sweet baby. Jesus Christ. He truly held me up and gave me the strength to do something that I never could have done on my own."

Ally had a few questions that she was hesitant to ask. Melanie seemed to understand and said, "Go ahead, Ally. I will be happy to answer any questions you have."

"Have you ever regretted your decision?"

"No." Melanie's answer was immediate. "No, I have never regretted the decision I made to place him for adoption. There have been times when I have missed him. In the beginning I missed him so much that it hurt, but as I have turned to the Savior, He has taken the burden of pain from me. I know that the little boy who grew inside of me is with the family that was meant for him. I am at peace."

"Are you . . . ashamed of the decision? I mean, I've known Hannah and been around your family for all of these years, and I never knew. You don't talk about it at all, like you don't want anyone to know."

"That's a fair question, Ally, and I'll give you an honest answer. I used to be embarrassed that I had gotten pregnant out of wedlock and didn't want anyone to know that I had made such a big mistake. For a while, I was ashamed that I had sinned. But, and please listen carefully, I have never been ashamed of the child I gave birth to, nor of my decision to give him a family. I know, as well as I know that I'm sitting here right now, that Heavenly Father's will was for him to be with the parents he has.

"Now that I'm older and maybe a little wiser, and have finally forgiven myself for my mistakes, I am no longer embarrassed about those either. The experiences I went through made me who I am today. You're right, though. I still don't talk about it much, but not for the reason you think. I don't tell many people about my experience for the same reason that we don't talk lightly about the temple: it is too sacred to me. Not secret, mind you, but sacred. I have never felt Heavenly Father's hand in my life as strongly as I did while going through the adoption process. Jesus Christ became very real to me as He gave me the strength to let my baby boy go. It was an incredible experience, and I don't want anyone to be able to make light of it. So I'm very selective about who I share it with."

"Wow, thanks for telling me all of that," Ally said. "I don't know what to say."

"You don't need to say anything, Ally. Like I said, I understand what a personal decision this is. What's right for one person might not be right for another. I don't know what you should do; Hannah and Amy don't know what you should do. Maybe your parents don't even know what you should do. They can help guide you, as can Bishop Jenkins and skilled social workers, but ultimately this is between you and your Heavenly Father. Don't forget about Him." Melanie smiled and stood up. Allison stood as well and Melanie gave her a big hug. "Good luck, Ally. If you ever need a listening ear, I'm here."

"Me too." Hannah grinned.

"Thanks so much! That really means a lot to me." It was all Ally could think of to say as she left, but her mind was buzzing as she walked slowly home.

Allison got home, said her prayers, and crawled into bed. She was exhausted, but her mind didn't want to shut down and go to sleep yet. Ally never would have believed that Melanie had once been in the same situation she was in right now. Even if she could have imagined that, Ally never would have dreamed that Melanie would choose adoption for her child. And yet . . . as Melanie told her story, Ally felt the Spirit. There was no doubting the peace in

Melanie's eyes, either. She made the choice that was right for her. Ally just didn't think that was the choice she would make.

She closed her eyes, trying to calm her mind. Melanie had an interesting way of looking at it. That she had given her baby a dad and a family. Ally would do just about anything to give her baby a dad, but she had to be the mom! Yes, Ally thought to herself, I will be the mom.

Ally's physical exhaustion was starting to win out, and she was getting close to sleep. The idea of counseling sessions sounded good, though. And Bishop Jenkins had said something about talking to other girls who were facing the same future she was. "Maybe it won't hurt just to go talk to someone at Family Services," Ally mumbled to herself. And then she was asleep.

CHAPTER SEVEN

It took Allison a minute to remember everything from the night before when the sun came streaming into her room around seven-thirty in the morning. But after taking a moment to orient herself, and then running into the bathroom to throw up, she was able to focus on the conversation she had with Melanie and Hannah last night, and the thoughts that had come to her after climbing into bed.

Ally went back to her room and looked through the stack of papers that had accumulated on her dresser during the last few months. She finally found what she was looking for and put the business card for LDS Family Services, that Bishop Jenkins gave her almost a month ago, on her bedside table before climbing back under the covers.

Her bedside clock said 8:15 when Ally woke up to her younger, twin sisters arguing over the bathroom. From the sound of it, Emma was inside with the door locked, and Elsie felt she had already been in there long enough. Ally forced herself out of bed and stumbled down the hallway. When Elsie caught sight of her, she stopped pounding on the bathroom door, and suddenly got very interested in a tiny crack in the doorframe. Emma, caught off guard by the sudden lack of yelling, opened the door to see what was going on, then dropped her eyes and mumbled, "Morning," when she saw Ally.

"Good morning, Emma. Good morning, Elsie," Ally said as she walked past. She had told her sisters and brother about her pregnancy a couple weeks ago. Charlie, her sixteen-year-old brother, took the news fairly well. He had asked a few questions about whether Ally and Brandon would be getting married, and did this mean that Ally wouldn't be leaving for college in the fall, and then went right back to being Charlie. He joked with Ally and teased her, and made fun of her when she would run into the bathroom to throw up. They talked about books he was reading, and he asked Ally when she would be too fat to fit into her pants.

It was nice. Charlie didn't tiptoe around and pretend she wasn't pregnant; he just kept treating her the way he always had. Ally appreciated that and told him so. Charlie responded with his usual honest nonchalance, "Hey, you're my big sister. I love you. We all make mistakes, right? It will all work out in the end."

The girls hadn't taken it so well. Being twelve years old, they were old enough to understand the mechanics of what had to happen to become pregnant, and they were mortified. They couldn't believe that their big sister would have done that. Then, as they started realizing that soon, everyone would know that Ally was pregnant, they got even more upset. They were embarrassed because their friends and neighbors and teachers and even the people they didn't like, would all know.

It all reached a boiling point when Elsie screamed at Ally, "Everyone is going to be whispering about it and talking about you behind your back, and then they'll wonder if me and Emma are like you!"

"Well, I'm sorry this is going to be so inconvenient for you two! I'm sorry that you're going to be embarrassed about me!" Ally hadn't meant to yell, and yet she was. "I'm sorry I screwed up, all right? But there's nothing I can do to change that now! Believe me, I'm going to be plenty embarrassed too!" Then Ally stormed out of the room.

That was about a week ago, and now Emma, Elsie, and Ally were very careful about how they talked to each other. The girls tried to avoid Ally as much as possible, and if they did have to say something to her, they had started staring at the ground while they talked. They would never meet Ally's eyes. After cooling down a bit, Ally really did feel bad for them. She knew that her choices had impacted her whole family, and that they were only at the beginning. So she was trying to stay out of the girls' way and just let them work through this however they needed to.

Ally arrived in the kitchen and started pouring herself a bowl of cereal for breakfast when her mother walked in. "Good morning, Ally. I heard you up earlier. Are you okay?" Julie was still upset about Ally's pregnancy, but she was trying very hard to put that aside and give Ally the support she needed.

"Yeah, I'm actually feeling pretty good right now. After I puked, I felt better and was able to go right back to sleep."

"I'm glad. I was just going up to break up Emma and Elsie's fight, but they seem to have quieted down."

"They just teamed up against a common enemy," Ally managed a weak smile.

"Give them some time, Ally. This is huge for them. But they'll come around. They love you."

"I know. Hey, Mom?"

"Yes, Ally?"

"I'm really sorry . . . about everything. If I could go back and change things, I would."

"I know. Let's just try to keep moving forward, okay?"

"Okay. Oh, speaking of that, I think I'm going to call LDS Family Services today."

Julie froze as she reached for the cereal. "Oh? I thought you weren't interested in talking about adoption."

"I'm not, Mom. I think it might be nice to look at all of my options, but mostly I want to talk to some other girls who are also single and pregnant." Ally shrugged casually. She didn't want this to be a big deal. This didn't change anything.

"Whatever you think, Ally."

"LDS Family Services, this is Amber, can I help you?" The voice on the phone sounded pleasant and helpful, but it still wasn't easy for Allison to choke the words out. She tried to swallow, wondering why her mouth was so dry. "Are you there? Can I help you?" the voice asked again.

"Yes, I'm here," Ally managed. "I . . . um . . . I wanted to make an appointment."

"I can help you with that. And have you been in to see us before?"

"No. I got your card from my bishop."

"Okay, and what would you like to talk about?"

Ally took a deep breath. "Well, I . . . I'm pregnant, and I'm eighteen, and I'm not married, and I just . . . I just wanted to talk to someone . . . about . . . that." Ally waited for a gasp or an awkward silence, but Amber didn't miss a beat and remained as pleasant as ever.

"Sure. In fact, let me check the schedule . . . yes, Barbara can meet with you later today. Will that work for you?"

"Yes, I can do that. What time?" Ally breathed a sigh of relief. That hadn't been so terrible.

"Could you be here at 2:30?"

"That will be great. Thanks."

"No problem. What's your name?"

"Allison Campbell."

"Okay, Allison. We'll see you then. You know where we're located?"

"I think so. It looks like you're on the north end of town? Just off the freeway?"

"Yes. You're set. We'll see you this afternoon."

"Great. Good-bye."

"Good-bye, Allison." Ally hung up and felt like a weight had been lifted from her shoulders. She was glad she had made the call.

By the time Allison arrived at the office of LDS Family Services that afternoon, the weight was right back on her shoulders, and heavier than ever. She was nervous and embarrassed to be confiding in a total stranger, but Barbara was supportive and pleasant. Ally was relieved that Barbara did not push adoption; only mentioning it briefly before Ally told her she was not interested. Mainly, Barbara listened, and Ally was grateful for that. Ally committed to attend the birth mother support group that would be held later in the week, and left the office feeling—not calm—but at least buoyed up. Not quite so alone.

CHAPTER EIGHT

Allison was at the end of her first trimester, and with it came a small measure of relief from the morning sickness that had plagued her. Ally was meeting regularly with Barbara, and the birth mother support group at LDS Family Services, and they were going well.

Ally cried when September arrived and she was not away at college as she had always planned, but she enrolled in some online courses and the school deferred her scholarship for a year. Maybe after the baby was born, she would be able to find a way to attend. If not, she would give up the scholarship and continue with online and independent study courses. It was more important now than ever to get an education so she could support herself and her baby.

Hannah had left for school, but Amy was still around and she visited Ally whenever her schedule allowed. She was supportive of Ally, but not of her visits with Family Services. According to Amy, her mom had managed without their help, and Ally didn't need them either. To Ally's surprise, her own mom agreed with Amy.

"I'm just not sure you need to be going and listening to those girls who are going to give their babies up."

"Place their babies for adoption, Mom." Ally corrected her.

"Fine. I'm not sure you need to be listening to these girls who are going to place their babies for adoption. You have already made your decision, and this is only going to confuse you." Julie was upset, as she always was when the topic of Ally's birth mother group meetings came up.

"It's not like that, Mom," Ally responded. They were in the kitchen peeling potatoes for supper. "Everyone is really supportive of each other. I'm not the only one who is going to parent her baby alone. Besides, I feel like going to these meetings is the right thing to do—like I've finally found the beginning of the path I'm supposed to be on." Ally stopped for a moment to see if her mom had anything to say about that, but Julie just kept peeling potatoes without meeting Ally's eyes.

"Mom?" Ally's voice cracked and she tried in vain to keep the tears from trickling down her cheeks. "I know you're upset with me for all of this, and I can't say that I blame you for it. I messed up. I disappointed everyone, especially you, and I'm so sorry. Please try to understand about Family Services. I don't know why I need to go or what's going to happen. I just need to go, okay?"

Julie's eyes were glistening and her jaw was set in a firm line, but she gave the slightest nod to show Ally that she understood. Then she went back to peeling potatoes.

Ally was glad when the cooler fall weather arrived. It gave her an excuse to wear her sweatpants, now that her jeans no longer fit. She was lying in bed one morning during the first week of October enjoying the fact that she did not feel nauseous and thinking about the idea that soon she would need to buy maternity clothes, when she felt a small flutter in her tummy. Ally gasped and dropped her hand on to her belly. The flutter came again. The baby was moving! This was the first time Ally was feeling her move; yet she knew right away that's what was happening. She started giggling as the fluttering continued. *Wow! Amazing! There truly is a little person in there!*

Tears began forming in the corners of Ally's eyes as she felt a surge of love for the tiny being moving around inside of her, and then the giggling subsided and the tears came in earnest as the overwhelming love was followed by a wave of hopelessness. Tears of love for her baby mingled with tears of sorrow for the mistakes she had made and ran down the sides of her face and onto her pillow. Here was a perfect little life forming inside her. The baby had made no mistakes, yet because of Ally's choices this baby did not have a dad.

Ally felt like she had been apologizing a lot lately, to her mom and dad, her sisters, her brother, Bishop Jenkins, Heavenly Father, but there was suddenly one more person that Ally felt the need to make amends with. "I'm so sorry, Baby. I'm sorry your daddy isn't here with me to celebrate this moment. I'm sorry that you will have to live with the consequences of my choices. I'm sorry I can't give you a complete family." Ally was sobbing now and cradling the small bulge of her belly. "I'm sorry, my sweet baby. I'm so sorry."

As Halloween approached, so did Ally's ultrasound appointment. Ally would be twenty-three-weeks along, and she was excited to confirm the gender of the baby. Ally had been calling the baby a girl almost since the moment she discovered she was pregnant, and felt quite certain she was right, but it would be nice to know for sure.

Ally was also ready to admit that it was time to buy some maternity clothes. The only thing she could wear was her largest pair of sweat pants, and even they pressed uncomfortably across her belly. She decided that this was a good opportunity for her to try and repair some of the damage to the relationship with her mom, so Ally asked her if she would like to come to the ultrasound appointment and then do a little shopping after. Julie was genuinely pleased and seemed excited about the chance to spend some time with Ally.

Ally was glad that Dr. Broadbent performed her own ultrasounds right in her office. It was easier that way; no new explanations about the "missing" father. She was waiting on the exam table while Julie sat nervously on a chair in the corner. Ally could only imagine how her mom was feeling. This couldn't possibly be the way she had imagined her oldest daughter's life going. Ally knew that her mom was working really hard to come to terms with the changes that had taken place, and she was doing her best to give her mom some time.

Dr. Broadbent entered the room with pleasant smile. "Hi, Ally. How are you feeling today?"

Julie fidgeted in her chair and Ally spoke as Dr. Broadbent

turned. "Hey, Dr. Broadbent. This is my mom, Julie Campbell." They shook hands and Julie tried to smile, but didn't quite manage it. Ally kept talking to try to cover her mom's moment of awkwardness. "And I'm actually feeling pretty good. A little tired, but not much nausea anymore."

"It's a pleasure to meet you, Mrs. Campbell." Dr. Broadbent's warm sincerity was not lost on Julie, and Ally was relieved to see her mom relax a little. Ally knew that Dr. Broadbent was not going to pass judgment on her or her mom, but she was quite certain Julie had been worried about that. "I'm glad to hear you're feeling better, Ally. It was pretty rough there for a while." Dr. Broadbent turned her attention back to Ally. "Now, are you ready to see your baby's first picture?"

Ally nodded and tried to keep her heartbeat steady while Dr. Broadbent lowered the lights, turned on a television monitor so Ally and Julie would have a view of the images, and then squirted some gel onto the ultrasound probe and began moving it around Ally's belly.

"Now, let's see. I think the baby is right . . ." Dr. Broadbent settled the probe onto the side of Ally's tummy and pushed lightly, ". . . here."

Ally gasped. She hadn't expected to be able to make out much of anything in the fuzzy black and gray images, but there was clearly the profile of a head, and what looked very much like a body with two little arms and two little legs.

"That's your baby, Ally." Dr. Broadbent began taking measurements on the screen and typing on the ultrasound computer. Then focused back on Ally and Julie. "Can you see everything?"

"I think so," Ally replied. "Does the baby look okay?"

Dr. Broadbent was slowly moving the probe around looking at all different angles of the baby. "Yes, everything looks good. Here's the heart, pumping away. Brain looks good, and the spine. Here's the face, that all looks great. Size is good. I think we'll leave your due date right where it's at. All in all, a very healthy looking little baby!"

Ally felt herself beaming while a few tears trickled out of the corner of her eye. A perfect little baby. Amazing! She forced her eyes away from the monitor to look at her mom, and she was pleased to see Julie smiling with tears running down both of her cheeks.

"Dr. Broadbent?" Ally brushed at her eyes with the back of her hand. "Is it a boy or a girl? Can you tell?"

"I thought you might want to know that," Dr. Broadbent grinned. "Let me show you." She moved the probe around again and then said, "There you go!"

Ally looked at the screen but couldn't make anything out now. "Um . . . I can't really see anything."

"Exactly!" Dr. Broadbent was smiling again. "This is the angle where we can determine the gender of the baby. I can see lots of things, but since you don't see anything, that means . . ."

"That means it's . . . a . . . girl?" Ally's heart was pounding now.

"Yes. Congratulations, Ally. You're having a baby girl!"

The maternity clothes shopping was going well, and for a moment in the dressing room, Ally and Julie started giggling and hugging about the news that the baby was a girl, and Ally got a glimpse of how everything with a pregnancy would have gone if she had been married and everyone's happiness was not tempered by her mistake and the reality of what the future would hold. These thoughts threatened to bring the tears to the surface again, but Ally was determined not to spoil this moment and went back to just enjoying being with her mom and buying some new clothes. The excitement of the day carried them through the rest of the week, and Ally was relieved that the tension between her and her mom seemed to have left.

CHAPTER NINE

Reality came crashing back down on Sunday morning, as the family was getting ready to go to church. Ally knew that people were whispering about her . . . how she was mysteriously not going away to college when everyone knew that had been her plan . . . how she looked a little pale and tired these days . . . and especially how she seemed to be gaining some weight. As yet, Ally did not think that anyone in the ward outside of her family, Bishop Jenkins, and Amy and Hannah and their moms actually knew that she was pregnant. As she pulled her new maternity dress over her head and looked in the mirror, however, Ally knew that there would be no doubt about the truth when she walked into church today. And she curled up on her bed and cried.

Downstairs, Julie had a similar thought, and was in a panic. Ally's dad, Steve, was trying to calm her down. "It will be okay, Julie. Today we need to be less concerned with what other people will think, and more concerned with our daughter. You've made a lot of progress with Ally this week. Don't let this fear of criticism from everyone else mess that up."

"I know you're right, Steve. It's just . . ." Julie seemed hesitant to continue.

"It's just what, hon?"

"It's just that . . . well . . . I never thought I would be taking my teenage daughter to church in maternity clothes! I never imagined that my baby girl would be in this situation." Sobs broke through Julie's panic, and Steve wrapped his arms around his wife.

"This is going to be a tough day for the whole family. I imagine it will be particularly difficult for Ally . . . and for you too, Julie. Let's just try to *not* dwell on the fact that she's in maternity clothes and what that means, and focus on the fact that she's still coming to church, and what that means." Julie took a deep breath and wiped her face. She hadn't thought of it in that light before.

"Ally's a good girl . . . and she's growing into a good woman. She's made some heart-wrenching choices, but she is also working very hard to overcome those and move forward. Let's help her. She needs us to help her. There will be plenty of people to gossip and stare and whisper and try to drag her down. It's up to us to help raise her up." Steve looked into the eyes of the woman he had loved for more than two decades and waited. Julie took a deep breath, wiped the remaining tears from her eyes, and nodded.

Ally did not want to walk down the stairs and face her family, but in the end, she knew that she had to. If she could make it through that, Ally was sure she could make it through whatever the ward members could dish out. She waited as long as she could, then made her way downstairs for something to eat. Her brother Charlie was in the kitchen. "Morning, Ally. Nice dress."

Ally was so relieved that she laughed right out loud. She threw her arms around her brother, who had grown taller than her in the last few months and said, "Thanks, Charlie. I needed that."

Charlie grinned. "Anytime, sis. Anytime."

Emma and Elsie arrived in the kitchen while Ally was sitting at the table eating a bowl of oatmeal. Ally tensed for an argument, but none came. The girls didn't smile or say anything encouraging, but they didn't roll their eyes and mumble anything under their breath, either. That was a big step.

Julie joined them and smiled, albeit rather shakily, and patted the bulge that now seemed so prominent on Ally's belly. Her voice, however, was clear and kind when she spoke. "It's going to be okay, Ally. I know you can make it through this."

Ally could only imagine what it cost her mom to say that and was very grateful for the support. "Thanks, Mom. Where's Dad?"

"You know, I'm not sure. He came out a minute ago, but . . ." Julie looked around and shrugged. As if on cue, the front door opened and Steve called Charlie to join them back in the kitchen. Steve's cheeks were red from the chill in the air, and he had some sticks in his hands. They were a little thicker than pencils and slightly longer. Charlie walked in and Steve handed him one of the sticks.

"Charlie, can you break that stick?"

"Oh please, Dad, at least give me a challenge." Charlie grinned as he easily snapped the stick in half. "What's this all about, anyway? It's not quite cold enough for a fire yet," Charlie joked.

Steve smiled but didn't comment. He passed sticks to Emma, Elsie, Julie, and Ally. "Can you guys break your sticks?" Snap. Snap. Snap. Snap. "Individually, it's pretty easy to break these sticks. It doesn't take much to splinter them in two." Julie looked quizzically at Steve. She didn't know where this was headed. He just smiled again, and continued. "But then, I got thinking. I wonder if we could make these sticks stronger, you know, able to withstand whatever force or pressure might be put on them?" He passed a second stick out to each of them as he spoke. "Then I realized something. Separately, they would always be easy to break, but if we put them all together . . ." Steve handed his own stick to Charlie and motioned for the others to do the same. ". . . then if we added a little more to our 'family' of sticks like the Savior, the Atonement, the covenants we each have made," Steve handed a few more sticks to Charlie and put a rubber band around each end to hold them tight, "I think it would be pretty difficult to break any of them now."

Charlie tried, unsuccessfully, to break the sticks, then he passed the bundle to Elsie. Each family member took a turn at trying to break the sticks. Julie was crying softly as her turn came, and so was Ally. Emma and Elsie's eyes were even glistening as Steve concluded. "Let's not forget that we are a family, and if we stick together and support each other, we can make it through anything." He waited for everyone to wipe their eyes and look back at him, and then he smiled. "Now, let's go to church."

The Campbell family walked into the chapel and made their way toward their usual bench. There were about five minutes left before the meeting started, and the chapel was more than half full. Ally tried to ignore the second glances that became stares as she passed. She also pretended not to hear the buzz of whispered voices that erupted after she sat down. Her pregnant bulge was obviously news. Julie sat next to her oldest daughter with her hand on Ally's knee. Ally caught her eye, and to her relief, Julie smiled and nodded. They could do this.

Ally noticed Hannah's family walk in—minus Hannah who was away at school—and when Melanie noticed Ally, she walked over and gave Ally and then Julie a hug and a smile before returning to sit down with her family. It was a small gesture, but Ally appreciated the support. Bishop Jenkins walked past on his way to the front of the chapel and greeted the entire family and shook each of their hands. "How's it going, Ally?" he asked.

Ally tried to grin and then shrugged. "I'll let you know in our meeting tonight."

"Fair enough," he replied.

Ally was glad when the meeting started and she could focus on the talks and the music. After the closing prayer, she hurried to Sunday School, not giving anyone a chance to talk to her.

Sunday School and Relief Society were uneventful. There were some more stares and whispers, or maybe Ally was just imagining that people were staring and whispering. It was hard to be certain. Julie stayed behind after the meeting to visit with the Relief Society president, who smiled at Ally and seemed supportive, but Ally didn't want to wait around so she headed down the hall. She was just breathing a sigh of relief that things went so well when she walked past the partly open door of a classroom and heard her name coming from inside.

"Well, I couldn't believe it when I saw her walk into sacrament meeting this morning!" It was the voice of Sister Chambers. She lived around the corner from the Campbell's and had a daughter two years younger than Ally.

"I know!" This voice was familiar, but Ally couldn't quite place it. "I was shocked when she came into the chapel—of all places— looking like . . . well, looking like she does! She should be ashamed!"

Ally was frozen. Part of her wanted to run away. Part of her wanted to open the door and confront these women, but she was rooted to the floor and couldn't move.

"She is clearly not the young lady we always thought she was," said Sister Chambers. "I wonder how long she's been sleeping around and fooling everyone."

"Probably a while," the voice replied. "Long enough to get pregnant, anyway."

"I can't believe that I used to use her as an example to my daughter and her friends of how they should act!" Sister Chambers again. "Clearly, I'm going to have to talk to them about this and tell them I have been wrong about Ally all along. On top of that, I think I'm going to tell the Young Women leaders to keep a close eye on Emma and Elsie. They may already be thinking about following in their sister's footsteps. Apparently Steve and Julie can't control their daughters!"

"Absolutely. Yes, absolutely."

Ally heard a nervous cough, and then a new voice, Sister Jasper. She had been Ally's Sunday School teacher when she was fifteen. "Maybe, ladies, we should just leave well enough alone."

"What?" Sister Chambers was annoyed.

"I said, maybe we should just continue loving Ally and leave well enough alone. We all make mistakes."

Sister Chambers wouldn't be sidetracked. "Well, I still say she should be ashamed. She has some nerve showing her face—and her belly—here at church right now!"

Ally's urge to run was finally strong enough to propel her down the hall. She didn't want to hear any more. She felt humiliated and belittled. She felt hopeless. She started to cry.

Ally heard the doorbell ring from her bedroom and had a good idea of who it was. After church was over, Ally came home very upset and cried most of the afternoon. When she finally confided in her mom what she had overheard, Julie wanted to call Sister Chambers on the spot, but Ally made her promise not too. She didn't want to stir things up any more than necessary.

After all of that, Ally did not want to see Bishop Jenkins tonight, and had, for the first time, skipped out on an appointment with him. The main reason she ditched was because a part of her believed that Sister Chambers was right. She had been having many of those same thoughts herself and trying to push them aside, but hearing them out loud and with such contempt, made them seem very true and even more ugly than when she thought them.

Ally could hear the murmur of voices in the entryway downstairs and then a soft knock on her bedroom door. She sat up, wiped her eyes, and smoothed her hair as she called, "Come in."

Julie poked her head in the room. "Ally, Bishop Jenkins is downstairs, and he'd like to talk to you for a few minutes." Ally didn't respond at first, and her mom glanced around the room nervously. "It sure can't hurt to visit with him," Julie offered after a moment. "It might even help."

Ally had to admit that her mom was probably right, so she stood up and moved toward the door. As she passed, Julie put her hand on Ally's shoulder and gave a comforting squeeze. A rush of love flowed through Ally. "Thanks, Mom. For everything."

Julie shrugged. "That's what moms are for."

Steve and Bishop Jenkins were standing at the bottom of the stairs when Ally came down. "I missed you this afternoon, Ally," Bishop Jenkins said. Ally couldn't quite bring herself to make eye contact. "Your dad was just telling me about what happened at church. I'd like to visit with you about that, if you don't mind."

Ally nodded. She was grateful her dad already told Bishop Jenkins everything. She didn't want to rehearse it all over again. Steve led them down the hallway to his home office and gave Ally a quick hug before he closed the door. Bishop Jenkins sat down in the black leather office chair and spun it away from the desk to face the armchair in the corner. "Do you want to sit down, Ally?"

Ally sat down but still did not make eye contact. Bishop Jenkins continued, "I don't think there's any reason to dwell on what happened this afternoon, other than for me to tell you that that was their opinion, and it is definitely not how I feel on the matter, nor do I believe it is how the Savior feels. I urge you to try and forget about it. It's unfortunate that it happened, but I think it would be best not to think about it any further."

Ally spoke but continued to stare at her hands. "Well,

that's a lot easier said than done. How can I just forget about it when . . . when . . . ?" Ally broke into tears again. She angrily rubbed her sleeve across her face. All of this crying was driving her crazy!

"How can you forget about it when . . . what?" Bishop Jenkins prodded.

Ally took a deep breath and set her jaw. "How can I forget about it when . . . they're right? I didn't hear anything that I haven't thought of over and over. I know how badly I messed up!" Ally's voice was agonized. "I know I disappointed everyone. I know that I've been a terrible example to my sisters and to all of my friends. And believe me, I know how I looked walking into the chapel today, and it was not easy. Maybe I should have stayed home. Maybe I don't belong there . . . at least not right now. Maybe after some time has passed . . . I just don't know anymore."

Bishop Jenkins let the silence settle before he asked, "Are you finished?"

"Finished? What do you mean?" Ally was surprised by his response and looked up at him for the first time. His eyes were searching her face, trying to read the emotions that were present there.

"Are you finished with your temper tantrum?" The bishop's voice was gentle but firm, and his eyes never left Ally's.

"My what?" Ally was mad now. She thought Bishop Jenkins would be on her side, not come in here and tell her she was throwing a tantrum.

"Your temper tantrum, Ally. Not that I blame you," he inserted as Ally opened her mouth to protest. "I understand that you are feeling some strong emotions because of what happened at church, but I want you to think about something." Bishop Jenkins waited until Ally nodded before he continued. "I want you to think about who these feelings, that you are feeling right now, are coming from." He paused to let his words sink in, and then said gently, "Do you think that Christ would want you to feel like you could not go to church? Do you think He would want you to feel humiliated? Hopeless?"

Ally shrugged.

"Come on, Ally, I know you can do better than that. Really think about what you know of the Savior, and then answer me. Do you think He would want you to be having these types of feelings?"

"Probably not," Ally mumbled.

"Absolutely not," Bishop Jenkins countered. "There is, however, someone else who would want to alienate you from the gospel, from church, from Christ. Someone who does want you to believe that you've messed up so badly that there's no coming back. It's Satan, Ally, and he wants you to feel as miserable and hopeless as he feels."

"But, Bishop?"

"Yes, Ally?"

"I walked in to church today, and everyone could see my sin. Everyone. They all knew what I had done; how I had messed up. Even though I only heard a few women, I'm sure other people felt the same, and it got me wondering whether or not I really belong there. I'm just not sure I do, at least not right now." Ally looked back into Bishop Jenkins' face, searching for an answer.

Bishop Jenkins sighed and rubbed his hands wearily across his face. Ally thought she had won the argument. She thought he was stumped, and then Bishop Jenkins surprised her. "My grandmother was an amazing woman."

"Excuse me?" Ally was more than surprised. She was confused by this change in the conversation.

"My grandmother. My dad's mom. She was an amazing woman. She died when I was fourteen years old, but I remember her so well. Quick to smile, quicker to love, and she always had a cookie in the cookie jar. Anyway, her neighbor was a woman about her same age, Mrs. Freeman. Mrs. Freeman hadn't been to church in years because she struggled with the Word of Wisdom. She smoked." Bishop Jenkins answered Ally's unasked question.

"She didn't feel like she belonged at church because everyone knew what her sin was. It was obvious. She always smelled like smoke." Ally nodded in understanding.

"Mrs. Freeman and my grandma were friends for many years, and one day my grandma told her that it was time for her to come back to church. Mrs. Freeman put up her usual excuses, but Grandma was having none of it this time. She told her something that I have always tried to remember. She told Mrs. Freeman that if everyone's sins had an odor, the stench would be so strong that we wouldn't be able to stand to be around each other."

"But I don't stink, Bishop."

"Don't be unreasonable, Ally, you know what I'm saying." His voice was still kind but was firm once again. "There's a reason Jesus Christ is called 'Savior.' It is because we all need to be saved from something. Right now, you need to be saved from your obvious mistake, and we all need to be saved from sin to some degree. But there are many, many more reasons that people need to be saved. Sorrow. Heartache. Pain. Anger. Hate. Hurt. Hopelessness. Fear. Ignorance. Despair. Perhaps the two women you overheard suffer from one of these, and that is why they behaved the way they did today." Bishop Jenkins paused to be sure that Ally was listening. "Sometimes we even need to be saved from ourselves. Ally, the way to healing will never, never be to turn our back on our Savior, and we are never so far gone that He will turn His back on us."

Ally was crying freely now, and even Bishop Jenkins's eyes were shining. "The gospel is not for perfect people, Ally. It is for all of us on this earth who are imperfect, who make mistakes, who struggle, who cry, but who have hope that through our Savior we can make it through this earthly existence and learn and grow and prepare to move forward. So if you ask me, the chapel is exactly where you belong. Right there with all the rest of us."

Ally sat quietly for a few minutes, thinking about what Bishop Jenkins had said. Warmth started flowing through her as the Spirit confirmed that Jesus Christ did indeed love Ally and that He wanted her to turn to Him and be forgiven. She felt the truth of the bishop's words that we all have a need to be saved and that Heavenly Father loves us, in spite of our weaknesses. Ally's tears were still flowing, but they were no longer tears of shame and anger and humiliation. There was still sorrow there; sorrow for the wrong she had done and for the hurt she had caused, but also an overwhelming feeling of gratitude and love for the Savior who was giving her the chance to make things right and move forward.

Bishop Jenkins allowed Ally all the time she needed to collect her thoughts. It was Ally who finally broke the silence. "Thanks for coming over tonight, Bishop. I really appreciate it."

"No problem, Ally. Don't give up. I know you're going to make it through this. Don't forget that Heavenly Father and Jesus are there to help you. They are as close as a prayer." Bishop Jenkins stood up and reached out to shake Ally's hand.

Ally tried to dry her eyes with her sleeve before returning the handshake. "Thanks again, Bishop, for everything."

"It's my pleasure, Ally. Good night."

CHAPTER TEN

The following weeks passed in a blur. Ally enjoyed Thanksgiving with her parents and brother and sisters, and even the cold weather and snow of early December were a welcome relief. With her baby girl getting bigger and bigger inside of her, Ally felt like she had her own built-in space heater. Ally was continuing her meetings with Barbara at LDS Family Services and she was also still attending the birth mother support group. Her parents even went to visit with Barbara a couple of times, and everything seemed to be going well. Julie and Steve were getting excited about the prospect of becoming grandparents, and even Emma and Elsie seemed to have forgiven Ally amidst the idea of having a little niece. Charlie was as supportive as ever, although in the moments when his family was chattering with excitement over the impending arrival of the baby, he often remained thoughtfully silent in the background.

Ally arrived home from a meeting with Barbara a few days before Christmas, and Charlie immediately noticed that she seemed a little unsettled. "What's going on, Ally? Is something wrong?"

Ally gave Charlie a weary smile. "I knew I wouldn't be able to hide this from you. You're so observant."

Charlie shrugged. "So what's up?"

"Today Barbara asked me if I have prayed about my decision

to raise my baby." Ally looked at Charlie as if this should explain everything.

"My mind reader must be broken, Ally. Why does that have you upset? You've been doing a lot of praying lately. Surely you have prayed about this."

Ally squished up her eyes and wrinkled her nose the way she had done since she was two years old and was caught sneaking a cookie right before supper. That sheepish look was Charlie's answer.

"So you haven't prayed about your decision?"

"Not exactly."

"What does that mean?"

"Well, I have definitely been praying for forgiveness and for help to be strong and be a good mom, and for the baby to be healthy and for everything to go smoothly with the delivery, and that mom and dad and you and the girls would still love me, but . . ." her voice trailed off.

"But you have never asked if you made the right decision," Charlie finished.

"No."

"And . . . you're worried about what the answer is going to be?"

"No, not really . . . maybe a little . . . sort of," Ally stammered. Charlie didn't say anything, so Ally felt the need to explain herself. "I mean, I think I'm making the right decision. I know that I love this baby. I know that I'm willing to do whatever it takes to take care of her. I know that I want to raise her and be her mom. I know that I want to feed her and bathe her and change her diapers and hear her say her first word and watch her take her first step. I know that I want to be the one who puts band-aids on her scraped knees, and pushes her in the swing, and kisses her good night." Ally's voice cracked and her eyes welled up with tears as she continued, "I know that I want to teach her to tie her shoes and take her to her first day of kindergarten and comfort her when she wakes up from a nightmare." Ally was crying too hard to say any more, so Charlie just put his arms around his older sister, and she held onto him and cried and cried.

After several minutes, Ally was able to gather her emotions and she looked up at her little brother, who didn't seem so little all of a sudden. He rephrased his question from earlier. "So what are you worried about?"

Ally thought for a moment before answering. "I'm worried that what I want will be different from what Heavenly Father wants."

"So what are you going to do?"

"I don't know, Charlie. I don't know."

To Charlie's credit, he didn't mention their conversation to anyone over the next few days. He told Ally that he knew she would do the right thing and left it at that. Christmas morning came bringing all of the usual excitement. Ally got a couple of cute baby outfits from her mom, but most of the focus was on Emma and Elsie, which was just how Ally wanted it. They ate a huge Christmas supper with ham, mashed potatoes and gravy, potato salad, and baked beans. Ally was just finishing a slice of homemade lemon meringue pie when Charlie sat down next to her.

Ally's parents were cleaning up in the kitchen, and Emma and Elsie had gone upstairs, so Charlie knew they could have a conversation without being overheard. "Have you decided what you're going to do?"

Ally was waiting for this. Charlie wasn't pushy, but he didn't let important things drop, either. She was prepared with an answer. "Actually, I have been thinking a lot about this, and I've made a decision"

"And . . . ?"

"And," Ally continued, "I'm going to pray about it. I really think that parenting my baby girl is the right decision. I've graduated from high school, I'm responsible, and I'm willing to work hard to make this work. Plus, Mom and Dad are going to let us stay here for as long as it takes me to get my life put together. I really think everything is going to work out."

Charlie smiled at his sister. "I believe you."

Allison went for a walk to try to clear her head. This turmoil in her mind was now as familiar as her own reflection. It had been a week since she sincerely prayed and asked Heavenly Father if her decision to raise her baby herself was in accordance with His will, and the words from a First Presidency statement Barbara showed her during their first visit kept floating around the corners of her mind.

Children are entitled to birth within the bonds of matrimony . . . When the probability of a successful marriage is unlikely, unwed parents should be encouraged to place the child for adoption . . .

Ally was doing a decent job of pushing these thoughts away, but she could not completely shut them out. Obviously, Ally had no chance of a successful marriage with the father of her baby, and so, according to the statement, she should consider adoption. But every cell in Ally's body rejected the notion of giving her baby girl—this baby who she knew, this baby who she loved —to strangers. *No!* She was going to be a mother to her daughter. She was going to take responsibility for this life she had helped create. She was willing to make the sacrifices necessary to do that. Even Ally's own mom had warmed to Ally's pregnancy and was excited about the baby.

No. Ally's decision was made. Barbara had been supportive of that and was helping Ally with information on being a single mom and the resources available to her. No one was pushing adoption or even discussing it lately. Ally had a plan, so she could not understand this fresh turmoil that had her mind boiling.

Ally shivered against the early January chill and stopped to tuck the ends of her scarf inside her jacket. She wasn't paying much attention to where she was heading as she walked along in her troubled reverie, but now she found herself at the city park. It was a place that held many fond memories from Ally's own childhood: kite-flying in the spring, summer afternoon picnics, and winter snowball fights. As she shuffled through the memories, her mind's eye seemed focused on one person. Her dad. He was laughing as Ally ran, string in hand, trying to will her kite into the air. He was stretched out on a blanket with the remains of lunch scattered around him while he watched her scuttle across the monkey bars. He was hiding behind the snow fort with Charlie while Ally fired snowballs over their haphazard shelter.

Ally stopped and rubbed angry fists across her eyes, forcing the memories back to their hiding places. *No! I can do those things with my daughter. I will do those things with my daughter. I will be a great mom, the best mom there ever was!*

But? Ally looked around, even though she knew the question was only in her mind.

But, what? Ally retorted. As far as she was concerned, there was no "but" in her sentence.

The thought came again, *But?*

And then the words Melanie had spoken the night Ally told Hannah and Amy about the baby, replayed themselves in Ally's mind. *I could not be a dad.*

Ally found herself on her knees, pleading. "No, Heavenly Father. No! Does it really matter? My dad will be around. She will have a grandpa . . . and Charlie! Charlie will be the best uncle there ever was." She was sobbing now and the words poured out through her tears. "I love her so much! I'll give her anything—sacrifice everything if I have to. Please!"

The answer came softly and lovingly to her mind. *Will you give her a dad? Will you give her a family? Will you sacrifice what you want, what you believe you need?*

Is there any other way? Ally couldn't speak the words aloud, but she knew it didn't matter.

There's always another way. You can always choose. I would never take that away from you.

Ally thought about the sweet baby girl growing inside her. She thought of the countless times she had committed to make any sacrifice necessary to give her daughter the best chance at life. She had never considered that maybe her baby girl's best chance at life would require the ultimate sacrifice on her part. She wrapped her arms around her belly, cradling her baby girl, and cried.

Ally didn't know how long she knelt, crying, in the snow that was covering the ground, but her pants were wet and the cold had penetrated her boots when she wiped her eyes, folded her arms, and prayed. She had done a lot of praying since getting pregnant, thirty-four weeks ago. She had offered some agonizing prayers, pleading for forgiveness. They were nothing compared to the emotions threatening to tear her apart as she managed the most painful words imaginable.

"Heavenly Father, I love my baby girl more than anything else on this earth. I want to raise her and hold her and be with her always. But," Ally's voice cracked. She paused and reached deep inside herself to find the strength necessary to continue. "But, because I love her so much, I will give her a father and mother who she can be sealed to—right now—right from the start. I'll need Thy help because I won't be able to manage this alone, but if it be Thy will, I will place my sweet baby for adoption."

The searing pain that flashed through Ally's heart at the thought of placing her baby into someone else's arms was almost more than she could bear, but at the same time, there was a soft warmth that was trying to break through to her soul. Amidst the darkness and confusion she had been feeling almost steadily for the past week, that warmth brought a glow—just a glimmer—of hope.

Hope was the balm for Ally's troubled soul, and as she instinctively turned her mind toward the source, the warmth filled first her heart, then her mind, and finally flowed through her body. She knew what she needed to do.

Ally managed to make it home from the park, and her dad was just walking out the front door in his coat and hat as she started up the sidewalk.

"Ally, we were starting to worry," Dad began. Then he looked at her wet clothes and red, puffy eyes and closed the distance between them in two bounds. "What happened? Are you okay?"

"I'm okay, Dad. Don't worry," Ally said, wiping her eyes with the back of her glove. "But I need to talk to everyone. Right away."

"Okay, but let's get inside, and you go change out of those wet clothes first. You don't need to be getting sick now." Dad followed Ally through the door and he promised to gather everyone into the living room while she put on dry clothes.

How am I ever going to tell them that I've decided to place my baby for adoption? Ally thought that nothing could be harder than telling her parents she was pregnant, but this was definitely right up there. She tried to remain focused on the peace she felt when the answer came while kneeling in the snow at the park. She pulled a dry pair of pants on and stretched a large sweatshirt over her belly. Ally considered stalling but knew that she needed to get this over with as soon as possible. Her family deserved to know.

Dad was true to his word, and when Ally walked into the living room the whole family was there—Mom and Dad holding hands on the sofa, Charlie sitting on the recliner in the corner, and Emma and Elsie on the floor at their parents' feet. Dad motioned for Ally to take the glider rocker across from him. As Ally sat down, she realized these were the same seats she and her parents were in the night she told them she was pregnant. With any luck, her dad would be as understanding as he was that night, and her mom would handle the news a little better.

"So, what's going on, Ally?" Julie was curious but not worried. After all, she could handle just about anything after the roller coaster of emotions connected with Ally's pregnancy. What could be more difficult than that?

"Well, I can't come up with an easy way to tell you this, so I'll just say it." Ally quickly looked at the faces of each member of her family, stopping briefly on Charlie, who smiled and nodded his encouragement. *He already knows*, Ally thought, and her eyes welled up with love for her brother and the support he was constantly giving her. Support that seemed way beyond the capacity of a sixteen-year-old.

Ally returned Charlie's smile and then turned to face her family. "I've been praying a lot this last week, and I've come to a decision." Once again, Ally had to dig deep to find the inner strength to say what needed to come next. "I'm going to place my baby for adoption."

A stunned silence filled the room as Ally waited for some response. Ally turned to her mom, and then wished she hadn't. Julie couldn't have looked worse if Ally had walked over and slapped her. The girls looked angry, and when Ally finally looked up at her dad, the sadness and confusion on his face were almost more than she could handle.

Charlie tried to come to Ally's rescue. "I think that's a very good decision, Ally."

"Yeah, right," Elsie muttered.

"You mean a very selfish decision," Emma agreed.

"No," Charlie countered, "I think that Ally is trying to do what is best for her baby." He looked at his dad, silently asking for a little help.

"Girls," Steve began, "Ally is an adult now, and even though we may not agree with her decision, there's really nothing we can do to change it." Charlie glared at his dad. That was definitely not the kind of help he was looking for.

Ally's tears spilled over at her father's cool reaction, but what hurt the most was when her mom got up and walked out of the room without a single word.

Book Three

HOPE

CHAPTER ONE

O livia and Michael's adoption file had been active since the first week of August, and they recently celebrated the New Year with no news. Of course five months was not very much time to wait. Although they met an adoptive couple through their classes at LDS Family Services who only waited three months for a baby, they also met several couples that waited close to two years, and one couple that waited five years. Even so, it was hard to be patient.

Olivia was immersing herself in her job at the hospital and looking for chances to serve, including volunteering to babysit Heather and Greg's children once a month so they could attend the temple. Michael just completed an undefeated football season with his high school team, capped by winning the state championship, and was becoming more and more excited about adopting a baby. As the football coach, Michael was very good at fixing problems. Whether it was the problem of how to stop the other team's star running back, or which play they should run on fourth down with four yards to go, Michael could analyze the situation and come up with a successful solution almost every time. He was really beginning to believe that adoption would be the winning solution for Olivia—and for him.

Although Olivia was starting to smile more and seemed to be feeling a little better about things, there were still quite a few days where Michael knew she was fighting the same old battles brought on by their infertility. In the first few meetings with their social worker, Kevin, he often reminded Michael that adoption wouldn't cure Olivia's sadness about her infertility, but Michael couldn't help but believe that it would help.

CHAPTER TWO

Ally walked into Barbara's office and before she lost her nerve or completely broke down, she announced, "I prayed about it, and I am going to place my baby girl for adoption."

Barbara raised her eyebrows. "Ally, are you sure? You have always seemed so confident in your plans to parent your baby."

"I was," Ally couldn't hold back her tears any longer, "until I prayed about it. It turns out that what is best for my baby girl is going to be the hardest for me."

Barbara nodded. "Have you told your family?"

"Yeah. It didn't go very well." Ally closed her eyes to the memory of the way her mom's face crumpled when she told her about the change of plan. "My mom is especially upset." Ally felt the need to explain, to defend her mom. "It's just that she was finally coming to terms with all of this and was excited about having a granddaughter."

"You don't have to explain to me," Barbara said. "Your mom's feelings are very common. She's welcome to come in and talk to me about it, if she wants."

"I told her that, but she's not interested, at least not right now. She thinks it was you and the birth moms I've met here who talked me into this." Ally sighed. "Little does she know that there's nothing on the planet that could've convinced me to part with my baby girl, if I hadn't received a witness from Heavenly

Father that this is what will be best for her."

Barbara nodded again. "Well, if she changes her mind . . . I'm always here. What about your dad and brother and sisters?"

"Dad isn't thrilled with the idea, but I think he understands the decision. I showed him the statement from the First Presidency about adoption. He really has a testimony of following the prophet, so I think he's trying to put his faith in the fact that it can't be a bad decision if the prophet has recommended it for someone in my situation. Emma and Elsie are pretty bent out of shape over it. They think it would be fun to have a baby around. They think I'm being selfish. Emma thinks I changed my mind because I'm scared to be a mom. Elsie thinks it's because I want to leave and go away to college and not have to worry about a baby." Ally's tears, which hadn't fully dried up yet, were flowing freely again. "They're both dead wrong, of course. They don't understand that my heart is breaking over this, and I can't seem to get them to see that I'm doing it out of love. I want to give my baby girl the best chance at life. I want her to have everything, and if that means removing myself from the picture . . ." Ally's voice broke and she couldn't say any more.

They sat in silence for a few moments, until Ally composed herself enough to add, "Only Charlie seems to understand. Once I made the decision and told him about it, he said that he had been feeling for a while that this little girl was meant to be in someone else's family. He didn't understand why he was having that feeling until the day a few weeks ago when I told him that I wasn't going to pray about my decision to parent my baby. He said that then he knew his job was to encourage me to pray about it so I could get the answer for myself." Ally smiled through her tears as she thought about her younger brother. "I guess I have been so focused on what I was going to do that the Spirit couldn't communicate Heavenly Father's will to me. Lucky for my baby, Charlie was listening."

"It will be the hardest thing you'll ever do in your life, Ally," Barbara said gently.

"I'm trying not to think about the particulars too much right now," Ally said, wiping her tears. "I'm just focusing on making it through the next few weeks."

"You're sure this is what you want to do?" Barbara questioned again.

"No. It's absolutely not what I want to do," Ally said, "but yes, I am sure of my decision." She squeezed her eyes shut again and tears leaked out of the corners. "I am going to give my baby a mom and a dad. I'm going to give her a family."

"You're due date is next month?"

"Yes. February eighteenth."

"Okay. If you're sure," Barbara paused and Ally nodded once, "then we better get started."

Julie opened Ally's bedroom door carrying a basket of folded laundry. She stopped as she looked in on her very pregnant daughter kneeling at the side of her bed, face buried in her hands, sobbing. The basket fell to the floor and Julie was at Ally's side in an instant. "Ally, what's wrong?"

Ally jumped at the unexpected interruption and then threw her arms around her mom's neck. Julie held her oldest daughter until Ally's sobs quieted. "Mom, it's been a week and I have looked at hundreds of adoption profiles, and I can't find the right mom and dad for my baby girl!"

Julie stiffened slightly. "Maybe that's because you're the right mom. You don't have to go through with this adoption you know." Ally looked straight into her mom's face, and although tears blurred her dark brown eyes, Julie could not mistake the conviction behind them.

"Mom, please try to understand this. I'm going through with this adoption plan. I have continued to pray about it every day, and the only thing I know for sure right now, is that Heavenly Father wants my baby girl in a family, with a mom and dad, right from the start. That's what is going to be best for her."

"And what about you?" Julie's voice quivered with pain and anger. "What's best for my baby girl? Do you think I like seeing your heart break each day? Do you think it's easy for me to think of you suffering through childbirth, only to have your baby wrenched away from you? That's not something that goes away, Ally. That's forever."

Julie and Ally both cried freely now. Julie expected further argument. Instead, Ally reached forward and took her mom's hands.

"Thank you, Mom." This caught her off guard. "Thank you for loving me so much. I'm so sorry that, once again, my actions are causing you pain. You haven't done anything to deserve this, and yet here I am, hurting you all over again, and I don't know if I can ever make that right. But you know what? There's someone else who hasn't done anything wrong. Someone that I love even more than myself. Someone who deserves the very best that life has to offer. Someone who deserves to have the same kind of amazing parents and childhood that I had. And I can make things right for her."

"But you've been talking so much about being a mom and raising your baby and everything that entails. You think you're just going to turn your back on all of that?"

Ally didn't answer right away. Instead she said, "Mom, my whole life you have been an amazing example to me of what motherhood is all about. You have devoted everything to making sure that your children have the best chances, the best opportunities. I know that you have sacrificed time, money, energy, sleep, and other things that you have wanted or could have done in order to be a mom to me, Charlie, and the girls. And why have you done all of that? Because that's what moms do. Moms are selfless. They love their children so much that they can endure anything to see their children happy and successful. So to answer your question, no, I don't think I am turning my back on motherhood. I think I'm being a true mother by loving my baby girl enough to sacrifice everything I want, so that she can have the family and the life that she deserves—that Heavenly Father wants her to have."

There were still tears on Julie's cheeks, and she didn't say anything. She just looked down at her hands in Ally's. She almost smiled. Steve was right. Their daughter was growing into an amazing woman. But that didn't make all of this any easier. "I guess you're right, Ally. Just give me some time, okay?"

Ally nodded and attempted a grin. "Fair enough."

"Now," Julie sat up and wiped her face. "What was the problem before I interrupted you?"

Ally's eyes darkened. "I'm just so frustrated! I know that there is a mom and dad out there for my baby, but I can't find them. And," Ally rubbed her belly, "I'm running out of time."

Julie took a deep breath, "Well, would you like a little help?"

Ally's tears started fresh. "That would be great, Mom. Thanks."

"Do you think we should say a prayer before we start?" Julie asked. "You said this is what Heavenly Father wants for your baby. If you ask, don't you think He will help you find the right family?"

Ally nodded and they moved from their sitting positions to their knees. Ally offered a humble prayer asking to be led to the parents for her baby girl, and for Heavenly Father to give her the strength to follow through and do His will concerning her baby. She closed the prayer and Julie gave her a quick squeeze as they headed downstairs to the office.

Ally sat down at the computer and turned it on. Julie pulled up a chair to the side of her daughter as Ally connected to the LDS Family Services website and logged in. She had several preferences for the adoptive family. She wanted the father to have served a mission, both parents to be graduated from college with at least a bachelor's degree, and for the mom to be planning to be a stay-at-home mom once they had a baby. She also wanted her baby to be their first child. Ally liked being the oldest in the family. She quickly filled in the appropriate boxes and hit the "search" button.

The search yielded nearly one hundred available couples. Ally sighed. "This is where I feel so overwhelmed! There's so much information here. How do I filter through it all?"

"With a little help," Julie replied. "Let's not pore over every file. Let's glance at the photos and quickly skim over the material. I think the Spirit will let you know who the true prospects are."

Ally agreed. "That will definitely be less stressful than carefully reading every word in every file and studying all of the pictures. That's what I have been doing, and all of the families seem deserving, but none of them seem right to me."

Ally looked over the first page of matches. "What do you think?" Julie asked.

"Well," Ally said, "all of these look like nice people, but none of them draw me in. These photos are beautiful, professional-looking pictures of lots of happy couples, but to me they feel too staged and a little fake. They don't tell me anything about the couple."

"Okay, moving on," Julie said as she clicked on the next page of matches, and then the next. They skimmed through a lot of wedding photos without stopping.

"I already know that all of these couples are married," Ally commented. "I want these to tell me something I don't know."

"I agree," Julie said. "And I don't really like all of these cruise pictures."

Ally nodded. "One or two vacation pictures are nice, but that's all that is in this file. It makes me feel that a baby is just going to put a kink in their vacation plans."

They continued searching through page after page of posed photos in relative silence. Then Ally exclaimed, "Maybe there are birth moms who would like these kinds of pictures, but I want a photo that shows me something—anything—about who these people actually are!" She was getting frustrated. "And a lot of these messages aren't any better. I have no doubt that all of these couples are good people who would be good parents, but nothing is speaking to my heart." Occasionally, a file sparked Ally's interest, and she would carefully read about some very nice people who really wanted a baby, but she didn't feel drawn to any of them.

By now, they had been looking through files for several hours. Ally was on the verge of getting upset again, and Julie wasn't far behind. Ally was ready to call it a day but felt impressed to keep searching a little longer. "Thirty more minutes," she told her mom, "and then I'm done for today."

Ally skimmed through several more files with no luck and was about to give up when a photo caught her eye. It appeared to have been taken at some sort of birthday party as there were people and balloons in the background, but the couple was front and center in the picture. They looked as though they had been talking and laughing together when someone called the wife's name and she turned to look at the camera as the picture was snapped. Her mouth was slightly open in a laugh and her eyes were happy. The husband was turned toward the camera but was looking at his wife with open, unrehearsed adoration. That was the only word that came to mind. Clearly, this man adored his wife. You couldn't fake that look on his face. She was the center of his world.

Ally's eyes flickered to the box next to the photo where the couples wrote their "first impression" message to the birth mom. This message was different from the others. It didn't say how they were ready and waiting to love a child, and there was no drawn-out quote about trials and adversity. It simply stated, "There is always hope through the Savior." Ally felt her heart skip a beat as the message echoed familiarly with her spirit, and she clicked on the link to see more about this couple.

Ally soaked in every word—about how these two met, what they each loved about the other, and about their struggle with infertility—like parched earth. She felt a thrill as she realized that the wife was a nurse by profession, just like Ally wanted to be, and that she would be a stay-at-home mom when a baby joined their family. She got excited about a photo of the wife playing basketball, and she really liked a picture of the husband obviously coaching a football team with his wife cheering from the front row. Ally thought briefly of Brandon and knew that, if he were here with her, he would like the idea of their baby's dad being involved in football like he was. The photo Ally loved the most, aside from the first one, was of the husband and wife cuddled up together on an oversized recliner, wrapped in a denim quilt, with each of them clearly immersed in the books they were reading. Ally couldn't see the title of the husband's book, but the wife's was *Jane Eyre*, one of Ally's all-time favorites.

They wrote with love and concern for the birth mother of the baby that would join their family, and the wife concluded the letter by writing:

"There is no way for us to understand the emotions you are going through or the sacrifice you are making for your baby. However, having been through a few ups and downs of my own, I am beginning to realize that there is Someone who does understand each of us perfectly. There is Someone who loves each of us perfectly, and there is Someone who can give each of us help and hope, no matter what we are facing. That Someone is our Savior Jesus Christ, and we have been praying that you will be able to feel the great love He has for you, and that He will sustain you and give you the faith and the hope that you need to make it through."

Ally didn't realize she was crying until her mom reached up and wiped the tears from her cheek. Ally couldn't define her emotions. Was it possible for your soul to be filled with warmth and light, and for your heart to be breaking at the same time? It must be, because that was how she felt as she spoke. "Mom, these are the people I have been looking for. These are my baby girl's parents."

Julie didn't trust herself to speak. She had been hoping that they wouldn't find anyone Ally liked and she would rethink her decision. But she had read the file over Ally's shoulder and watched her daughter's reaction. She was feeling the Spirit confirming Ally's decision. There was no mistaking that Ally's prayer was answered. Julie wrapped her arms around her daughter and cried with her.

CHAPTER THREE

Olivia was enjoying a relaxing morning of lying on the couch reading a book, when the telephone rang. She reluctantly unwrapped herself from her favorite quilt to go answer the phone.

"Hello?"

"Hello, Olivia? This is Kevin with LDS Family Services."

"Oh hey, Kevin, what's going on?"

"I was wondering if you and Michael could come over to the office this afternoon."

"Yeah, I think that would be fine. Michael should be home around 3:00 so we could probably be there by 3:30. Will that work?"

"That'll be fine. I'll see you both then. Bye."

"Bye." Olivia hung up the phone and was utterly confused. What was that about? Kevin had called a couple times since their file had been active, but they always discussed whatever he was calling about over the phone. She and Michael had been to the office several times, but that was for Families Supporting Adoption meetings, and Kevin hadn't called them about one of those since the first one back in August, right after their file was approved.

Suddenly an idea flitted across Olivia's mind, and her hands were shaking as she dialed Michael's cell phone number. She hoped he wouldn't be in the middle of teaching and could answer. She had to talk to him. The phone rang once, twice, three times, and then, "Livvy, is everything okay? You never call me at school."

Olivia tried to talk, but she was crying and couldn't get the words out.

"Olivia, what's going on? Are you all right?" Michael was worried now.

Olivia took a deep breath. "Michael, I just got off the phone with Kevin from Family Services."

"And?" A hint of excitement crept into Michael's voice.

"I don't know!" Olivia laughed through her tears. "I don't know why I'm crying! He just asked us to meet him at his office today at 3:30. That's all he said. Only, I can't help but wonder . . ."

"If a birth mom has picked us?" Michael finished for her.

"I don't know, maybe," Olivia admitted. "I mean, what else could it be?"

"Don't get too worked up yet, Livvy," Michael cautioned. "It could be lots of things."

"Like what?"

"Like, oh, I don't know, but let's try and relax until we get there and find out what's going on. Maybe they just want to . . . uh . . . update our file, or something," he finished. Olivia wasn't convinced.

"Well, maybe," she said, "but it's too late to not get excited. I already am!"

"Fine," Michael laughed. He liked the sparkle he could hear in his wife's voice. "Just try and contain yourself until we know for sure what's happening."

"Okay, I'll try," Olivia agreed. "Hurry home this afternoon."

"I will. Bye."

"Bye. Oh, wait, Michael?"

"Yeah?"

"I love you!"

"I love you too, Livvy. See you later."

Olivia hung up the phone, but she couldn't stop smiling. It felt like this was it. It felt like she was, finally, going to become a mom.

Michael and Olivia arrived at LDS Family Services ten minutes early, and luckily, Kevin could see them right away. Olivia had been anxious all day and now she felt like her heart was about to jump right out of her chest. Kevin invited them into his office and motioned for them to sit down in the two chairs facing his desk. He smiled, and said, "So, I guess you're probably wondering why I asked you to meet with me today."

"Yes," Olivia replied. She was sure Kevin could hear her heart pounding. "I've been a nervous wreck all day."

"Well, I won't keep you waiting any longer then." Kevin reached into his desk drawer and passed Michael and Olivia an envelope with their names printed carefully on the front. It wasn't sealed, which was good because Olivia's hands were shaking so hard she could barely get the card out as it was. There was a short, handwritten note on the inside, which Michael and Olivia read, and then reread.

Tears were running down Olivia's cheeks, and Michael was grinning from ear to ear when they looked up at Kevin. Olivia was searching for words, but for the moment, she was speechless. Kevin smiled brightly at them and said, "Congratulations! A birth mom has picked you. You're going to be parents!"

Olivia looked again at the words on the card—the words that had just changed her whole life. They were from an eighteen-year-old young woman who introduced herself as Allison. She briefly explained that she was single and pregnant and that, after much prayer and soul-searching, she felt that adoption was the best option for the baby girl that she was carrying.

Olivia looked up at Michael as the words sank in. "A baby girl, Michael! We're going to have a daughter!" She was laughing and crying all at once. She focused back on the card where Allison went on to tell them that she had searched through hundreds of adoption portfolios and was praying to be led to the family that her baby girl was meant to be with, when she found their file online.

"I knew immediately that you were the right parents for my baby, and it has been confirmed again and again as I've prayed over the last few days. While my heart aches at the thought of not being the one to raise my sweet baby girl, I feel hope and comfort in the knowledge that she is meant to be your daughter and that you will love and care for her and give her everything that I can't provide. I look forward to meeting you, and hope that we can have a face-to-face meeting before the baby is born."

Michael was reading the letter again along with Olivia, and he asked Kevin, "When is the baby due? She doesn't say."

Kevin smiled. "Yeah, her social worker told me she didn't want to put her due date in the card, in case it freaked you out. Apparently, she has been planning throughout her whole pregnancy to single-parent her baby, and only just really prayed about it and came to the decision to place her for adoption. She's due pretty soon. February eighteenth to be exact." Kevin's smile became even wider at the surprised looks on both Michael and Olivia's faces.

"Wait a minute," Olivia managed through her tears. "You mean that our baby girl," Olivia paused and slowly shook her head in wonder, "is going to be born in about three weeks?"

Kevin laughed right out loud now. This was clearly his favorite part of his job. "Yep. If she goes all the way to her due date. Apparently at her last doctor's appointment, Allison's body was beginning to prepare for delivery. The doctor thinks there's a good chance the baby will be born several days, if not a week, early."

Michael leaned over and hugged his wife and they laughed and cried together for several minutes. Kevin was content to let them have their moment, and then said, "So, we should get the face-to-face meeting scheduled as soon as possible."

"Where is Allison at?" Michael asked. "How soon can we get there?" Olivia squeezed her husband's arm, excited about his enthusiasm.

"She's a little over two hundred miles away, but still in-state. It should only take you a couple hours to drive down there," Kevin replied.

"We could go the day after tomorrow, right, Livvy?"

"Yeah. I'm off work for the next three days, and you'll need tomorrow to get a substitute to fill in for you at school. That will be perfect." Olivia had stopped crying and was now beaming.

"Great!" Kevin said. "I'll call Allison's social worker to get it all set up, and then I'll call you with a meeting time and place as soon as I know."

Olivia and Michael stood up and shook Kevin's hand. They were floating out of his office when Kevin said, "Oh, I almost forgot, I need to give Allison's social worker your official answer. I think," he smiled again, "that it's safe to say you would love to adopt this baby girl and that you're very excited about it?"

"There are no words to express how excited and happy we are," Olivia said, and she and Michael walked out of the door hand-in-hand.

Olivia spent the rest of the day alternating between laughter and tears. She began calling family and friends to tell them the exciting news, crying each time she told someone that they were getting a daughter. Olivia had a special moment when she told her grandma.

"I'm so happy for you, Olivia," Grandma said through her tears. "I knew you would figure something out. Your great-aunt Elizabeth would be so happy."

"You mean she is so happy," Olivia said. "I can feel that she is."

"Yes, I believe you're right," Grandma agreed.

Heather wanted to throw a baby shower right away, but Olivia convinced her to wait and have it after the baby was here. Olivia knew from their classes at LDS Family Services that until Allison signed the relinquishment papers, she could still change her mind, and she didn't want to have a big party until she was positive the baby was theirs. "Besides," she told Heather, "then I can show her off to everyone." After all the phone calls, Olivia and Michael went out to celebrate by going shopping. They purchased a bassinet, some baby clothes, and a few of the essentials.

The day ended with Michael and Olivia kneeling together in prayer, as they had done nearly every night of their marriage. Olivia often thought that was one of the things that had helped keep them together through all of the intense emotions and frustration and anger of the infertility. It was Olivia's turn to say the prayer, and she thanked Heavenly Father for sending them a baby. She started praying for "their" birth mom, as they had been doing for months, but now that their birth mom had a name, and an identity, the prayer became more fervent. "Please help Allison to know how thankful we are, and how much we, already, love her for this choice. Please bless her with hope. Please help her to feel of Thy love for her, and please bless her with the strength and the courage she will need to make this amazing, loving sacrifice for her baby girl."

Olivia ended the prayer, and she and Michael climbed into bed. Olivia adjusted herself into her favorite cuddle position with her head lying in the crook of Michael's shoulder and his arms around her. "It's really happening," she whispered. "We're going to be parents." Michael squeezed her closer, and Olivia closed her eyes.

CHAPTER FOUR

Two days later, when Olivia's alarm went off, it took half a breath to orient her mind, and then she remembered that today was the day they were going to meet Allison. Kevin called early the morning before to confirm the appointment for 1:00 today. They would be meeting at Allison's local Family Services office, and not only would Allison be there, but her mom and dad would also be joining them.

Michael stirred next to her, but she was too distracted to notice. When he rolled over and said, "Good morning, Livvy," she was so preoccupied that he startled her and she jumped half out of bed. Michael focused in on her face and then grinned.

"What?" Olivia demanded.

"You look terrified!"

"Well, I am. I already told you that last night! What if, when Allison meets us, she decides that she doesn't like us and she changes her mind? What if her parents don't like us and they convince her to change her mind? What if, now that we are finally getting a baby, we get in a car wreck while we're driving down to see her and one of us is killed?" Olivia was on the verge of hysteria.

Michael wrapped his arms around his wife and then started laughing. "Livvy, calm down. Everything is going to be fine. Allison is going to love you. Her parents are going to love you. We will be fine on the drive."

She started to protest, but Michael stopped her with a long, slow kiss. "Now, as much as I hate to say it," he said, smiling at his wife, "it's time to get up. We've got to get going so we won't be rushing to get there."

The hot shower managed to calm Olivia's nerves a little, and she was able to keep them under control through the morning as they drove. She and Michael visited about how they thought the face-to-face meeting would go, and they started talking about what they would name their daughter. Olivia loved the name Elizabeth, and ever since reading her great-aunt Elizabeth's journal, Olivia had the desire to pay tribute to that amazing woman who taught her so much and helped her start on the road to healing.

"Hmm. Elizabeth. You know? I like it!" Michael told her. "Yeah. That's definitely at the top of the list."

Olivia had worried that the car drive would drag, but instead it passed in a blur, and as they exited the freeway, the butterflies that laid dormant for most of the ride, rose in Olivia's chest with a vengeance. Michael first drove to the Family Services office to make sure they knew where it was, and then, since they had arrived on schedule—over an hour early—they went to get some lunch. Olivia tried to eat her sandwich, but couldn't, and Michael just kept smiling and telling her to try to relax. After lunch, they went and picked up two bouquets of flowers: one for Allison and one for her mom, and then drove back to LDS Family Services.

They parked the car at ten minutes to one. Michael got out and went to open the door for his wife. She looked like she was going to be sick. "Livvy, sweetheart, breathe!" Michael joked. "You're not going to make a good impression if you go in there and throw up on everyone."

Olivia looked horrified for a moment, but then the mental image that popped into her mind made her burst out laughing. That was just what she needed. "Okay, okay, I'm fine," she said as she got out of the car. "Let's go."

Michael gave Olivia a quick hug and then they walked into the office. The receptionist looked up when they opened the door, and when she saw them holding the bouquets of flowers, she gave them a big smile. "Are you Michael and Olivia?" she asked.

"Yes, we are," Michael said.

"Great. Barbara is expecting you. I'll let her know you're here. She'll be with you in a few minutes."

"Thanks." Michael and Olivia sat down in the waiting area. They couldn't help but smile at each other, and Michael kept rubbing Olivia's arm telling her to relax. Everything was going to be fine.

They waited about five minutes before a door opened and a middle-aged woman with smile wrinkles around her eyes stepped toward them. "Michael, Olivia? I'm Barbara. It's nice to meet you."

"Nice to meet you too," Michael said as they stood and each shook Barbara's hand.

"Let me quickly tell you how this is going to go today," Barbara said. Olivia relaxed. She was relieved that she would have a little information and wouldn't be walking blind into this meeting. Somehow that helped her feel better. "Allison and her parents are waiting for us in my office. You should know that her parents, especially her mom, are having a difficult time with Ally placing her baby." Olivia threw a worried glance at Michael. Barbara didn't miss it. "Don't worry, though. I think you will find that Ally is very sure about her decision and feels strongly that the baby girl she is carrying is meant for you two. Just be sensitive to the feelings of her mom and dad." Michael and Olivia both nodded as Barbara continued. "The birth father is completely out of the picture; Ally hasn't seen or heard from him in months, so be sensitive in asking any questions about him as well." Barbara stopped, thinking. "Yes, I believe that's everything. The five of you can visit as long as you want, and I'll be with you the whole time. Now, are you ready?"

Olivia nodded and Michael took her arm and smiled. "Let's go," he said to Barbara, and they followed her back to her office.

They opened the office door, and the first person Olivia noticed was the beautiful young woman with blonde, wavy hair and big brown eyes. *Allison.* The man sitting next to her was obviously her father. Their eyes were exactly the same. On the other side of the father sat a very pretty woman with blue eyes and the same wavy hair as Allison, although there were a few strands of gray emerging. Her arms were crossed and held close to her chest, and even from across the room, Olivia could see that her jaw was clenched tight. This must be Allison's mom.

Barbara followed them into the office and closed the door behind her before she spoke. "Allison, Steve, Julie, this is Michael and Olivia. Michael and Olivia, this is Allison, her dad Steve, and her mom Julie." Barbara seemed to melt into the background as Olivia crossed the room and Allison stood to meet her. They hugged each other and when they stepped back, both women had tears in her eyes.

"It's so great to meet you, Allison," Olivia began, and then laughed softly. "I can't believe I'm crying already."

Ally grinned. "I'm so excited to meet you too. I hardly slept at all last night."

"Me neither," Olivia confessed.

Michael stepped forward and stuck out his hand, but Allison gave him a hug too. "It's great to meet both of you," Allison said.

"And you," Michael said. There was a brief pause as they all surveyed one another, then Michael broke the silence as he smiled and handed Allison her bouquet of flowers. "We brought these for you. Important days should be celebrated with flowers."

"They're beautiful," Ally said. "Thanks."

Then Michael turned and took a step toward Allison's mom. "Julie, these are for you. Thanks for raising such a remarkable daughter. Livvy and I will always be grateful." Olivia nodded her agreement.

Julie appreciated their thoughtfulness, and her eyes misted up momentarily as she murmured her thanks. But she couldn't think of anything else to say. Steve rescued his wife from her discomfort by standing and reaching out to shake Michael's hand. "We've all been a little nervous to meet you. Ally is hoping you guys don't change your mind about the baby after meeting us." He chuckled nervously.

Michael laughed right out loud. "Olivia's been beside herself worrying that Allison might change her mind after meeting us."

"But," Olivia jumped in, "we're not going anywhere. We couldn't be more excited—or thankful." She smiled at Allison and the nervousness evaporated.

"You don't have to worry about me," Allison assured them. "I know this is the right decision."

Michael and Olivia walked out of LDS Family Services nearly two hours later feeling joy, hope, peace, and relief! Allison was terrific! She was a wonderful young woman, who was at peace with her decision to place her baby girl for adoption with them. She cried as she told them of the confusion and darkness that filled her mind until she decided to make an adoption plan for her baby, and of the hope and peace she felt as she read about Michael and Olivia and knew they were to be the parents of her baby girl.

Ally explained to them that she was unsure about the amount of personal contact she would want after the adoption, but that she would definitely love to exchange letters and pictures. She asked Olivia about being a nurse and shared with them her plans to go to school and become a nurse herself. She spoke briefly of the birth father and told them that he wasn't a bad person; he was just scared and didn't know what to do. When Ally told them his name, she cried when Michael said that he knew of Brandon White. Although their teams never played each other, Michael had kept an eye on one of the most recruited football players to come out of the state last year and noted that he had a great season as a true freshman in California.

Ally asked Olivia if she had thought of any names for the baby, and Olivia told her they were considering "Elizabeth," and told the story behind it. Ally liked the name and she seemed to like the story about Great-Aunt Elizabeth even better. Ally talked about her childhood and her hopes that her baby girl would experience many of the same things she had, such as playing basketball with the family, swimming lessons and picnics during the summer, having a big cup of hot chocolate after building a snowman in the winter, and having water fights on the fourth of July. The most emotional part of the visit was when Ally asked them to please let "our" daughter know how much her birth mom loves her, and that the only reason Ally could bear to part with her was so that she could have an amazing life with a mom and dad right from the start—the life that Ally would not have been able to provide.

Allison's parents, Steve and Julie, said very little throughout the afternoon. They both seemed to be watching Michael and Olivia very closely, and Olivia could only hope and pray that they would pass inspection. Julie's eyes welled up several times as she listened to Ally speak of placing her baby, and Steve's eyes were shining when Ally asked Michael and Olivia to teach the baby about Jesus Christ, and to take her to church and help her gain a testimony of the gospel.

Michael and Olivia were both lost in their own thoughts as they got into their car and started heading for the freeway. After a few minutes, Michael spoke, "That was amazing!"

"I know what you mean," Olivia agreed. "The Spirit was so strong and Ally is incredible!"

"Did you notice how she kind of cradled her arms around her belly when she talked about the baby; like she was holding and cuddling her now. It's obvious that she really loves that baby girl." Michael was waiting for a response, but none came so he glanced over at his wife. He was surprised to see her eyes welling up, and when Livvy blinked, the tears spilled down her cheeks. "What's the matter, Livvy? I thought everything went great!"

"Everything did go great. It's just that, well, of all of the emotions I imagined feeling when I met our baby's birth mom, jealousy never crossed my mind."

"What do you mean?"

"I mean that I expected to feel love and gratitude and joy, and I did feel all of those throughout the meeting, but feelings of jealousy kept creeping in, even though I was trying to push them away. I did notice the way she kept cradling her belly, and all I could think of was how I will never know how it feels to have a life growing inside of me." Olivia shrugged. "It just seems so stupid to feel this way. I'm overwhelmed with love and excitement about our daughter joining our family, and I can't even explain how thankful I am for Ally and the decision she is making. I just thought I was putting a lot of this old baggage behind me, and I'm frustrated that some of it is still hanging around."

Michael thought carefully before he answered, because he didn't know what to say. After a moment, he spoke. "I think those feelings are perfectly normal, Livvy."

Olivia was surprised. "You do?"

"Yes, I do. All of your 'baggage' has been being packed for years. I don't think that's something that just gets put away all at once. You've been working hard and making really great progress, but only the Savior can completely take those feelings away. You just have to believe that He will do it when the time is right."

"But don't you think that it's crazy to be feeling this way now that we are going to have a daughter?"

"No. You didn't say you are angry that we are adopting. You feel amazed and humbled and overwhelmed that Ally would choose us to be the parents of her baby girl. It doesn't matter how our baby joins our family. She is our daughter and we already love her. I think we have effectively put away the pain of not having a baby, especially now that we are going to be parents in just a few weeks. Maybe the thing we need to focus on now is turning the pain of not having the experiences a pregnancy would bring over to the Savior."

Olivia chuckled as she wiped away the tears. "You know, Michael, that actually makes sense."

"Try not to sound so surprised."

"I just hope that the Savior really will take those old feelings away from me. I don't need to be carrying them around forever."

"Well, Livvy, hope is a great place to start."

Barbara left the office with Michael and Olivia, and Ally turned to her mom and dad. "They're perfect! I knew they would be. I can picture them as parents. They're going to be amazing!"

Steve smiled at his daughter. "They did seem great. I liked that they were really interested in and concerned about you. Even though they are clearly excited about having a daughter, they seem to care about your well-being also. And you were right about them being everything you wanted for your baby. She will definitely have a very happy life."

Julie knew that Ally wanted her to say something, but all she could manage was, "They did seem nice."

"What about the story behind that picture of the two of them reading? The one in their portfolio that I loved so much. I can't believe their social worker tried to talk them out of putting that one in because their faces weren't perfectly clear in it! That picture really spoke to me. It was one of the reasons I chose them."

Steve added, "Well, when Olivia said that they prayed and prayed about it and felt strongly that they should include the picture anyway, that was a real testimony builder to me that Heavenly Father is truly involved in this work of adoption. He knows who your baby girl is meant to be with, and what would draw you to them." His voice choked up as he finished speaking, and Steve wiped at the tears forming in his eyes. "It all seems like a miracle."

"Well, I think the miracle would be if Ally changed her mind and we could all stay together and I could have my granddaughter instead of sending her off with strangers!" Julie's emotions finally got the better of her. Ally and Steve fell quiet, and Barbara entered the room to find an uncomfortable silence. She sensed there was a problem immediately.

"What's the matter? I thought that went great. Didn't you like them?" Barbara asked Ally.

"I loved them," Ally said. "The meeting couldn't have gone better. It's just that Mom is still . . . having a little trouble with my decision."

"I see," Barbara said. "Well, Julie, I think it's time that we talked about this. Clearly, you don't approve of Ally placing her baby for adoption. Is that because you don't agree with adoption in general?"

"No," Julie said. "I think adoption is a great choice for girls who are still in high school or girls who don't have any help or support or girls who wouldn't be able to be a good mom. But Ally, well, she is already graduated. Steve and I are willing and able to support her financially until she can get on her feet, and she will be a terrific mom. She is responsible and mature and a hard worker. Plus she has me! I can teach her everything she needs to know about taking care of a baby. Besides, this is my granddaughter we're talking about! My first granddaughter!"

"So, if I'm hearing you right," Barbara clarified, "adoption is a good choice for other people, but not for Ally, because . . . ?"

"Because she is different!" Julie snapped. "Okay, fine, I admit it. I think she's different than lots of girls who get pregnant. She wasn't sleeping around or doing drugs or being a troublemaker. She just made a mistake! That's all! One mistake! Why do we have to be punished because of one mistake?"

Barbara waited until Julie finished, and then spoke firmly. "I'm afraid I have to disagree with you, Julie. Every young woman that comes in to my office because she is single and pregnant is in that situation because of one mistake. Some have made other mistakes as well, others haven't, but in the end, it was one choice that resulted in pregnancy."

Julie started to protest, but Barbara stopped her. "I've worked with birth moms for a lot of years, and I've learned a few things. First, anyone—and I do mean anyone—can get in trouble by allowing themselves to get into a compromising situation, and then choosing not to leave, and it can happen in half a heartbeat. It doesn't mean that they are a bad person; it just means that they made a poor decision. Who of us hasn't done that at one time or another? Second, Heavenly Father does not love His children any less because we make mistakes. On the contrary, I have felt some of the most amazing manifestations of His love when one of His daughters turns to the Savior amid her struggles and finds the hope, and eventually forgiveness, that the Atonement promises. Third, the babies that are conceived out of wedlock are completely innocent. You asked why you should be punished. I assume by 'punished' you mean not having your granddaughter with you?" Barbara paused.

"Yes, that's exactly what I mean," Julie said.

"Well, what about her? What about Ally's baby girl? Should she have to live with the consequences of this mistake? Should she be denied the blessings of living under the sealing covenant? Of having a mom and a dad?" Barbara's voice had become gentle but remained firm. "Finally, I have learned that these young women who place their babies for adoption are some of the very most loving, unselfish, responsible, caring people that I have ever had the pleasure of know- ing. They are willing to sacrifice everything that they want to provide the best possible chance for their baby. There is no greater love than from a young woman who can hold her newborn infant and hug her and kiss her and sing to her, and then say good-bye through her tears, and break her own heart in order to give her precious, precious baby all of the best opportunities this life has to offer."

Barbara stopped to wipe the tears that had trickled from the corners of her eyes, and then passed around a box of tissues when she noticed that Ally and her parents were all crying as well. "Julie, I'm going to tell you the same thing that I tell all the birth moms. I don't know what you're going through. I can't completely understand the emotions you are feeling, but Christ can. He has suffered all, so that we don't have to suffer alone. Ally has made an amazing decision, and the Savior has given her hope and comfort and the knowledge that she is doing the right thing. If you will turn to Him with a truly

open and humble heart, I know that He will do the same for you."
Barbara smiled and reached over to hug Julie.

"I hope you're right," Julie said.

"I am," Barbara replied, "but don't put your hope in me. Put it in the Savior, where it belongs."

CHAPTER FIVE

Ally woke up with a cramp in her lower back. She wasn't surprised. Her back had been hurting quite a bit over the last couple days. As she rolled over to try and rub the spot, she glanced at the calendar on her wall. Today was February fourteenth. Valentine's Day. A day for love. She laughed in spite of herself and patted her huge belly. "Well, it's just you and me, Baby Girl. What do you say we treat ourselves to a nice warm bath this morning?" Ally didn't get up right away. It was so hard to move these days! But when the pain in her back didn't go away, she decided it was time for that bath.

Ally was just sinking into the tub when there was a knock on the bathroom door, and her mom spoke. "Ally, are you okay? It's only 7:00. You're usually still asleep."

"Yeah, I'm fine, Mom. Lying in bed was making my back sore, so I decided to get up. I'll be out in a little bit."

"Okay," her mom replied. "Holler if you need anything."

"Thanks." Ally was so glad that Julie was taking Barbara's advice to heart. Ally had seen her mom several times over the past two weeks kneeling beside her bed, praying and crying. Ally knew she was seeking the hope that only the Savior can provide, and it seemed to be working. Julie was still sad at the thought of not having her granddaughter, but she didn't seem to be so angry now. Ally hoped that would last. She was going to need her mom's support through her labor and delivery, which was fast approaching. She was nervous and a little scared, and Ally couldn't believe that her due date was only four days from now!

Ally knew from an email that Olivia had finished her last day of work and that she and Michael had been busy painting and decorating the baby's room. Olivia attached a photo of the finished room. It was painted in soft pinks and greens and decorated in flowers, butterflies, and rainbows. Ally smiled. She loved rainbows. Michael and Olivia were excited and nervous and still amazed, humbled, and forever grateful that Ally found them.

Ally shifted in the tub, but the pain in her back wasn't getting any better. In fact, it seemed to be getting worse. She closed her eyes and tried to relax. She turned her thoughts back to Michael and Olivia. She felt much the same way about them as they did about her. She was so thankful that she had been led to them and that they were going to be such amazing parents for her baby girl. She knew that they already loved her and that they would take especially good care of her. Ally's baby was going to have a wonderful life, and that knowledge comforted her.

Ally stayed in the warm water a while longer, but she was becoming increasingly uncomfortable, so she decided to get out and see if walking around would make her feel any better. She stepped over the side of the tub, being careful not to slip, and started drying off. She had finished and was wrapping her robe around her when her legs were suddenly wet again and she was standing in a puddle. Only a second passed before Ally realized what just happened. She closed her eyes, took a deep breath, and offered a quick but fervent prayer that Heavenly Father would help her make it through what was coming. Then she called out, "Mom? Can you come here, please? I need you."

Olivia was standing in the center of the baby's room smiling. She had been dreaming of fixing up a nursery for so long, and now, here it was! This was her baby daughter's bedroom, and Ally was due in only four more days. Before this week was over, Olivia was going to be a mom! She had been praying so much lately, that at the thought of Ally, one naturally began in her mind. *Heavenly Father, please give Ally the strength and courage she will need to follow through with her decision. Please bless her with comfort and with peace. Help her to feel of our love for her and the gratitude that we have at the precious gift she is offering us.*

Olivia jumped when the telephone started ringing. She laughed and ran to answer it. She was still smiling at the way the ring startled her when she said, "Hello?"

"Hello, Olivia?"

"Yes."

"This is Barbara with LDS Family Services." Olivia could tell from her voice that Barbara was smiling too.

"Hi, Barbara. Is Ally okay?"

"Yes, she's okay. She is actually settled in to her hospital room, and her doctor says that things are progressing nicely."

Olivia felt warmth wash over her. Her tears came before her voice did. "Do you mean . . . is Ally . . . ?"

"Yes, Olivia. Ally is in labor. Her water broke a little after seven this morning. She had been having contractions before that, and they started coming more heavily after. Call Michael. You guys better head down here. It looks like your baby girl is going to be born today."

Olivia was laughing and crying, and she could barely manage to get out, "We'll be there."

"I'll call you in an hour or so, once you're on the road, with more details."

"Sounds good. Thank you so much!" Olivia was still crying.

"Oh, and Olivia? Congratulations!"

"Thanks, Barbara. See you soon."

Olivia hung up the phone, and once again her hands were shaking as she dialed Michael's cell number. He answered after one ring. "Livvy? Is Ally okay?"

"She's in labor, Michael. Barbara just called. It's time. Ally is having our baby today. We've got to go." Olivia could hear the joy in her own voice.

"I'll be there in ten minutes. I love you, Livvy."

"Love you too! Bye."

Barbara called at ten o'clock in the morning, and Michael and Olivia were on the road by 10:20. Olivia had their suitcases packed and was standing on the front porch waiting for Michael when he pulled into the driveway. The rest of the morning was a blur. Olivia and Michael laughed and talked and cried and laughed some more as they drove south. They thought often of Ally and prayed that the delivery would go smoothly and that both Ally and their daughter would be healthy.

True to her word, Barbara called to give them an update. Everything was going well, but it would probably be later that evening before the baby was actually born. Ally wanted Michael and Olivia to call Barbara when they arrived in town, and they would make a plan from there.

Olivia's head was spinning when they finally exited the freeway. She called Barbara and was surprised when she started giving them directions to the hospital. "Ally is far enough along that they've been able to give her an epidural, and she is fairly comfortable right now. She wants to see you before the baby's born."

"Sounds good. It shouldn't take us long to get there," Olivia said. Then she asked the question that was gnawing at the edge of her mind. "She . . . hasn't changed her mind, or anything, has she?"

"No, no. Nothing to worry about. We'll talk a little more when you get here. I'll meet you in the lobby of the hospital."

"Okay. See you in a minute." Olivia hung up the phone. She was trying hard not to be nervous as she directed Michael to the hospital, but her familiar butterflies were churning more than ever as they parked the car and walked in to meet Barbara. She was waiting for them by the information desk.

"Hi, you two," Barbara said as she shook Michael's hand and gave Olivia a hug. "Everything is going really well, and Ally is looking forward to seeing you. I just want to let you know what to expect over the next couple days, and then we'll go see her." Olivia nodded nervously, and Michael squeezed her hand.

"In a few minutes, I'll take you up to Ally's room. You can visit for half an hour or so, and then I'll ask you to leave and go check into your hotel. Ally has asked that the delivery, and the time between the baby's birth and the placement, be her time with the baby."

Olivia nodded again, but Michael said, "Sure, no problem. We are happy to do whatever helps her feel more at ease." Olivia agreed wholeheartedly with this, but she was still nervous. She knew that nothing was certain until after Ally signed the relinquishment papers. Up until that point, Ally could change her mind at any time.

"After the baby is born," Barbara continued, "I'll call and let you know. Then, state law gives Ally a minimum of twenty-four hours before she can sign the papers. Depending on what time the baby arrives, we should be able to do the placement either tomorrow evening, or the next morning. That will take place here at the hospital, and then you'll be able to leave and take your daughter home." Barbara smiled at them. "I know this is a very nerve-racking time for you, but have some faith in Ally. She's an incredibly strong young woman. I think everything will move forward as planned." She gave Olivia's arm a quick squeeze. "Now, let's go see her."

The three of them wound their way through the corridors of the hospital and up the elevator. After a few minutes, they arrived in the maternity ward. Barbara greeted the nurses as they passed. Olivia was determined to maintain her composure and not let her nerves show. They turned one last corner and saw Steve standing outside a closed door. He smiled and walked forward to give Michael and Olivia a big hug. "Well, today's the big day," he said. "Are you two ready to be parents?"

"Absolutely," Michael said. "How is Ally doing?"

"She's actually doing really well. She's such a trooper. The morning was a little rough, but she's feeling better since she had the epidural. The doctor is checking her progress right now, so we should have some news any minute."

Olivia remained silent, and Steve seemed to sense her nervousness. He put his arm around her as tears filled his eyes. "Olivia, I can't tell you how happy we are that our baby girl is going to have such an amazing mom. Ally knows, and so do I, that you and Michael are the ones who are meant to be this baby's parents. She belongs with you. I won't pretend to understand why things happen the way they do. We probably won't ever understand—at least not in this life—but I do know that the adoption plan Ally has made is in accordance with

Heavenly Father's will. Both for Ally's life, and for the baby's."

The tears that Olivia had been fighting were now streaming down her cheeks. "Thank you, Steve. That means a lot to me."

Steve wiped his own eyes, then said, "Even Julie has felt that confirmation. It's still going to be extremely difficult for her to let her first grandbaby go, but she has come to the understanding that this is how things are supposed to be." He looked at Michael and smiled. "She knows this baby needs a dad, and especially a dad who is sealed to her mom and holds and honors the priesthood."

"Thanks, Steve. We'll do our very best."

"I know you will. You'll both be amazing."

Dr. Broadbent opened the door and smiled at the four of them. "How's she coming?" Steve asked.

"I'll let Ally tell you. You can all go in."

They walked in the room, and Olivia was relieved to see Ally smiling at them from her bed. Julie was sitting next to her, and she also had a smile on her face. This melted away the worries stewing inside Olivia, and she went right over and gave Ally a big hug. Ally spoke first, "I'm so glad you guys made it! I really wanted to see you before the baby is born."

"I'm glad we're here too," Olivia said. "How are you doing? Is everything going okay?"

"I'm doing good. I can still feel the contractions." Ally grimaced slightly and put her hand over her belly while a contraction passed. "But the epidural has taken most of the pain away. And actually," now Ally grinned again, "Dr. Broadbent says I'm dilated nearly to nine centimeters. She's going to be born in the next few hours!"

"You know what that means," Julie said to Michael and Olivia. "You're going to have a Valentine's baby!" She smiled. It was her way of telling them that she wasn't angry with them. They understood and smiled back.

"Well, I can't think of a better expression of love, or of a more tender gift, than what Ally is doing," Michael said. "We'll never be able to thank you enough," he said to Ally. Then he turned to Julie and Steve. "Or you. Thank you so much for raising your daughter to be so loving and unselfish." His voice cracked and Olivia was crying and nodding. "Saying thank you doesn't seem like nearly enough, but I don't know what else to say," he concluded.

By now everyone was crying, and it was Barbara that finally spoke. "Well, Ally, if you're all the way to nine centimeters, maybe Michael and Olivia should go and get checked into their hotel."

"Yeah, okay," said Ally. She reached up to give Olivia one more hug. She said, "I just wanted you to understand about why I want you guys to wait until the placement to see the baby. Don't worry. I'm not going to change my mind, or anything. I just really want this little bit of time with my baby girl before she becomes your daughter."

"I understand, Ally. It's okay." Olivia smiled. It really was.

Olivia was anxiously pacing back and forth in their hotel room. There was an indoor pool, and Michael tried to convince her that they should go have a swim, but Olivia couldn't be distracted right now. It had been almost two hours since they left the hospital, and she knew that the call could be coming at any moment. She was praying almost constantly that everything was going well, and that Ally and the baby would both be fine. Michael was sitting at the desk trying to read a book, but his eyes kept flickering to his watch, and Olivia knew that he was just as anxious as she was.

They both jumped when Olivia's cell phone started ringing, and since she was already holding it in her hand, she answered it before the first ring even ended. "Hello?"

"Olivia, it's Barbara. Congratulations! Your daughter is here."

Tears were already streaming down her face and Michael's arms were around her before she could say anything.

"Is she okay? Is Ally okay?" Olivia asked. Michael leaned his head close to the phone so that he could hear Barbara as well.

"Everyone is doing great. The delivery went very smoothly. She was born about fifteen minutes ago—at 4:33 p.m. to be exact. She weighs six pounds, five ounces, and is nineteen-inches long. She has lots of curly blonde hair and is absolutely beautiful!"

Olivia was crying and nodding until she remembered that Barbara couldn't see her and she would have to actually say something. "That's terrific," she managed through her tears. "And Ally is fine?"

"Yes, she is. She wanted me to tell you guys 'Congratulations.'"

"Well, give her a hug from us," Olivia said.

"I will," Barbara said. "Since the baby was born this early in the evening, we will probably be able to do the placement tomorrow evening. I will give Ally some time, and then I will go and talk to her about what she wants to do. Then I'll give you guys a call around 9:30 tonight and let you know what the plan is."

"That sounds great, Barbara. We'll look forward to your call."

Olivia didn't remember hanging up the phone, or it dropping from her fingertips. She was only aware of one thing. Her daughter had been born! She was here and she was healthy! She whispered, "Thank you, Heavenly Father. Thank you!"

"Amen," said Michael. Then they held each other and cried.

CHAPTER SIX

A lly was sitting alone in her dimly lit hospital room cradling her beautiful baby girl in her arms. It was 3:00 in the morning, and she had just finished feeding her. Time seemed to be racing forward in these moments when she wanted, more than anything, to slow it down.

Charlie, Emma, and Elsie had visited earlier and each took a turn holding the baby. They all had school tomorrow, so when they left, they had each said a tearful good-bye to their baby niece. Charlie gave his big sister a hug and said, "I know you're doing the right thing, Ally, and I'm really proud of you."

"Emma, Elsie?" Ally said. "I'm sorry that I wasn't a better example to you two, but I want you to remember that now I am doing the right thing, even though it is the hardest thing I can imagine."

The girls gave their sister a big hug and Emma said, "We're sorry we were so hard on you."

"Yeah," Elsie added. "We were just embarrassed, and then a little mad that we wouldn't even get to tend the baby that started all of this." She shrugged and tried to smile. "But we love you a lot, Ally."

"We really do," Emma said. "And we're proud of you too." Ally could only smile through her tears.

Julie had spent the evening sitting beside Ally in her bed with her arms around Ally and the baby, and Steve had tenderly held

Ally's baby girl and whispered to her as he ran his fingers through her golden curls.

Hannah had called offering her love and support, and Amy stopped by. She believed that now that the baby was born, Ally would give up this "crazy idea" about adoption, give in to her own desires, and decide to raise the baby herself. Amy was angry when she left, telling Ally, "I never thought you would actually do it. All a baby really needs is love."

Ally cried as one of her best friends stormed out. She felt betrayed, but she thought, *I wish that were true. Love alone can't give my baby girl a father, or a full family, or security, or stability, or a mom who is home every day with her, or the sealing covenant. But I can give her all of that. And I will. Because I love her enough.*

Barbara had come in and made plans for the placement. Ally wanted to do it tomorrow evening, and so they had planned it for 6:30 the following night.

Julie had just finished the baby's midnight feeding, when Ally asked her mom and dad to go home and get some sleep. Her mom objected, but Steve could see that Ally needed some time alone with her baby, and he persuaded Julie to leave with him. Ever since they left, Ally had been talking to her baby girl. Telling her all about her own life and childhood, and about all of the hopes and dreams for both of their futures. She told her about her birth father, and the night Ally got pregnant. She talked of the darkness and hopelessness and misery she felt at first, and of the Savior's overwhelming love, which she was now feeling. Ally's tears dropped on the pink blanket swaddling her baby as she spoke of the night she knew that she was not meant to raise her sweet baby girl, and of the turmoil of trying to find the right parents, and the peace she felt when she finally found Michael and Olivia. Ally told her baby about the love she felt for Olivia and Michael, and how much they loved both of them.

Ally finished burping her baby girl, and as she began telling her daughter how much she loved her, she was suddenly overwhelmed by the depth and power of the love she felt. She knew in her mind that this sacrifice was going to be difficult, but her heart and soul were unprepared for the overpowering emotions of maternal love that were sweeping through her. A sob began building deep in her chest and by the time it escaped her lips, Ally was clinging to her daughter. "I can't do it, Heavenly Father. Please, is there any other way? I don't want to let my baby go. Please! Please! I don't want to be alone! I don't want to be left here all alone!"

Ally sobbed harder and harder over her sleeping angel, and despite all of the good intentions she had nurtured over the past month, her resolve began to waver. "Please, Heavenly Father," she cried, "Please don't let me be alone! I can't do it! I'm not strong enough! I need some help! Please send me some help!" Ally pressed her baby girl into her chest, hoping that the baby's touch would stop the pain that was threatening to tear her apart. "How can I ever do this?" Ally whispered, and she closed her eyes trying to shut out the ache that was building, eating her from the inside.

Ally may have drifted into an unsettled sleep, she was never sure, but then images began flashing through her mind. Images that she had seen in pictures many, many times throughout her life, only now she seemed to be watching them as if they were happening just now, at this very moment. They began with a newborn baby boy being held by his young mother in a stable surrounded by animals. Her loving husband was standing over them—watchful, protecting. It occurred to Ally that this man was not the baby's "biological" father, but he loved the infant fiercely and would raise him as if he were his own flesh and blood. The scene shifted and the baby was now grown, although still a young man. Ally knew He was only just past the age of thirty, and as she watched she saw love personified. Over time He taught, He healed, He wept, He loved. And then, He was alone. Alone on a garden path with the weight of His burden pressing down on Him like a vice. Ally heard him speak, and her soul recognized the agony in His voice, "O my Father, if it be possible, let this cup pass from me: nevertheless not as I will, but as thou wilt."

Ally was still crying, for she recognized this man, this Being whom she had come to know and love more than ever over the last nine months. Her Elder Brother, her Savior who offered her the hope of a new beginning. She felt that through her own experiences and emotions, she had been given a tiny glimpse of understanding into Christ's ultimate, and most loving, sacrifice. Her tears continued, as Ally realized that she had heard her own answer through the Savior, and her thoughts echoed, *Not as I will, but as thou wilt.* In her dream—or was she awake?—her mind called out, *But how? How did you do it? How can I do it?*

Ally felt a hand on her shoulder and looked up into a pure, perfect, loving face. There were tears streaming down His cheeks as well; tears that Ally knew were for her own pain and suffering, and she felt His answer. *Through love. I loved my Father's children—I loved you, Ally—too much to fall short in what I had to do. You don't have to be alone. You never have to be alone. I have already carried your burdens. I have already felt your agony. I know your heartache and your pain. I will always be here to give you strength. You can do it through the hope and peace I can provide. I will never leave you alone.*

Ally opened her eyes as her baby girl stirred in her arms. Julie was sitting in the chair next to the hospital bed, and Ally smiled at her mom.

"Rough night?" Julie asked. "Your eyes are all red and puffy," she said in response to Ally's surprised look.

"Sort of," Ally replied. "But I had an amazing . . . dream . . . or something, and I know that I'm going to be okay. I know this is the right thing for my baby girl, and I can do it. I can do it because I love her that much. I can do it because the Savior will give me the strength I need."

Julie raised her eyebrows in a question. "A dream?"

"I can't really talk about it right now," Ally said, "but I promise I will tell you all about it soon. For now, do you want to feed the baby?"

Steve arrived shortly before noon, and Ally and her parents spent the day holding the baby, taking pictures, crying, hugging, and crying some more. Ally tried to memorize each part of her baby from her tiny pink lips, to her ten little toes, to her new baby smell. She didn't want to forget anything about her.

Bishop Jenkins stopped by and told Ally how proud he was of her and that she could come see him anytime she needed to talk. Before he left, he kissed the baby on the forehead and said with tears in his eyes, "You're very lucky to have so many people who love you so much. I know you'll be very happy."

The clock was racing forward, and before Ally knew it, it was time to sign the papers that would relinquish her rights as her baby girl's mom. She asked Barbara and her parents to give her just a few more minutes alone with the baby first.

Ally carefully dressed her baby in the fuzzy, pink sleeper she had picked out for this moment. Her tears fell on the little hat that she tenderly placed over those blonde curls that were just like Brandon's. Ally wrapped her in the blanket that she and her mom had made, and then she held her sweet baby girl close to her face and whispered, "I love you, Baby Girl. I won't be seeing you again any time soon, but please just remember that I love you. I gave you life, and now I am going to give you the best chance in that life. Your mommy and daddy love you so much, and they've waited a long time for you. They are amazing people, and they will teach you everything you need to know. You will always be in my heart. Good-bye."

For a moment, Ally felt her heart quiver, but as she turned her mind to the Savior, hope came pouring in, and with it came the strength to move forward. "Mom, Dad, Barbara," Ally called loudly enough for them to hear. "I'm ready."

CHAPTER SEVEN

Michael and Olivia were pacing in the hospital lobby. Michael carried an infant car seat in one hand, and Olivia had a packed diaper bag over one shoulder. Olivia was trying to keep her eyes dry, but the tears kept sneaking out anyway. At 6:45 Barbara came walking down the hall. "It's time," she said. "Ally has signed all of the paperwork, so we will go up now and she will give you your daughter. She has asked that we keep it fairly brief, and when we are done, she would like you to leave the hospital with the baby first. I will see you off, and after you have left, Ally and her parents will go home as well." Michael and Olivia nodded, and then Barbara continued. "By the way, what are you going to name her? I know you talked about Elizabeth. Is that what you decided on?"

"Actually," Olivia said. "We've had another thought that we wanted to talk to Ally about, before we decide for sure."

"Okay," said Barbara. "Let's go."

They walked to Ally's room in silence, Michael and Olivia clasping each other's hand. When they arrived, Barbara knocked, and Steve opened the door. Ally was sitting in a rocking chair with a tiny pink bundle in her arms and Julie was standing beside her. Olivia's tears broke through and Michael started to say something, but the words caught in his throat. It was Olivia who broke the silence. "How are you doing, Ally?"

Ally smiled. "I'm going to be all right. Do you want to see her?"

"Yes!" Michael and Olivia both said at the same time. Ally carefully unwrapped the blanket and turned the baby so she was facing the people who were now her parents, for the first time. "Oh, Ally, she's beautiful!" Olivia exclaimed.

"She really is," Michael added. Ally took off the little hat and smiled again as Olivia laughed at all of the curls.

"Her hair is curly, just like yours," Ally said to Olivia. They all smiled as Olivia wiped her tears.

"We have a little something for you," Michael said as he set the car seat down and reached into the diaper bag. He pulled out a small blue jewelry box and handed it to Ally. She carefully opened it and pulled out a beautiful, gold, heart-shaped locket.

"I love it," Ally said.

"Open it," Olivia told her. Ally did and found that one side of the locket contained a small picture of Michael and Olivia. The other side was empty for the moment. "We thought you could put a picture of you and the baby in the other side, because our hearts are always going to be connected from now on."

Ally's eyes welled up, but she smiled. "I love it," she said again. "That's a great idea!" She had Julie help her put the necklace on. Ally looked down and smiled at her baby girl. "So, what did you decide to name her?"

Michael smiled at Olivia and nodded, encouraging her to tell Ally. "We talked a lot about that last night and today," Olivia began. "As we thought of everything we have been through in trying to have a family, we became more and more humbled and thankful for you . . ." Olivia broke off as tears choked her words. She took a deep breath and tried again. "It's been a long journey to get to this point, and some parts of it were not very pleasant, but because of Jesus Christ we have been able to find healing and peace." Olivia paused and fingered the three stone ring Michael gave her several Christmases ago. "And now because of you, we have been able to find hope for our future. We have prayed, and will continue to pray, that you will also find hope for your future, through the Savior, and we believe that as our daughter grows she will also have hope and joy in her life because of the sacrifice you have made for her." Olivia seemed to be gaining strength as she spoke. "As Michael and I talked about all of that, we came up with an idea of what to name your sweet baby girl, our daughter. We want to name her Hope. Unless you have a strong objection, her name will be Hope Elizabeth."

Ally thought of all that she had been through over the past year and the times of darkness and despair, and the light that had come through the Savior. She thought of her baby girl's future and could envision love and laughter and happiness. Ally could see herself moving forward and continuing to learn and grow. She could see her baby girl growing into a child and then a beautiful young woman. She could see Michael and Olivia kneeling with their daughter in prayer and going swimming together and playing basketball out on the driveway. Ally could envision the day when she would have a family of her own, and the love that they would share. Among these thoughts, Ally could see a common thread running through it all like a spark of gold. That thread was hope. Hope in Jesus Christ and the knowledge that we can overcome anything with His help.

"I think that Hope is the perfect name for her," Ally said. "It's just perfect." Ally kissed her baby girl one last time, then held her up for Julie and Steve to kiss. She whispered, "Good-bye, Hope. I will always love you." Then Ally stood up, walked to Olivia, and passed her baby girl into the arms of her mom.

Everyone was crying again as Olivia hugged her daughter to her heart. Michael put his arm around his wife and they gave everyone one last hug. As they got to Ally, Michael told her, "We'll take good care of her." Ally nodded. She knew they would.

"We love you," Olivia said. "We can't thank you enough. You've given us a future."

"Well, you're giving Hope an amazing future, and I can't thank you enough for that." Ally smiled through her tears.

Ally began to miss her baby the moment Michael and Olivia walked out the door. As tears filled her eyes, Ally thought she felt a soft touch on her shoulder. She looked up. She couldn't see anyone, but her heart burned within her, and she knew that even though she was hurting now, her own future was also in good hands.

Author's Note

I have had many people ask me if this book is based on my own life, so I thought it would be helpful to address that here. The short answer is that this is a work of fiction. The characters and events are not real. However, because I wanted this book to feel real, I tried to be very honest and truthful with the emotions—and those do have a base in my real-life experiences. There you go. In case the short answer doesn't completely satisfy you, I'll include a little more about my own experience of creating my family. If you're interested, read on . . .

Several years after marrying my wonderful husband, Shane, it became obvious that it was going to be difficult for us to have children. We began fertility treatments. In the beginning there were lots of tests and monitoring and some minor hormone therapies. That moved on to more extensive monitoring and hormone shots and more aggressive treatments, including about six months of IUI. Fortunately for us, the doctors were able to diagnose the causes (yes, multiple causes) of our infertility. I won't bore you with all of the details here. Suffice it to say that one of the major issues is that I have endometriosis, along with several other smaller diagnoses. I had a surgery trying to clean everything up, but it wasn't very effective. My husband also had some fertility issues that required two surgeries to correct. These were much more successful than mine was.

Shortly after we began fertility treatments, we felt strongly impressed that we should continue with treatments *and* try to bring children into our family through adoption. This was a fairly easy decision to come to, once the idea occurred to us. I know that is not always the case, but it was for us. At the time, we knew just a handful of people who had adopted their children, and I immediately called one of them on the phone and asked, "So how would Shane and I go about adopting a baby?" She was surprised but extremely helpful. She told us about several agencies and recommended one that she thought would be a good place for us to start. And start we did.

After feeling helpless over our situation for so long, this was something I could really sink my teeth into. We attended the required classes immediately and worked very hard to get the mountains of paperwork completed. (Today, most of the "paperwork" is done electronically, but when we started, there were literally mountains of papers spread all over our kitchen table.) Then one day, our hopes and prayers were answered when we got a call from our social worker explaining that a birth mom had picked us. She was having a baby girl and was due in about a month. We were thrilled, overwhelmed, excited, happy, grateful, and in awe of the amazing sacrifice this remarkable young woman was going to make that would give us a daughter.

We met her once before the baby was born and got to see her briefly in the hospital before she delivered. She gave birth on a Friday evening, and on Sunday morning she placed our beautiful daughter into our arms, giving Shane and I, as well as this precious child, a forever family. From the time we had first called an agency until our daughter was placed in our arms was about fourteen months.

There was a bit of legal risk with the adoption (which we knew going in) and it took a little longer than the normal six months before we could finalize, but our daughter's birth mom never wavered in her decision and was very supportive of us throughout the entire process. When our sweet girl was eighteen months old we were able to finalize. She was born back in 2002 and adoptions were more or less closed at that time. During the last couple years, we have been moving toward more openness in our adoption, which, I think, is a wonderful thing for everyone involved. Today, many adoptions are open from the beginning, which is great!

Once our daughter's adoption was finalized, we started trying to adopt again. We had a few more ups and downs this time around, coming close to having a second baby join our family several times, but not quite happening. Meanwhile, we had been continuing with our fertility treatments. One week before our daughter turned three years old, we found out that the latest treatment had been successful. After five years of fertility treatments, I was pregnant! We were cautiously excited. We decided to wait until the end of the first trimester before making any big announcements or adding it to our adoption profile, just in case I had a miscarriage. We still wanted to continue with our plans to adopt again, but figured we would put that on hold until after the baby I was carrying was born.

Just a few weeks short of the 3-month mark, we got a call from our social worker. A birth mom was considering us. She lived over halfway across the country so we couldn't meet with her right away, but she had a question or two for us before she made her final decision. I quickly answered her social worker's questions, then told him the news that I was pregnant. I told him that it didn't change the way we felt about wanting to adopt, but that this birth mom should have all of the information before she made her final decision on a family. He thanked me and hung up the phone. I didn't think that we would be hearing from him again.

I was surprised when the phone rang two days later and it was our social worker asking us to come down to his office. We made the arrangements and got there as quickly as possible. He handed us an envelope that contained a faxed copy of a letter written by a young woman. She had chosen us as the family for her soon-to-be-born baby boy. She didn't care that I was pregnant; she felt strongly that we were the family for him. We were ecstatic! I had always wanted twins and it was fun to think that these two babies would be just six months apart! She was due in a couple of weeks, so we began preparing to have our son join our family and make the long trip out to pick him up.

We got a call late one Thursday night that she had gone into labor. We had been planning on leaving in the next day or two anyway, so I already had all of the suitcases packed. We loaded into the car at ten o'clock at night and started driving. We didn't make it there before he was born on Friday but got a chance to meet his sweet birth mom on Saturday, and spend some time in the hospital with her, and her parents, before meeting our new son. The placement was on Sunday, and I was overwhelmed once again at the love of a young woman for the baby she had just given birth to, a love that was so strong and pure that she was willing to sacrifice her own wants and desires to give him a family. This time it took twenty-one months from the time we started the process until our son was born.

After about a week of waiting for all of the interstate compact papers to go before a judge, we were approved to leave the state and we headed home with our daughter and her new baby brother. The story almost ends there, but not quite.

When our baby boy was three months old, I developed a severe case of toxemia with my pregnancy. My blood pressure shot sky high and my kidneys started shutting down. I had a mini-stroke. Additionally, the cord was wrapped around the baby's neck three times, so my doctor performed an emergency c-section in order to save both of our lives. Our youngest son was born three months early and life-flighted to a nearby Neonatal Intensive Care Unit. He stayed there for sixty-one days and had several blood transfusions, a surgery, and a few other big scares before he could join us at home. My boys ended up being only three months apart, and we felt our family was complete with our beautiful daughter and two sons. Shane and I love all three of them more than we ever dreamed possible!

It was a long journey getting my family here, but I wouldn't trade the things that I learned for anything. I learned that it's okay to grieve for lost opportunities and experiences. I learned that after the grieving process, it's time to heal. I learned that healing and hope are possible—no matter the circumstances. I learned that selfless love and sacrifice can still be found in this world, and I learned that families are created not by blood, but by love.

Acknowledgments

I want to thank everyone at Cedar Fort for making this book a reality. Special thanks to Angie for taking an interest in the story and for answering every question I've had along the way; Angela for your beautiful and touching cover design; Emily for all of your effort and hard work; and Laura for helping me navigate the marketing world.

I wouldn't be who I am today without the love and support of my family. A great big thank you goes to my parents. To my mom, Jodie, for showing me what a mother's love is all about, and to my dad, Nick, for teaching me to take a big bite out of life. To my brothers and sisters and their spouses, thanks for being willing (and even excited) to spend the family camping trip reading and critiquing my book. Matt, Nicki, Josh, Beth, Sarah, Jonathan, and Jesse—I can't think of a better bunch of bibliophiles. Your feedback was invaluable. To George and Donna, thank you for raising an amazing son and for your support and excitement about this book.

Thank you to all of my wonderful friends (you know who you are) who have continually encouraged me. Karen and Becky, your responses reminded me why I decided to write this in the first place. Special thanks to MaryAnne. You have helped and supported me through every one of the ups and downs of this long process. I will always value your opinions, and especially your friendship.

ACKNOWLEDGMENTS

To my three beautiful children, Isabella, Tyson, and Jay. Thank you for inspiring me to find my story. I love each of you more than 128 humpback whales.

Thank you to the two amazing women who were strong enough, loving enough, and selfless enough to place their newborn babies into my arms. I think the best places in heaven are reserved for birth parents.

Above all, thank you to my best friend, Shane. Life can be a crazy ride, but there's no one else I'd rather take the journey with. I love you.

About the Author

Jennifer Holt was raised as a farm girl in Enterprise, Utah. An avid reader since age four, she always enjoys a good book. Jennifer graduated Cum Laude from Brigham Young University and shortly after, began her journey through infertility and the miracle of adoption. She lives in Boise, Idaho, with her husband, Shane, and their three beautiful children. She likes wakeboarding and going to the zoo with her daughter and two sons.